RUSTLING
OF THE
CHALENT

THREAD 1: HELLO WORLD

RUSSELSTILTSKIN

https://twitter.com/Russelstiltski1

https://www.instagram.com/Russelstiltskin_Chalent/?hl=en

russelstiltskin@gmail.com

TABLE OF CONTENT

HELLO WORLD-1 (LUCAS)

Lucas bounded through the corridor, fast as a sprinting leopard. He was but a blue and black smear, hair pushed back by the wind that his movements made. The guards never saw him coming until it was too late.

"Who's there?!" one screamed when he heard the flurry of beating boots on the pretentious carpet rolled over the floor. There were only three of them.

But they weren't human. They were Purebloods, they were Serperins.

The Serperins were renowned for their beautiful scales that refracted the light into a thousand shades and transitioned with natural gradients. Their scales came enameled like jewels and they padded onto each person's skin like armor plates onto a knight. Their front was made of hard skin, coarse as leather, but the rest was a work of art.

They were dressed in black and white suits with ties, and the vest tucked under the suit made them puffier than they actually were. And then armed with an arsenal of weapons. Lucas would expect no less.

5

But, them being Serperins nor bodyguards did not make them any less easy to kill. He had ended so many of their kind he could complete this mission with muscle memory alone. When you were basically made for it, nothing really hindered you.

The one who screamed tried to draw out a gun, but after a flicker of light arced past, his hand was gone, and so was the gun. The blade was so thin he couldn't see but the reflection of its edge by the light that showered him when it passed. It was dimly lit by the lamps fixed by golden hands protruding from the walls, as were all hotel corridors. So that helped. When the blade sunk into flesh, the slash was smooth as a knife cutting into melted butter. Even bone didn't provide much resistance. It severed almost as easily.

The hand flew away to his colleague and smacked his head with a revolting mushy noise. Residual blood brushed on his lips as the hand slid and dropped the ground. That one stumbled back, both disgusted and frightened. He didn't faint, but that was only expected of a trained bodyguard. He had probably seen a lot worse.

While the hand had the unfortunate fate of flying onto a face, the other two guards should have been pleased the gun merely clattered harshly on the ground, its gears inside rattling.

Blood was splattered over the lavish wallpaper and the doors of the corridor, following the whip of motion from the blade. They weren't smooth, patterned with coarse lines and the blood that painted a new coat of red on it followed. Its grainy surface was perfectly outlined, with nothing concealed. The blood quickly streamed down from their blobs. Lucas knew under the chilly air-conditioner of the corridor, the blood would coagulate quickly. And it did... or it could just be his nerves. *Shut up,* he told himself. The Serperins were easy pickings, but it was a bad habit to allow his mind to wander off mid-battle.

The cut was so clean that the Serperin required a moment before he realized his hand had been chopped off, even with all the blood spurting out like a rogue water sprinkler. But before he could scream, Lucas helped him with his trauma by ending his misery all at once. Another flicker of light and a swing of his arm and the head was gone. The head flung onto the wall and made for a heavy collision. "You should be glad. At least you wouldn't have to adjust with living your life as a cripple," he snarled.

The headless body hadn't had the courtesy to answer, however. It dropped to the ground, soft and sudden.

The rest didn't put up much of a fight. How could they? Even a veteran soldier would fumble under the element of surprise, and definitely under the element of Lucas. He lunged on each of them the same ferocious way as he had done the other. The first tried to draw a gun like the first, but Lucas only needed to recycle the same movements from earlier and he had another head bouncing on the ground. A thick soup of red was bathing the carpet by then.

The last was smarter. He knew long ranged weapons were useless in this range, and especially since Lucas operated so swiftly. He had time to sheathe a knife out, as much good as it would do him. Lucas could tell even he was thinking that, eyes quivering like his hands. His yellow eyes like a cross section of a fruit, the slits that made his pupils were seeds, and the bands that grew out from the pupils were the fibers.

Lucas indulged him for a while, letting him slash and prod at Lucas. Lucas evaded or parried them all condescendingly. When he decided to stop messing with the Serperin anymore,

7

he smirked and all hope drained from the Serperin's face. He stepped forward when the Serperin made a final desperate thrust out, just inches away from the knife so Lucas' chest brushed on the fabric of the Serperin's suit on his arm. One sudden flash of his blade and his head was gone as well.

He killed all his guards, of course, and anyone and anything who might live to tell the tale.

It was necessary, it was for the greater good, as was drilled into him.

His boots squished into the blood sodden carpet and he kicked away a hand blocking his way to the door. He knocked on the door. He was taught to be polite. It would not do if he just barged in if the occupant was in the middle of something.

"Room service!" he shouted lazily. He looked down at the pile of bodies drenched with blood and frowned. "Oh, he would have heard. Never mind then. At least I tried to be courteous. No one can question that." When he paused, long enough to make sure the occupant was ready, he kicked the door open.

The blur of motion his leg made, the force on the door, and the clamor the door made when it swung and hit the wall at the end of its rotation added into a promise of action that wasn't fulfilled. It ended in a disappointing silence when only an empty room greeted him. The room looked like it had not been occupied. The sheets were neatly folded, the desk was clear of clutter and the stationeries and papers stowed at one side. The chair was tucked into the desk. The curtains were drawn out to unfold the magnificent view of the bustling District below and the azure sky above and then the sea that started not too far after a few rows of buildings after that.

Lucas allowed himself to enjoy the tranquil waters, swaying gently in half a hundred different shades of blue as it rose and fell under the power of the sun. The sea went on till the sky met it on a line thinner than Lucas' blade. It was so peaceful, it was something that was in scant supply nowadays, so he was loath not to take it in.

The glass panel that stood between Lucas and the view was soundproof so the room was exempt from the noise while its occupant could still enjoy the view.

It had just enough of modernity and nature to represent themselves while still harmonizing impeccably so they completed each other instead of competing for the limelight. It was perfect for a quiet afternoon with a cup of piping hot coffee at the side. To top it all off, there was no luggage or clothes to be seen anywhere. The occupant had been diligent.

The ploy would have worked if Lucas hadn't walked in… or if his prey had not shrieked in shock when the door slammed open.

Lucas snorted and shot out a hand into the room at the side of the entrance the door wasn't hinged on. His hand fumbled for a while until he found the familiar cold and hard surface of metal, forged into a shape even more familiar. Lucas grabbed onto a gun and yanked at it from below to snatch the chance of peril from being aimed at him.

A shot fired at an angle up, but Lucas' hand was underneath and far from harm. The bullet pierced through the gorgeous door and sent a shower of splinters fluttering at the other end. Lucas clicked his tongue in annoyance.

It was high quality material, intricately carved so its haphazard texture was pleasing to the eyes. "Hey, that door was nice!" Lucas complained. He wrenched at the gun harder and it came loose. He threw it behind him and pounced into the room. His other hand shot out to grab the Serperin hiding behind the wall by his neck.

The Serperin stretched his neck, baring his fangs as long as daggers as he tried to make Lucas' arm a sumptuous snack to chow on, but Lucas jerked his hand down promptly before he could have a maul at it. He shoved the Serperin away.

"C'mon, you can do better than that!" Lucas quipped as the Serperin's tail grappled for reprieve on the ground. Serperins had tails for legs. One would be mistaken if they thought they could slither slower than people with legs could walk.

The problem was that they weren't very good at catching their balance when they lost it, especially when it was as pregnant as an actual snake that had swallowed a rabbit whole. When he failed to regain his posture, he fell onto the bed.

"Help! Help!" the Serperin screamed, flailing his arms like a newborn unable to sit up on his own. This particular one was wrapped in bath robes. It was wrapped over his body loosely, and yet it still clung and took the shape of his bulging belly.

"You're too fat to fight, why did you even try?" Lucas laughed. "You should have surrendered the very moment you heard fighting outside your door. I am in quite the good mood today, so I could have made a special arrangement to spare them from their gruesome fates… as long as they promised me they wouldn't talk of this."

Lucas flung his head back to pretend that he was thinking. Then his cunning eyes fell back on the squirming Serperin. "And they would. They surely have knowledge of my identity. Yes, I think that would be sufficient to scare them." His face hardened. "Unfortunately, that offer has expired. They're too dead to accept it now."

"And me?" the Serperin whimpered still on the bed. He had partially given up trying to get off the bed. His movements sedated and he laid still, panting after just a few moments of what little form of action and what little fight he tried to oppose Lucas with. "It's not too late for me, right? You've not said that you have rescinded your offer either," he begged, all the indignance and dignity fled from him.

"You?" Lucas almost burst out laughing. "C'mon, don't act so oblivious. I came for you, why would I compromise for you? But there was still something in it for you," Lucas leaned in and stated in a lower, firmer tone.

The Serperin's eyes lit up for just a moment, but quickly sunk back when Lucas answered him. "At least you could free yourself from all this cardio," Lucas sneered at last. "Did you almost think you had a way out? C'mon, don't be so naïve."

"You mock me, child! How there you reduce me to such a state!" the Serperin jerked suddenly and Lucas nearly got anxious. He jolted to a defensive stance but the snake was just thrashing about trying to find the strength and angle to hoist himself up. He eventually slid down from the bed and used it to support his back as his rose.

"Nimble, elegant" Lucas smirked. He relaxed his shoulders and untensed his muscles. Though he left his blade attached to his hand. *This one is no threat. Even if he has a weapon, he'll be too slow to the draw.* Lucas' eyes flitted to the side for a second, noticing the open door and proceeded to close it.

He knew it wouldn't do much to dispel suspicion with the litter of bodies marked outside, but it would at least give the

11

semblance of privacy. This was nasty business he was involved in. A few more splinters from the bullet hole had rained down behind him. The bullet itself had torn through it completely and was firmly wedged into a wall at the end of the room.

"Who are you? What do you want?" the Serperin continued mewling.

"Trying to buy me?" Lucas said, intrigued. "How much would you offer me?"

The Serperin froze, surprised it would have been so easy. He did not even think to be skeptical of the sudden offer. "A million?" he muttered.

"No. Don't think you have the upper hand on the terms just because I suggested it first," Lucas retorted firmly. "But another zero behind that figure and I shall consider. I've looked at your records, you have far more than you reveal." He said it casually, as if bargaining for a second-hand item.

It seemed to give the Serperin the impression he truly was considering it. "Then we shake on it," the Serperin said tremulously, raising his hand. "No hard feelings."

"That's too easy, Baron. Really, you thought you could buy me? You did not even think that I was playing you? Do you think I'm stupid? Once I leave with your money, you'll just buy another gang of hitmen on me. As useless as they would be against me, it would be an inconvenience." Lucas narrowed his eyes. "And I'm hurt, Baron. For you to think you could buy me at such a low price, it only means you really weren't feigning ignorance. After all this time, you don't recognize me?"

"Who are you?" the Serperin squinted his eyes trying to recall.

Lucas sighed again. "I thought you would know me," he grumbled his disappointment. "No?" Lucas raised his brow. "Fine. I'll be blunt with a name you'll surely know. I'm the Ace."

"No! No!" The Serperin wriggled back again, but when his back touched the bed once more, he turned and steadied himself so he would not fall for the same thing twice. And then he tried to skid past Lucas towards the door. With his large and slow frame, he was easy to catch and shove back into the room.

"Really?" Lucas taunted. "You're trying to escape? Where will you go? Take the lift down? Or the steps? Can you even walk down steps? What foolish hope manifested in your stupid head to think you can outrun me? You cannot outrun death more than you can escape me, creature," Lucas said scornfully.

"You can go to hell!"

Lucas shook his head and pretended to let the words affect him. He made his next words clear he thought nothing of that offense. "You know, I'm still a little peeved that you just took all the fun out of this. You actually thought I was some run of the mill assassin people can just hire? But even that is more than you desire, scum." His face and tone darkened all at once.

The Serperin screamed again, an ululating, high-pitched one that would have sent a flock of birds flapping away from all over the District if not for the soundproof walls. Lucas' ears had to take the brunt of the scream spearing into his eardrums. He winced. After so many battles and injuries, he would rather take another stab than experience that again.

"Like your voice, Baron, my patience is running thin," Lucas seethed through clenched teeth. "Scream all you like, no help is coming. I do not intend to make this look like an accident. In fact, quite the opposite. I'll make this a brutal murder that would shake the country. Not that they will care. They will rejoice more than would be disgusted. Though if I were you, I would not prod on my temper any longer. The manner of your death will heavily depend on how much you continue to irritate me."

A smirk crawled up his face as if the Serperin thought of something brilliant that might save his life. Lucas let him wallow in his hope before he would take it all away. "What's so funny? Care to share?"

"There are cameras," he said. "They will catch you. And you have prominent features, beautiful blue eyes, a shaggy mane of brown hair, and those ludicrously large ears, and a prominent name besides. If you leave now, I will promise in my family's name I will forget this."

"No," Lucas acted shocked. "Your word and promise mean as good as dirt," he spat.

"It is the best you have. And generous, far more than you allowed me. The tide has turned huh?"

Lucas' face sloughed back to indifference. "Cameras which I disabled. Again, you insult me!" Lucas whined. "You know my name, but you still continue to put out idiotic suggestions. Are you desperate or truly stupid? Or have you not heard of me? You know I'm not careless."

The Serperin's stupid face snapped back into shock and his earlier desperation. "No, please! I did not mean to insult you. Please, let me live."

Lucas shrugged. "You know you should have put more guards; at least pretend you care for your life. Not that it would matter, I would still kill them all, but at least it will prove more of a challenge? No, a harder exercise. This was an appetizer.

And you know how unsatisfying having a meal is if you have an appetizer without the main course and then skip to desert."

"Desert? What are you talking about?"

"Yes, well, desert is you. Don't you know what I'm talking about? I'm taking my time in reveling in you, can't you see? Why do you think I'm delaying your death? Now, back to…" Lucas frowned. "Ah, never mind. Makes no matter what my woes are, I shouldn't be complaining. Some people don't get to eat at all even in this Era."

"This is against the law!" the Serperin tried to implore to the righteousness in Lucas' heart, but someone should have told him it was futile. The Ace did not balk. The Ace was heartless. He should have heard it all enough from the rumors. It only annoyed Lucas even more that the Serperin hadn't heard of them.

"They have found me innocent! I was found innocent abiding all the laws of this land, by under every regulation required of me. You saw it, you saw I was pronounced free, fair and square!" the Serperin begged and screeched, his voice rising and falling like a turbulent tide.

That did it. The words cut deep into Lucas' anger and for a moment, he lost himself. A flick of the blade and a pounce later, he found himself on top of the Serperin, one hand at his neck and the other with the blade pulled back so the tip was perched gently on his chin.

"You call that farce a fair trial?" Lucas whispered at first. "You call being tried under a panel of no good charlatans and sheep to be a fair trial? In a court you manipulated every inch of? You bought them all out! The sentence was a sham! And I will not accept such perversion of law!" Lucas' anger erupted

15

all at once. "So right now I'm taking it upon myself to do what the bunch of them don't have the mettle to. I will be dealing the judgement."

"Just because you don't like it doesn't mean you come crying or go on a killing spree! Power does not let you do that," the Serperin sobbed.

"Power lets me do exactly that!"

"Why would you do this? How can you be so merciless?"

"You have murdered, you have butchered children and women, some when they thought they were safe in their homes. Innocents! Innocents who had no stake in your fight! Where was the mercy for them? Tell me?!" Lucas raged, vaguely aware a flush had risen into his face to turn it into a deep crimson color, veins swelling at his neck. "And you are crying? Even you must see the irony. You have the presumption to kill your victims like this, then you must have the courage to fall the same."

No more dumb words rolled out the Serperins' lips. He gulped. His face sagged, knowing there was no other choice but to accept his defeat.

"And I remembered you have the nerve to call them collateral. Well, the smug smile you had then if washed off clean now, huh?" Lucas gloated.

The Serperin's eyes were filled with terror, even a hint of contriteness, and he knew the Serperin could see his wrath.

When the Serperin finally realized who Lucas was, he widened his eyes. "I see. It's you. Yruf sent you, didn't he?" his voice had become starkly soft.

16

"He didn't. But he would have if he knew. Don't worry, I would tell him all about how you met your end in disgrace; begging and squirming pathetically."

"You would inflict such humiliation on a royal family? This is not a good way," he murmured. "Go on, do it. The days where we Serperins were once considered a threat to be reckoned with are gone."

"No," Lucas differed, "it's only you who are weak. It's the reason your damn Region cast you out in the first place."

Lucas still remembered the damned creature's eyes. It was onyx, like two cracked, faceted crystals studded onto his sockets. Before the last light was snuffed out from it, it shone with detest and fear, though far less than before after he had accepted his fate.

Lucas could not decide which was stronger, nor did he dwell on it long.

Eventually, Lucas thought it rude if he continued playing with his food. A clean slice at the neck was all it took to end him. Lucas watched him writhe, claw at his neck, his tongue wriggling like a live flame as he sunk down as if he was melting.

He still remembered why he had not given the Serperin the mercy of a quick death. *You caused the EMA so many lives and so much trouble, so much headache, and then you have the audacity to make me wait in a charade of a court.* He didn't deserve to be put out of his misery, he deserved a slow, painful death, so Lucas made sure of it.

From the slit where Lucas opened, crimson seeped in, it looked watery at first, like the viscosity of prune juice, but soon it deepened into a majestic color and soaked the carpets. The blood flowed down in thin streams at first, then it cascaded

17

down in gushes. He could still hear the choking and ghastly gurgling sound the Baron made as he died. It was noisier than Lucas could have liked, but Lucas would be lying if he said he didn't revel in every moment of it.

Even when the Serperin was on the ground, he spasmed and still refused to let go of his dear life. Lucas made sure he eyed him as he died. He wanted the Baron to know he was not going to let him off the hook. If there was even the slightest chance that the Baron would be saved, Lucas wanted the Serperin to know that Lucas would not allow it to happen.

The Serperin was done, and there Lucas smelled the harsh and metallic scent of despair as he had seen a million times when people faced him. When the Baron had taken his last breath, all the tension in his muscles released. Then came the nauseating stench of bowels being unleashed. Brown and red that bloomed through the bath robes and the floor merged into a sickening color.

But that wasn't the worst part. The unease of his heart fluttered, tickling the cavity of his insides. He had done this so many times he thought he would be numb to it by now, but it seemed he would never be. The Emissary of death, he was once called.

But it was required. It was just. Yruf said so, so that was that.

Once he made sure the deed was done and the Serperin was fallen, he wiped his hands off the scene and left as stealthily as a spy would.

HELLO WORLD-2 (LUCAS)

Lucas had tried to sleep, but the voices wouldn't let him. The eyelids that glazed over his eyes fumbled and twitched as he tried. It was a nuisance he could barely tolerate. He knew full well the more you tried to sleep, the more your mind would resist you. No one ever won the wrestle with your mind for sleep.

He decided to give in and open his eyes. But when he did, a sudden rush of clamor erupted all around him. A throb in his brain sought to plague his peace and he winced. So much went around. Great beams of metal rose and curled towards each other, converging on a strip that went further than Lucas' eyes could compete. They were secured onto each other to form a structure that looked much like the skeleton of an ancient monster so large that it swallowed all the people around Lucas in it. If so, he was in the belly of it.

Glass panels covered the gaps between the metal beams allowed sunlight to pass through. The sun was at its zenith, it had climbed to its throne and so had its power, and about now it wanted to boast just how powerful it was. An aureole skirted around the sun, a blazing halo that sprouted out from the main sphere to make it larger than it should be. Lucas could not see the dancing flames on it, but he could sure see the surge of radiance it produced. The sun was frantically intent in making sure everyone could see that.

Where the light could not lance through, blocked by the opaque metal beams, it turned the beams into dark silhouettes when juxtaposed under its field of glory. If it could not pass, it was sure to remind anyone of its wrath. But the darkness was not merely saved for the metal. Even thin lines skirting around the metal streaks, the light never really touched, so darkness ruled.

The light ate the rest of what it could chew on, however, bursting through the windows and splashed onto the floors. The windows sparkled, decorated with bands and arcs of little rainbows. The dried water stains where a cleaner had just wiped shone in dull streaks, then water dappled on surfaces glistened wetly. The light threw itself onto the floors, walls, anything it could lay its noble fingers on, and was as bright as it was unforgiving. It left patches glowing onto the surfaces, some marred with reflections and distortions, others blotched with the mist left by the cleaner's towel.

A patch was cast just before Lucas' feet, and even here he could feel the warmth from it, slowly rising. He even caught one of the fibers of the carpet smoldering, but when he blinked it was gone so he decided it was just a trick of the eyes. Heat radiated from the floor, shimmering the air above, and that wasn't a trick of the eyes.

He could only imagine how hot the outer surface of the airport was if it was already scorching in here.

A flurry of activity surrounded him, which unfortunately, he had already been aware of when he had closed his eyes. His other senses compensated for what his eyes left a hole in. He

20

could taste the air. It was sterile and dry which if he sucked in too quickly, it made his lips arid and crack. He could hear the cacophony of noises. A few minutes ago, he could still make up some of their conversation. His busybody mind made it easy to shift from his thoughts to another and zoom in on other people's business, with a bizarre lust to understand what they were saying. It was mostly an annoyance than anything else. It meant that in crowded places he could never truly focus and have his mind to himself.

Slowly, the cool air from the air-conditioning was overwhelmed by the heat the sun above had put down on its subjects. If he could just switch off all his senses when he closed his eyes, it would have been a fantastic, nifty trick. But he couldn't and shouldn't. It would do well for him here, but on the field where a single vibration to reach your ears or a shift of the shadows or an odd smell could mean life and death. He had to be alert even in sleep and plugged senses was not a luxury he could afford.

The waiting gates where people boarded their planes lined along a large hall so it saved the airport from having to provide more screening areas than necessary. It was a long walk all the way till the end and it would have been tedious for the people who needed to go there without the conveyor belt to carry them there. With half of the people here overweight or out of shape, hauling or dragging their baggage all the way there would have been akin to running a marathon.

Where there were people, shops gathered.

Between both sides that flanked the conveyor belt were rows of shops that lined till the end selling overpriced souvenirs made of the cheapest materials and shoddy craftsmanship even by machine standards. Slotted among them were the customary cafes and posh food stalls. Other shops sold merchandise, shirts and books, but most related to the Region this airport stood in in a bid to milk what they could from tourists.

Some were just basic, ordinary shirts weaved in a mass-produced factory and stupid trinkets people would just chuck away but printed with the simplest designs that weren't even that nice to act as honey for customers. Shirts like those broke way too easily, and their threads jutted out after just one use which tickled and served only to annoy.

They were captioned with printed famous catchphrases of the Region or cheery quotes and a whirl of colors and famous landmarks to draw in tourists in the holiday mood willing to spend more money overseas. They were all flagrantly and shamelessly sold at inflated prices, knowing tourists who were desperate to find a last-minute gift for a family or friends at home would still spend.

Most shops had a modish design to it, simplicity was key and the colors alternated between hard black or unsullied white. Some decided that a more rustic or traditional design to swank with the customs and styles familiar to the Region would do better to attract customers who wanted a break from shops they could well see back in their home. Those had more wood and less metal and glass, and their interiors were more ornate, and decorations handmade and carved out.

There were several cafes serving typical café food at exorbitant prices with small portions and didn't even taste good. It attracted the most pretentious of people, and slowly Lucas could predict who would go in. Those with families, especially those who wore utterly bland clothes like they were going for a casual day at the mall refused to patronize such an establishment.

Those who were ludicrously dressed or clad in more skimpy attire walked in when they first caught sight of it. You had to be either of those, there was never any in between. Patrons included those wearing sweaters with turtlenecks, business people, old folks who looked ready to hit the beach in their aloha shirts and sagging jowls and half-dead eyes. A rare few with dreary or featureless looks who could actually use a cup of coffee was rare. But by far the most popular of them, and perhaps most ludicrous of all were kids the age of Lucas who he knew full well did not have the kind of money with them that should have anything to do with such extravagance.

They just want to show off, Lucas reflected. Especially among girls, boys did not even think twice before incurring such an expense. He had to admit that it was a classy place, however, looking through the glass panels that curtained the café. It was dingy as all cafes were, painted in all shades of brown that gave the atmosphere of sophistication and somber elegance.

Some studied there, some simply chatted over cakes and small dishes. Most ordered coffee. He was tempted to go in, by far the ambience here was rowdier than inside. But he wasn't hungry. He thought he was, but his stomach had been silent and defiant even after much coaxing.

A woman dropped her fork and it clattered on the ground, business people spoke seriously on their phones, wannabe artists holed up in their corners trying to concentrate with half a drink left in front of them which only the heavens knew when they were going to finish.

Most of them had probably been there for ages, they only took sips at a time on their straws. What was a cup that Lucas could gulp in a second became cups with pits that ended when they wanted to. They could stay there for an eternity if they wanted, a neat trick to grant them immunity from getting chased out. Otherwise, they would have spent too much on something Lucas knew would have taken a fraction of the cost to make.

Conversations broke out and ended at the same time. Some were loud and boisterous, howls of deep voices, sharp voices that were basically screams on itself, and then the dull but continuous blabbering. People seemed to be able to drone on and on while they chattered on frivolous topics. All the voices competing to overpower the next one, but in doing so they merely melded into a single mess of static that formed a particularly irritating peripheral.

His attention split to every direction the noise came, and it scared him stiff. Anxiety laid its keen, stiff claws on him, cold and harsh, and then it seemed to burrow into his body like icy tendrils, knifing a chill through his system. *Never put a soldier in such chaos, it distresses him, it reminds him...* Lucas decided closing his eyes were for the best after all.

He liked it when he closed his eyes. Sure, sometimes light would seep in and irritate the darkness, but for the most part, it was tranquil; nothing happened here and he was left alone with his thoughts. No one could trouble him, disturb his thoughts, nor could anyone attack him in here. Now, however, he wished his thoughts weren't with him, or at least have the grace to leave him to his own devices.

He deserved it, the respite from all the chaos he had faced today and the day before and so many that came before it. The line of work he was in entailed this, he knew well, but it never was any easier. Day and night would become fluid, sometimes weeks became a day and a year would fly by as quick as he could blink. He was there before dawn and battling with his fatigue at the twilight. So much happened, so problems grew like weeds in a garden; too many to eradicate and too few of him. No matter how you tried to cull them, they never truly went away. And when you took even a step back, the field would suddenly be swamped by them as if your hard work previously had meant nothing.

He didn't want to think about anything, but his consciousness refused to leave him, it refused to wander in the magical land of dreams. Instead it stubbornly stuck with him, and with it, everything he thought of. Then the voices came. He had once downplayed it as part of growing, another of the strange afflictions puberty cursed on him, but he knew now it wasn't that.

For one, it wasn't as forgiving as the pimples that would go away, nasty red spots filled with yellow pus. At least they had the decency to leave when they were done with him. Nor was it hair on the strangest, more obscure areas he could get used to. Nor was it… more queer thoughts that seemed to rouse something in him. Nor his broken voice, or the sudden shyness that took him when he spoke to other people, suddenly conscious of so many other variables he did not consider before.

Knowledge is a curse, he reflected drolly. How belittling for him to use such a profound statement on this juvenile context.

No, it wasn't puberty. These were more than that. It was merely a coincidence they had come at the same time four years ago. Even without confirmation, he had a sneaking suspicion of how it all came about. There was once when he was a tad more outgoing, a point in his life where the people who knew him would have said it was drastic. But then the incident happened. What rose so quickly, fell. Betrayal was rife and friends turned enemies. Enemies he thought as friends had been enemies

25

lurking and prowling around him, searching for weaknesses. The bitterness still lingered on his tongue.

In short, he had hit his head really hard. But Lucas would rather not think too much of it, he had spent those four years trying to forget it, why would he resurface them after all that. That birthed the voices.

Lucas, baby, are you awake? We love you.

It was more than he could handle. It disturbed him, and nothing much disturbed him in this world. *Not after what I have seen.* The voices always started the same. Laughter, a pure, blissful one of a man and a woman. Their faces never truly appeared in front of him, but it did not stop him from imagining how they looked.

Oh, you like that, don't you? You sweet boy. What a hunger! The voices were tender and gleeful. Sweet and rhythmic and smooth as honey.

In his mind, they were beautiful. He knew who they were. They were his parents. Who else could it be? Lucas never forgot a face or a voice, never. And he didn't know whose voices they were. So, the conclusion was natural.

You're going to grow up just like mommy. I bet you'll like sushi as well.

He had never seen them, but if he had blue eyes and brown hair, they must have had some resemblance to those features.

He never knew the context to what they were saying. But he always understood them, curiously. Then again, his parents probably didn't expect a baby to understand them. Their words probably didn't concern him, and if they did, it was always dumb-downed, soppy words. Plus, he did not need context to feel their love.

Towards each other, they always spoke in scientific jargon, playfully arguing or… arguing for real. They spoke of names he did not know too, and of office politics and people they admired and hated. They were *very* vocal when it came to people they abhorred.

That man is a jerk. I see him every day in the parking lot. I've got a thought that might one day cause me to run him over. The temptation! They would always notice Lucas was around to hear and then giggle nervously, hoping he would not understand. It was a reasonable optimism, he was a baby after all.

They must have spent a lot of time together, since their conversations had piled quite a backlog in his mind. And every time their conversations flowed into his head, the subject was always different. They must have loved each other a lot with the time they spent. It was rare if the two could spend more than an hour without professing their love in some sort of cheesy way that made Lucas cringe. It seemed the romcoms he found himself drawn to recently weren't exaggerating. What he thought couldn't have possibly existed in the real world did in his head.

I love you.

I love you more.

You hang up.

You hang up first.

Yet, sometimes Lucas didn't mind. He even longed for it at times. Such cloying sweetness was at times the best thing in the world, and at other times there was nothing he abhorred more. It only oscillated between that duality, never in the middle.

They spoke of the marvelous, miraculous world, its quirks and strengths, and the diversity and its ability to overcome hardship, and how it never failed to bless the world with brand new creations that spawned every Era.

They spoke much of how lucky everyone here was here too. There was much truth in that, with everything happening behind the scenes, Lucas didn't know how mortals could have survived till now. Either a celestial force was interfering with their lives, or it had simply been a string of lucky incidents.

Lucas yearned for them. A deep melancholy always settled in his stomach whenever the gush of voices came. He wished he could be with them; not merely as an audience to their joy, he wanted to be part of them. He wanted to feel his mother's love, he wanted his father to teach him baseball like all the other kids he watched in the movies, he wanted to complain to them, tell them of his day... but he knew it was a forlorn hope.

What strange powers of past Eras that could have made it possible were out of his grasp, and those who had presumed to invoke such unnatural forces always had consequences caught up to them. His ancestors had dealt with that Eras ago, he would not wish for this one to experience the same.

Now, he could only sit and cry hopelessly.

No matter how much he heard, they seemed a loving couple. They fought, but they reconciled every time. They gave each other names of endearment, they teased each other, and more importantly... he loved him. He knew that when they called his name in their tender voices. *Lucas, Lucas. We love you.* He would imagine them caressing his face. His dad would be a hunk, with burly arms and calloused hands. His touch would be rough, but with no less warmth than his mom. His mom was an elegant beauty, slender and sweet, with such soft, supple hands it smoothened his cheek to bring him warmth and affection. Such fondness had been so distant to him before, and yet now it was so close... so close... just a fingertip more to reach out... yet so far and impossible to reach.

The hairs on him ruffled as if someone was truly touching him, and they stood as goosebumps swelled. There were times he loved this, when he was lying on his bed with nothing to do, it was a great break from the tumult of the world. He did that once during an especially boring meeting, but Yruf didn't appreciate it at all.

Lucas disliked the feeling to disturb him when he was attending to matters; least of all paperwork, but most of all during battle. It just would not sit right in him, like he had eaten something funny.

In public though, this was the latter. It was shameful, he knew, it wasn't the right time to sort out personal matters, but he didn't care, nor could he remedy it anyway. He sniffled and allowed a tear to come running down his cheek, thin streaks blemishing his face, one of them had the audacity to curve into the side of his lips. It was salty as he expected, but the bitterness and his parched tongue overshadowed the taste quickly.

If you loved me so much, then why did you abandon me? He had no recollection of their faces since he had been given up before his brain had grown enough to discern how they looked. *If you loved me so much, couldn't you have at least spared a thought for my future?* Being abandoned was not the worst of it, they subjected him to a sort of life a child should never go through, not that he was any bad at it.

Hate trickled in him, forming powerful gushes of molten magma into his heart then flowering out. He did the usual. Many a times he had to face this, and he had learnt to

29

circumvent it. A simple grit of the teeth and coiling of his fists and it would go away, but this time it didn't. It hurt. It did. He wanted to whimper, and he could feel it rising into his throat, but a ring caught it just in time.

His eyes burst open and he whipped out his phone. The caller wasn't someone who liked to wait. He answered the call swiftly. "Hello, Sir? Is there a problem?" he spoke respectfully. He wiped his cheeks with the back of his hands as if the person on the phone could see him. Of everyone, he could not look weak in front of him, not to someone who had lived his whole life despising weakness.

It was Yruf, his mentor, his guardian, if there was only one person he knew he could truly trust in the world, it was Yruf. There were no secrets Lucas kept from him, he consulted Yruf whenever he had troubles and let everything he thought be liberally discussed with him. And Yruf seldom turned him away even in his busy schedule. He was not even his superior, or above that, or even above that, he was far higher than Lucas, the highest in fact, he was the Overall Commander of the EMA, an organization tasked with keeping the peace among all the species that lived in the world. If needed, it would use force, and Lucas often acted as his front line.

He liked to think himself Yruf's right hand man, Yruf deserved at least that shred of obedience from him after what he did. He took him in when his parents deserted him, and nurtured him with unconditioned, unreserved love Yruf knew to offer. While Yruf was a rigid, firm man by nature, a trait most important in his position, he tried to show his tender side when guiding Lucas and Lucas appreciated that. Behind Lucas' back, he was called all sorts of names; dog on a leash, slave, Yruf's middle finger he waved at his enemies. But he didn't mind. He took up the names with pride, he owned it, and soon all the names evolved into one that seemed almost reverent; Ace, a title usually reserved for the head of a pack of dogs, the alpha, the leader, the top dog. But silently, everyone knew it was meant to mock him.

"Lucas, after all these years, haven't we become closer than that?" the phone rattled in his hand. Yruf's voice was deep and resonant even coming from a phone, but it was this timbre that commanded respect from the people in the EMA. "Haven't I told you, son? In official matters and hours in the compound among other Agents, yes you should accord me by my rank. But unofficially, you can just call me by my name."

Lucas let a smile creep up, his lips bending into a crescent. "Yes, Yruf," the words sounded and *felt* wrong as it rolled off his tongue and touched his lips. He imagined it must have felt like addressing your teacher or parent by name to ordinary kids his age.

"You sound tired, are you ok?"

Lucas craned his neck forward and let his hand support his forehead. He wasn't sweating, but a varnish of oil had formed on his skin, another irritating affliction of puberty. He did not know what it was good for, or the dozen other weird growths that blighted him. Sometimes he felt like his body was just messing with him to make life harder, as if it wasn't already. He sighed. "It's... yes, I am quite exhausted. It's been a trying day."

"I expected it. But it's why I sent my most trusted man to the job. Harder than fighting, huh?" Yruf's laugh was a lion's roar.

Lucas nodded, knowing full well Yruf wasn't there to see it. "Yes, sitting still while waiting for the court proceedings to end is a torturous mission. Yruf, please don't send me for another."

31

His words had lost the force in them, and they all came out as a pant. There was some truth in his voice, a beg if not. But Lucas knew if Yruf sent him for another, he dared not defy him.

"Alright, maybe for a while," Yruf sniggered.

"I should have left after the mission was over. Isn't that why you sent me? To end the little rebellion?"

"Yes, that stupid… what does he call himself again?"

"Baron Von Selmy." Lucas groaned at the name. He was a goggle-eyed man with a stature of a child. He had only wisped of hair hovering over his head of brown patched that fluttered at the slightest breeze like a cone of cotton candy. But it was not his physical frame that made him terrifying, it was his mind. He had the size of a common rat but the charisma of a lion, and when he spoke, he bellowed like one as well. "How did that idiot rack up so much trouble?"

"You do not have to be smart," Yruf intoned ponderously, "all you need is a large enough mouth and a vigor in your voice and the masses will follow. Speak with enough passion, and it dulls the senses of even the sharpest of people. When enough people follow you then you can wreck the havoc this *Baron* did," Yruf made much effort to stress the word to show his contempt for the Serperin.

"Yes," Lucas admitted. Sometimes it was not the power of a single enemy that posed problems, sometimes it was the quantity.

"I severely underestimated that miniature doll of a man, I really did," Yruf grunted contritely, "but no longer. From now on, I will take each case with more… interest. I should have sent a squad to eliminate him when I had the chance." His voice was wrought with indignance.

"It's not your fault, Yruf. He tricked us, all of us."

Yruf's voice turned harsh and cold. "Yes, he did. But you forget, Lucas. I am not most men, I cannot be, for the peace of the world I cannot be. I should have seen it coming. Their deaths were on me. I should have known it wasn't just a normal protest. I should have sent more." Each word came out with more strain, more pain.

When the Baron's numbers grew large enough to be prominent enough for the EMA to notice, Yruf had simply sent a squad of agents down at the behest of the world, thinking it was enough to wipe them out. Instead, they proved far stronger and wiped the squad of Agents. Furious at the defeat, Yruf unleashed his Ace out, and Lucas took care of it quickly.

"He had an annoying voice to boot, too," Yruf said. "That was the icing on the cake. But I'm glad it's done. I could not have stood for more losses on the EMA's part. Our recruited numbers for this term have been worse than dismal. We are suffering a shortage, Lucas, and that would only mean you would have to take more trips." Yruf did not mince his words, whether he was being blunt to his underlings or nurturing to Lucas.

"I understand," Lucas replied. He should take it as an honor to work harder for the man he so respected, but part of him loathed more work, the human side.

"I'm glad we have you, Lucas boy. I fear we may be in a much worse situation without you supporting us to this extent. You certainly are more than an army yourself. The most portable, destructive army in the world," Yruf bellowed in pride. It made Lucas' heart swell up in the emotion as well. It was seldom Yruf complimented someone, and Lucas knew to cherish each one.

"So, was it difficult?"

"The battle?"

"No," Yruf snorted, "you already told me of the battle. And it was so long ago to still harp on it. You still gloated at how easy it was and beckoned to have me send you immediately when another one struck instead of delaying my hand. You said of how they wielded sticks and batons, a pistol here and there. You eradicated them easily, you said."

"It would have been faster if there were no civilians around. And it would have been easier if you gave me the permission to kill on sight. Many surrendered. Cowards," Lucas sneered.

"Well, to be honest, I don't blame them. You are ferocious. As expected, your abilities were nursed from me," Yruf boomed. "So, how many surrendered and how was your kill count again? It's all over the news, but I think it has more meaning if it comes directly from you."

"Hundreds," Lucas answered without a blink of an eye. It was a common number for him. Yruf liked to save him for the most dreadful of wars, and it only meant he easily racked up hundreds of kill counts. No one used a nuclear weapon to cut fruits, as was Yruf's justification for reserving Lucas' time to only dire battles like this. "But double the number survived. And you specifically told me not to harm the Baron, so I didn't. You should have heard him whimper, Yruf."

Yruf chuckled gleefully. "Ah, yes I too wish I was there with you, son. Alas, my combat days are over as age slowly catches up to me. No matter how strong, time will bring even the strongest person to heel. My limbs ache and sore, my joints are no what it used to be, and my instincts rust. Imagine if we

34

fought together, our battles would be glorious! We would be more undefeatable than we already are!"

"We would," Lucas reflected in dejection. He could only imagine now. Many times, he had tried to entice Yruf to join him, like how a son would ask his father to watch him play in a baseball game, or even get the chance to play with his dad. This was better though. "You were right. The noisiest of them are always the most cowardly. He did not even have the courage to take his life at the embarrassment of defeat. A pity I could not take him out quicker than I liked. He did not deserve so long of my time."

Their recent battle was the second time Lucas had clashed with the Baron's ragtag bunch, too impoverished to be even called an army. It had started in the Baron's hometown of the Serperin's Perch in the European Continent, renowned for its liberal laws, perhaps too liberal for it drove the disparity between the rich and the poor to form a gap larger than any other Region in the world.

The Baron was a distant relative of the royal house there, a blood of the lesser branches of the main family that occupied the upper caste, but still important enough to be named a Baron. Even if he had the right of it, pressing for equality among the rich and poor, he did it in such an unscrupulous way it didn't matter what he stood for. He murdered, in cold blood, people who disagreed with him and fought with fear rather than hope.

When he had become irksome enough, the EMA involved itself or there were fears it might fester into an international situation. After all, rebellions weren't dangerous for their powers, but their infectiousness. And the world was done with more rioting. As issues between the Purebloods, non-human creatures, and humans were a touchy subject, only the EMA could step in.

And then Lucas was sent forth to bring the storm.

When a whisper glided into the Baron's ears that the Ace of the EMA was coming down all guns and blazing with the wrath of the EMA, he turned and ran with his tail between his legs... not that he had legs to begin with. He slithered once he knew his cause was done for.

And Lucas did as he was reputed for. He set alight to all the Baron had worked for and culled any hint of rebellion from the people's minds. The battle was easy. Lucas was used to fighting well-trained soldiers who had earned their spurs and put many years and achievements on their belts, but these were mere civilians who happened to have weapons. It didn't change how they died anyway, blood still flowed out the same when their life drained from them. *Well, I guess they died more noisily.* The Baron ran to the Orc Nation of the Oriental Continent, a strict Region renowned for its authoritarian laws. But the Baron was no fool, he knew the Orc Nation would give him amnesty for the hostility they bore for the Serperins.

And so, they did, just for a chance to spite the Serperins for disallowances for trade and disputes of territory, they allowed a known war criminal in.

Yruf laughed again. "Ah, you're starting to resemble me. When I was your age I was as arrogant as you. Not that it's bad, don't listen to the haters, look what I've become! I would imagine the courtroom was a mess today? What was the verdict?"

"Yeah, I came here just for a stupid, long-drawn process. Well, at least they were fast in setting the court up... it really makes you wonder if this all had been planned beforehand, huh? Well, I was awake for all of it, but it doesn't mean I paid any attention to any of it. Anyway, the result was bad, Yruf," Lucas frowned.

The trial was at the top of the priority list by the Orc Nation since it had suddenly exploded into an international incident. "They just wouldn't extradite him. It only was made worse with him being acquitted by the court. Most likely he had resorted to bribery and threats against the jury. It was all just a farce to appease the First Federation. He had more than enough savings stocked up to pay off everyone in the room and still live a decent life here... a luxurious one even."

The Serperins were the richest of the Purebloods since the Perch was the most open to trade and tourism to humans out of all the Sanctuaries, a special connotation for Pureblood Regions. If even a lesser branch of the royal family held brimming coffers, Lucas could only imagine how rich the top of their society were.

Yruf groaned. "The Serperins must be livid. It would sure cause a problem for us."

"It has been solved," Lucas' voice turned starkly hushed and grim. "I... solved it for us. I knew the problem would arise and cause more problems in the future, so I took it upon myself to act..." The scene was still fresh in his mind as if it had just happened a second ago. The blood, the entrails leaking out, the dead body sprawled on the brown carpets that sponged up all the blood. A vacuum would not be enough to wash away the stains, Lucas knew. He still remembered the stone of hate weighing in his chest, and the fear emanating from the damned creature's onyx eyes and blood as it was life seeping from him. "As you taught me. It should be on the news soon."

He heard Yruf gulp. "I see. I was thinking why you had not booked the flight directly from the Orc Nation, but now it makes sense."

"Once I had done the deed, I doubted that the people there would treat kindly to a murderer... no matter how dangerous or renowned. Their law compels them to have me apprehended. So I saved them some more deaths, and wasted no time in crossing their border straight to the nearest human Region."

"Then you did well," Yruf said, matching Lucas' tone. "It might be shady, but I'm sure even the Madam President of the First Federation would sigh in relief. The problem is resolved. That's all that matters now." The Region of the First Federation was the largest in the world, taking up close to a whole Continent by itself, and it was the most powerful even among superpowers of the world. Conceived at the same time when the EMA was when the treaty was signed, it was the judge the world required to see that the world's laws were upheld.

"Yes, sir."

"Were there any complications? Did he... prove to be any trouble in the fight?"

"Not so much as bringing a knife to a gunfight," Lucas mocked. The fangs were less than useless to him. And what poison was stored inside had long been given the treatment of an antidote. Ultimately, he had nothing against Lucas. "He was a poor fighter. What could you expect? All the true Royalty the Purebloods have been wiped clean off this Earth."

"Yes," Yruf agreed, "and thank the Treaty for that." He sighed again and Lucas heard tapping off the tip of a pen onto some sheets of paper. The thuds reverberated down onto the wooden table that supported it all. "Well, I suppose I have to cover it up for you. Do not doubt that they will not suspect you even if you left no traces to be found."

"Even if I did, can they?" Lucas gloated. "No one has ever pressed charges even when I was at my most careless."

Yruf snorted. "I guess they can't. They are more afraid of you than the naïve notion of justice in their head. But I suppose you have the right here, even if your reasoning is not. The Serperins will be elated, I assure you. Once a person's need outweighs their silly notions of justice, they will celebrate. Most like they might even start to worship you. The Orc Nation would never raise a finger for their poor ally knowing they face forces stronger than they are. They are not the gambling sort. Practical, just the sort I like. And the First Federation would ignore it... as it usually does. Still, rumors in the public will spread to besmirch the good name of the EMA. And I will still have to do some corrections on that. Some of the Baron's followers might come for you, you do know that right?"

"I do not have a lack of enemies already. A few hundred more will make no matter," Lucas replied blithely. He almost yawned. "Let them come, I will even encourage it. It's been so long since I've been in a real battle where my heart pumped." Sometimes it was as if Lucas' life was simply a game simulation with no real threat to my life and all the hacks he would need. There was no more... thrill. "When will you give me something worth fighting, Yruf?" he jested.

Yruf roared in laughter. "Very well, then you forced my hand. Next time perhaps. But now, you rest. You earned it for closing this irksome case for me. But Lucas, I sense a little... uncertainty in your breath. It is a little disconcerting. Is something wrong?"

Damn it. Lucas knew what it was. The nostalgia from his parents' voices still lingered in his mind, wallowing his heart in a pensive energy that rendered to his voice. "Yruf I…" *Never mind would not cut it. He would know. Yruf is sharp. But why am I even hiding this from him?* It was a rhetorical question, he knew. Yruf had once told him his parents were homeless people too poor to support Lucas. They abused and beat him until they gave him up for some money to spend. Or so to hear from Yruf.

The voices told otherwise, however. His parents loved him, their voices as sweet as songs and birds chirping in the distance would not be amiss. They spoke about sushi and plans for the weekend, they laughed and cared. It was the opposite of what Yruf told him. *But why would he lie? He must have a good reason to.* He decided not to say. Yruf might get angry at the lack of faith for him. Before he could sort out truth from delusion, he must not let himself slip.

"You're right, Yruf. I'm a little disappointed. The Serperins… couldn't the law have been made better so people like him would not be let off scot free? Why couldn't he be triad in the First Federation where we live? I'm sure they are more just there. I'm sure they will find him guilty and extricate or even execute him." He voiced his concerns. It was a lie of course, but half of it. The concerns were real, but they veiled his true intentions. The best lies always had a hint of truth.

"I see, I could sense that much disappointment in you. But know this, Lucas. What you did was a just thing. It was right, for the good of this world and all the people in it. Was he an evil man?"

"Yes."

"Then he deserved to die," Yruf said coolly. "There are always injustices in the law, and it is up to people like us, people

40

with power to rectify it where weaker people cannot do anything to," Yruf explained. "I have said it many times, but I'm sure it is a hard concept to grasp for someone so young."

"If the law cannot dispense justice, then why call it the law then?" Lucas challenged.

There was a moment of pause. "Do you ever wonder why there is a board of lawyers to sort out the righteous lawyers from the wicked rejects... and yet there are still unscrupulous lawyers?" Yruf shot back with his own question.

"Because people make mistakes."

"Yes, and people are flawed, so naturally the things they create are flawed. The system is broken, it always has been. People are reduced to percentages in order to maximize the number of criminals caught and minimize the number of innocents punished. But what if you are that tiny percentage?"

"You have no choice but to accept it," Lucas said glumly, a sour taste in his mouth. At least his lie had worked, but he was beginning to think his cover up had less fluff than he had originally thought.

"It has long been broken, and people still want to cover it up. You want justice, take it in your own hands," Yruf decreed. "You understand, boy?"

"I do." *I've subscribed to that belief for a long time coming.* "But is there more I can do? There has to be," Lucas pressed. "This Baron... and many others I faced, are just small pickings, just a small puddle of wrongs to a larger pool. There are some things that I can't see, that I don't know. How do you propose I solve that?"

"There are always things you can't see, so don't sweat it. You're not some all-seeing deity, Lucas," Yruf said.

"So it's hopeless?"

"Maybe I have the answer, maybe I don't. Who knows? I have many ideas, and too little time to try them all. And it should be abundantly clear that for those I did, it failed. If I was so certain of the answer, do you think I would be someone who sits idle?"

"No."

"Yes. I would not stop until my vision has completely materialized. That is who I am, and who you are, I know. You take after me."

Lucas beamed.

"Bottom line is that an idea that has not been experimented with will always stay an idea. You have to keep trying new ideas, Lucas. That is the only sure way to be sure that they are useful or not. I would even take it a step further and say that a failed execution is still better than an idea. At least you know it failed, and that will be one less item in your checklist. Those who succeed aren't usually the smartest, they are the most stubborn ones who refuse to be disheartened."

Yruf sighed. "Ah, let's stop talking about such depressing topics. It has tired me tremendously. I had wanted to tell you this before you came back, but it seems you are in dire need of something uplifting. Your promotion is in order, Lucas. I managed to convince those grizzled old geezers, as obstinate they may be, to allow you to jump up two ranks instead of one. You deserve it, after all the feats you have accomplished for us... and in such a short time too. Congratulations Lieutenant Lucas, effective immediately, you are no longer a cadet. You are named an officer of the EMA. Your official letter will be given to you at a later date, but you can go ahead and flaunt your rank now. Anyone who says otherwise will have a stern talking down from me," Yruf said with the slightest semblance of pride. He often did this so Lucas wouldn't get too ahead of himself. Teenagers were... fickle.

Lucas grinned. It was good news, but under all the worries that clouded him, it was a mere taste of sweetness in the mouthful of bitter. He still tried to be happy though. For the longest time he had desired for this, and finally he was given it. *Oh, how my trainers will wail now that I have surpassed them,* he smirked evilly. "Thank you, Yruf. That is indeed... very happy news. I don't know what to say."

"Then don't say anything. Now enjoy your flight and rest well. You deserved it." Yruf hung up first as he always did. Lucas figured it was just some odd power play move. He slid the phone back into his pocket and reminisced about recent events. Things always seemed to move slow when he was at the moment, but thinking about it after, he would never fail to question how things got to this point.

It was like he had been a different person entirely from the Lucas just yesterday; one with feelings. *It should not have been so easy,* he reflected. It always made him wary when things were too easy for fear it was just a curtain to hide the true malice. But as he grew older, he started to get used to being at the top where no one could reach. He was powerful, and he single-handedly propelled the EMA to a threat far beyond any army in the world... except perhaps for the ones underneath the sea; though no one truly knew what occurred below. Not even the EMA.

A cursory flash on his hands revealed them dripping with blood. A pool had formed on his palms each and they congealed into a sort of slimy jelly. Some where it ran thinner on his hands traced the web of prints grooved naturally on them. He shook it and it went away. *I washed them already, they don't even smell, but they will never truly be gone.* Yruf had warned him of that, and he was wary to lapse into despair.

He glanced back longingly at the kids he first noticed at the café, teasing and making jokes on each other, laughing... yes, laughing, laughing and blushing and letting the hormones rush through them as they sought comfort with people their age. Fortunately, they had not left so Lucas could continue admiring them.

That was where he belonged, being merry and worrying about whether a girl liked him or if his crush reciprocated to his feelings, to have his worst fears only be having a test coming up on Wednesday. Not inundated with all these conundrums. Their postures made it obvious who liked who, and who felt awkward to another. Yruf would have called it silly, giddy, superficial talk, and the logic in Lucas liked to agree, but his feelings betrayed him.

Lucas narrowed his eyes and his mind. He could not think of such things. He closed off the ticklish feeling blossoming from his heart down to his legs. He assumed a stony expression. The thoughts of the voices still clouded him, however. *Must you plague me till world's end? Can't you leave me just for an hour? I deserve that, don't I?*

He reached into his hair and grabbed full clumps of hair and shook it wildly. He had a full tousled perm by the time he was done. He must have looked like he had just awoken. This mess only formed because of that incident four years ago. Yes, he was betrayed by one he called his friends. He was just another kid like him. *How could he?* Once, Lucas had been sorry for having to dismiss the boy, but now all sympathy for him had left Lucas.

It had been a gruesome, vicious fight. In the end, Lucas won though; but not without grievous injuries. A good hit on the head had resulted in all these troublesome voices. Lucas wondered where that boy was now. *Of all the individuals in the team, why must he be alive?* Assuming the boy was, then he might well be Lucas' only rival on this Earth. He was sure Yruf had not completely left the boy off the hook, but he dared not ask such a touchy matter. He clenched his fists and pressed it hard onto his thighs. The coarse fabric of the jeans prodded his supply skin. *Doesn't matter. If he comes out, I will just kill him like the rest. No one will stop me from supremacy. No one will stop me from delivering the EMA's justice.*

As his thoughts trained on, it broke when a pleasant alarm of his gate rang. It announced for the passengers to board the plane. Of course, the deeper the pockets, the faster you went in. And Lucas had sat right beside the counter just for this moment. He stood up quickly and shuffled towards the counter where a queue formed behind him rapidly. He had no such patience to wait for the leisurely crawl of old and obese slugs.

The stewardess had a full face of makeup powdered on, so much she must as well have worn a mask. Her uniform was blue chased with white stripes that sat on her frame nicely to give it a sultry, high-pitched accent. Lucas wasn't moved though. He had enough problems of his own, and the whimsical obsessions of the people his age were the last of his agenda. *I'm not them, I will never be. The road to glory is often paved with sacrifice. And I will accept it.*

The stewardess glared at him suspiciously as he handed his passport and ticket wedged inside. He couldn't blame her. He did not dress the part. Opulence did not appear in his wardrobe. He had worn a simple shirt and jacket. And he was only sixteen, besides. To everyone else, he looked just like any other teenage boy.

Most importantly, no one knew his identity, his true identity. It was for the better. Never had he been tempted to be some sort of celebrity. The truth of it was that there were no heroes in this world. No one was powerful enough to be one. Those who tried had long rotted to become soil. Either that, or they were, and they had no interest in using their powers for gaudy, heroic bluster. Lucas liked to think he was in between. He wanted to help, but too bloody a past trailed behind him.

The stewardess inspected the ticket and the passport he gave carefully as if she was about to certify jewelry. She smoothened the ticket and placed it close to her eyes. When she could not find any of the clues she wanted, she grunted, stamped the ticket and tore it reluctantly. When she was done, she folded it back into the passport and gave it back to Lucas, not without a final stern look.

"Well, everything checks out. I can't see how you ever got the money to buy the ticket. Aren't you a little too young to board on your own? Did you steal money from your parents? It's first class, you know. That costs quite a bomb," the stewardess said it more as a rebuke than a question. The people from the Oriental Continent had a distinct accent that was both elegant and hard to understand. They had a flair for making their voices sound so sweet and haughty at the same time.

"I know how it looks, but I'll handle," Lucas shot back courteously, but with a hidden annoyance that said not to pursue the matter. Usually, he would fly back to the First Federation by himself with his powers. But this time he had been so weary

Yruf allowed him a commercial flight in the highest class as befitted his role in the EMA. It was his first time flying, but if the price was getting stared daggers at every time and being second guessed by people who were meant to mind their own business and serve him, perhaps next time he might stay for a while before heading back on his own.

The stewardess did not take the hint, however. She pressed on. "You must be one of those social media models. Look at you, made so beautifully. Brown wavy hair and deep blue eyes, and muscular to boot. Your ears are a little big, but I guess that's part of your charm."

It was all Lucas could do not to groan. Being nagged at by his trainers was far more tolerable. When he was younger, he was often teased for his elephant ears. Now, after they had seen the carnage he could bring, he wasn't anymore. It had been so long since he heard that insult that it disturbed him a little. She wasn't worth spilling his secrets out anyway. "Yes, that's how I did it. Very astute," he said it with a spice of sarcasm.

She didn't take the hint again. "To earn so much, you must have shaken the world when you became famous," she complimented.

Lucas' lips curled up dryly. "That's one way to put it."

HELLO WORLD-3 (LUCAS)

The man went through the cardboard box of old nothings as he spun his office chair from side to side. He was a lanky guy so his lab coat hung on him loosely like a monk's robes. He was harassed with a receding hairline so his forehead was as shiny as a polished fine china. His hair was tainted with strands of white that silvered under the light. He had humongous ears that sat disproportioned at the two sides of his head. His eyes were the color of the ocean; blue, unwavering, determined, but had its junctures of mischief and volatility as well.

And he was busy sorting out items in a box. The items looked old and musty enough to have come from a previous Era of scientists; legacy items left by his predecessors of those who had worked in this very same lab. Old Cassette tapes, some equipment, stacks of grubby paper that were so dry they could crumble from a touch. The man tried not to, of course, but human error was inevitable.

His nails were smudged with yellow and his fingers smelled sour from the dust and slimy stuff he would rather not think about.

Lucas recognized this place. He had been to it often from young till now for his regular checkups and work related to his powers. There was still much unknown about the power in him, so they had to be careful. Even a small spike of hormones or a flare of emotion had to be closely monitored. As Lucas grew up, he went there less and less as he got better at controlling the powers.

At first glance, Lucas could tell that the man was a scientist in the research division lab of the EMA headquarters in the First Federation Region. The lab was retrofitted with the latest technology, stuff you saw in the movies. There were rows of tables lined with old research equipment, then sprawled all over with paper. At the back of the room were shelves and laboratory furniture lined neatly. Some of the shelves had spines of books facing outwards, others more irritatingly placed the opposite way where the pages faced. The rest of the shelves held scores of equipment and other subjects they were waiting to experiment on.

Most of the time, the scientists had more stuff to do than time allowed, so many research items would sit there as decoration for generations of scientists just to collect dust. It did not stop the EMA from churning out more projects for the scientists though. But while the work piled on, so did the money. It was good that the resources that were given to this lab were almost limitless.

The male scientist in the room, however, did not look like he was doing particularly important work. In fact, the task that had been set on him looked fatally boring. He was just cleaning up his area. He was shuffling through the old, musty items, then organizing and packing them into boxes which would then be transferred into crates. Or if something intrigued him, he simply put it aside. Stuff.

"Why are we doing this again?" the man complained as he closed the lid of his box. His brown hair was neatly combed and his blue eyes glimmered with pent up anger. He looked down at his laboratory clothes to make sure they were still white. "We are scientists for heaven's sake, why are we doing such menial labor?"

"Because our superiors said so? It is rare they all agree on one thing, especially this one ridiculous one. But it makes it all the more important to finish it, otherwise we risk spiting them all," another voice called. This time, it was a feminine one. Soft, graceful, but there was a dour tone in it. The woman was just beside him so she was within view.

While the man had his back turned to the side where Lucas could perceive his features, the woman had her back turned against Lucas's view. Either way, none of them knew he was there.

This wasn't real. It was a dream. He couldn't put a finger on what made his dreams and reality different, but he just *knew*. There was some elusive trait deprived of dreams that made dreams different, that made dreams so flat and stiff, mechanical and psychedelic.

But this wasn't a usual dream. His corporeal body was missing, and so were tons of other senses he had come to take for granted. He wasn't invisible, he wasn't even there. People said dreams had meaning, but if Lucas' body wasn't even present to be tortured, then what meaning could this one have?

Was it from memory then? No. This could be a memory of sorts, but it wasn't *his* memory, Lucas could tell. He didn't feel all that intimate with this memory.

This wasn't familiar… yet familiar. A sort of queer déjà vu. Something about the setting and the voices made Lucas' insides tingle. So it wasn't even a memory. *Then, what is it?* His thoughts were broken when the woman finally turned to face the man after he said "well, so what? We shouldn't follow every stupid order blindly."

She was beautiful. A face freckled brown on a dewy skin, white as milk. Her pupils were gold on white, and her lips were so thin her mouth was a slit. She eyed him incredulously. "Cole, shush," she said. *So his name is Cole.*

"No!" he cried like a child throwing a tantrum.

"Will you keep it down? What's the point of complaining, it just makes the job more dreadful!" she complained.

"Can't we just ask the privates to do it? I mean, isn't that why they are here? To do this?" the man named Cole ranted while pressing his hand on something cold and gooey. "Goodness, I just touched something…" He raised his fingers and smelled it. "Ketchup? Really?"

The woman broke into a giggle, the back of her right hand muffling the sounds.

Cole groaned. "Gah, fine. But can we at least take a break? We've been at this for hours. My hands are sore and I'm sick of sorting through Dr. Jared's research on fungi, goodness what were they thinking? Fungi? He must have gone into depression straight after he realized his work was worthless."

The woman shook her head. "You're mean, and you complain like a child."

Cole slouched and pushed away the box, causing a dent on the side of the box. "You know what, Colleen? You married this child." He smirked coyly.

"Fine," the woman named Colleen softened, she pulled out a CD from her box and shook it. The cake of dust on it cascaded down to the floor. "We're going to need to mop this place after this. But!"

"That must be the most advanced piece of equipment in this pile of junk," Cole sneered.

Colleen ignored his snarky comment. "Yeah, and it is our history lesson for today. You remember this?"

Cole leaned forward and his eyes tapered as he studied the article. His eyes widened suddenly. "Is that what I think?"

"It is." Colleen grinned. "It's our initiation video, the original one, the one they used for our batch when we first came. Of course, now they have switched up the video to a slightly more interesting one after all these years, but who could forget Dr. Rickman's delightful voice!"

"You mean his hoarse, guttural voice?" Cole sniggered.

"Now don't mock him, Cole." Colleen wagged a finger with a cheeky look. "Dr. Rickman is a revered member of our scientific community. It will be your mistake if someone hears of your snide about him. His voice, the honey covered onto butter, the one every single person employed in the EMA gets the pleasure to hear," she sang with infinite sarcasm.

Cole shook his head. "Pleasure, yeah right," he laughed. "I can't believe someone still kept this, though."

"Does it matter? It's for our benefit."

"I suppose so." Cole's head shimmied. "You want to watch it? Now?"

"Why not? Weren't you the one who said you were bored?" Colleen's brows pulled into a mocking curl.

52

Without a better idea, Cold shrugged and yanked it from Colleen. "Alright. I will set up the television. The CD reader has not been used for so long, I doubt it would work though."

"Sure, hotshot," Colleen melted onto her chair and spun around playfully while Cole fiddled with the console below the TV attached to the wall. When Cole opened the slot for the CD, a gust of smoke erupted out. He turned away in disgust and allowed the dust to settle before he dug his fingers back in. His eyes quivered in place as he focused on brushing off the dust and cobwebs inside. He placed the CD on the holder and the console ate the CD up.

Cole sighed and slumped back on his chair. "Gosh, that concludes my exercise for the day," he joked.

"Well, then that's one more than your usual," Colleen jeered.

"Ouch," Cole winced, though unable to refute the claim. The television let out an ear-piercing screech and static buzzed onto the screen of the television.

"Great...now even our source of entertainment is..." Before he could continue, the TV hissed more aggressively and black and white dots filled the screen. The screen lit up and a grizzled old man appeared on the screen. He was an old frail man with a badly trimmed white mustache and a beard and hair above his head that puffed up in a shaggy mess.

He sat on a table and before a wall that was all washed with white. His face was gaunt and wrinkled, his lips parched and his skin patchy with brown spots. The mark of the old video was made clear by its yellowish, spotted quality marred with a grainy texture fizzing like bubbles on a soft drink and distorting every few seconds. A continuous but low hum sought to further prove its age.

"Ah, our glorious, solemn Emeritus," Cole's eyes lit up and declared in feigned reverence. "You know, he doesn't look so frail in this video, in fact he was pretty good looking."

Colleen could only giggle. "Very funny. I guess you can say the same for you too," she joked and received a look from Cole. "Your turn to shush, let's enjoy this for once." Colleen rolled her eyes but did as he was ordered.

"It happened long ago, so long even our historians have trouble discerning when exactly it happened. Some say half a million years ago, some say just a hundred thousand years ago, but we can all agree it happened around there," the Doctor read in a gingerly tone, soft, raspy, yet in an imposing volume. He paused for dramatic effect every once in a while. "After a long and brutal war, the tribes of the world agreed to end the war by signing the Treaty of Civilization. This treaty provided an explicit set of rules which promoted peace among the various species and allowed all the races on the planet to coexist and live together.

"Many of these rules prohibited the Purebloods from fashioning new machines or birthing people for war that gave them their superiority in the first place. In doing so, there was a sacrifice of much culture and ancient practice, both ones that were vicious and obsolete, and ones that were good.

"Most, however, thought that it was a worthwhile tradeoff. Even if some good was lost in the midst, if more heinous ones than good were cut down, the overall direction will still be progress. And if not, the reclamation of virtue will let new ones flourish.

"That was what happened, and it was what shaped the modern world.

"Vampires and Werewolves stopped all hostilities, Angels could once again roam the lands and the people under the oceans were welcomed to walk among the surface dwellers for the first time.

"While the diplomacy was rocky at first, it gradually smoothened. Soon, interbreeding between species happened. However, interbreeding among our various ancestors did not create super-beings with multiple powers as prophesied by the sears and magicians of their time. The dilution of bloodlines caused species to lose their individuality, forming beings with no wings or horns or teeth that could suck blood from prey. It created an entirely new species with no distinct defense mechanism. A species so weak no one thought would survive.

"Alas, we did. And we called ourselves humans.

"Presently, 90% of the Earth's population is made of humans. We have split into Regions and that bloomed a myriad of exciting cultures… and unfortunately, disastrous wars as well. As weak as beings with little to no abilities might seem, our propensity for violence did not diminish. Sadly, we have not yet grown out of this horrendous habit.

"At the same time, the rest of the more conservative Purebloods lapsed back into obscurity seeing that their numbers were slowly diminishing as the world began to overrun with humans. They segregated themselves once again, ironically, at the height of the Earth's diversity. Those beings who remained chaste kept their blood pure. They remained in their own Regions, with little to no contact with the rest of the world. Lucky for us, we are all slowly coming back together to restore our former glory.

"But peace amongst different species is always a fragile one. Thus, the EMA was conceived, dreamt to be the paragon of peace for all the species in the world to bow down to. Our first intent has always and will always be to protect these primal species and keep them from squabbling among themselves. At the forefront of technology and science, the EMA serves to provide a considerable force to maintain peace. They act as the mediator between humans and Purebloods, making sure that contact between the two sides is minimal.

"They have done such a good job most humans have little knowledge of Purebloods. Some even regard them as myths or conspiracies by the government to scare off opponents. However, my good friends. If you are here, then you must be very aware that these creatures are real. Do not fear them, for they are just like you and I.

"Don't trust me? I don't blame you. You may say I'm biased, of course I would take their side when I have worked and gained their trust all my life. But you forget that I once sat at the same spot as you are now, facing toward yet another old geezer pontificating. Then, I must confess, I had thought all the EMA was good for was to suppress these creatures.

"But not long before I met the first Pureblood that my perspective changed. She was a Wildcat, with a majestic mat of fur of pure white as snow. She had fangs, ears were at the top of her head, and her eyes seemed to be rheumy with malice.

"Stripes corded her fur here and there, though I couldn't see much as she had been covered with clothes. More specifically, draped with a robe, to preserve her modesty just like we do. Ah, I still remember well." The man on the screen lifted his gaze and stared wistfully away, eyes glassy and plaintive. A coquettish smile drew out when his eyes went back down to face his audience. But it was not the tasteless and salacious sort, there was a nostalgic delight in it, happy that he had just relived those memories.

"She was a head taller than me, and shoulders twice as broad as mine; though I must admit I am not what you would call a fine specimen of a human, heh.

"As one from another species, I did not feel physical attraction to her. But she was slender and her features were sharp, so she could be popular to her own species. Even so, the claws on her paws were so sharp they could have stabbed me there and then. She looked so devious, so sinister like what the rumors my seniors spoke about. I was afraid, and at first, I dared not approach her.

"However, when she spoke, her voice was crisp like a freshly split cracker. And she was intelligent. Her laugh was infectious. She was very funny, very lively. She saw I was uncomfortable with her claws so she retracted them no problem. And suddenly I didn't see her as another species, as if she was some zoo animal I had to take care of. She was just another person like you and me, with thoughts and feelings. I didn't see our differences, her claws, her diabolic eyes, her ears, her fur... no, instead I focused on our similarities.

"And once I overcame that, I shocked myself. They were just like us. She didn't look like a peculiar creature anymore. And of course, I would speak of her in such endearment, I married her, heh. And we had three beautiful children. I would be lying if I said that we didn't struggle. Relatives and friends gave us a hard time, society did not accept our relationship. We were teased and mocked. But I would say that it was worth it. I had to often remind them that this was how humans ourselves came about, and what we were doing was nothing new. In fact, I was the only following tradition.

"And I like to think I played a little part, however small it was, in restarting a new Era that would shine as bright as the more inclusive Era before.

"But before we delve into the marvelous possibilities of the future, let's get back to the part to where we started. How did the Treaty of Civilization come about? Who were the brave heroes who came to save the day? So many Eras, so many layers to explore. My friends, we are about to find out—"

The television made a splutter, the flickering lines fizzled to their demise. "Alright, we have had enough," Colleen said as she stood up to turn off the television.

"Why?" Cole whined, "It was just getting to the good part!"

"We have things to do," Colleen growled sternly, "like pack this place. Don't you remember?"

Cole sighed. "Yeah, yeah," he mumbled. He spun his chair just to relieve his indignance. It stopped when he faced Lucas and his eyes glittered. He looked straight at Lucas and smiled. *He can see me?* Appalled, Lucas wanted to turn and run... but where did his legs go? Wait... he couldn't even turn his head. He was paralyzed. *No, I'm not even in my body.* It was an odd feeling, like he was some wraith who had become an audience to these two people.

"Wait," Cole said. Lucas' heart did several flips.

"Wait what?" Colleen turned to match the direction of her husband's eyes and Lucas realized the words had not been directed at him. "Why not have some fun with you, first? It's been a long time since we fiddled with it, after all," he picked Lucas up. No matter how much Lucas tried to squirm or thrash his way out, Cole's hands did not seem to feel it. Oddly, Lucas could not feel himself being picked up. All he could do was *see*.

58

Cole brought Lucas close to his face to inspect him, so close Lucas could see the pores on his skin. A zit was about to explode at the right edge of his forehead hidden by a canopy of hair. It was yellow at the tip and engorged red at the base. He turned to Colleen. "What do you say?"

Colleen shrugged. "I don't think anyone's going to check up on us anytime soon anyway," she allowed. "Why not."

Over Cole's shoulder, Lucas could see himself on the glass panels that forded the laboratory to partition it from the walkways outside. A reflection. But what he saw had no semblance of a face. *It is not me.* Instead, he saw a rugged Cube with the texture of hardened lava, with the black rocky parts protruding out and the fissures between the outer chunks glowing blue. It looked like a meteorite, but the organized blue tessellations streaked on it made clear it was designed, and not a mere product of nature. It was something alien, if not to the humans… then to the world.

Lucas recognized it instantly, no… he recognized everything and everyone in the room… and his heart skipped. He wanted to get out of there fast, but no matter how hard he squirmed, he was but the mere Cube.

Lucas' vision switched to black in a second as if it was a television screen. His eyes burst open and they quickly went to work to absorb all of his environment, a habit to discern if there was any immediate danger to him. He rubbed his eyes to make sure they were real eyes, and then flailed his arms wildly like a psychotic person to make sure his arms caught the drafts of air.

Yes, it was real enough. At least the throbbing headache and the stinging in his eyes was real enough to convince him so. It was only then he realized. The dream he had were full-blown dreams, when before they had just been voices.

59

He took a while to collect himself before he allowed his eyes to wander.

He was in his own little cabin seat, he could discern it well now. His mind was still foggy as he tried to remember the order of episodes that led to this moment. He had been at the airport, he was ushered into the tube into the plane then straight to his seat by a personal attendant, bestowed with all the proper courtesy a person who paid extravagant amounts of money would expect. Then hadn't he wanted to enjoy the amenities afforded to the First-Class passengers? He supposed he hadn't had more energy after that.

He tried to dig harder, but he surmised there was so little of it that they were irrelevant anyway. Most likely he had drifted off into a deep sleep right after he had sat down.

His seat was wrapped with a fine leather, burnished and smooth, not like the dry and flaky texture cursed onto lower quality ones. And it had that rich, earthy scent that Lucas loved so much it could well be an addiction. Lacquered wood acted as his seat rest and table in front, so shiny it would have been glossed with a layer of glass. The wood was a mahogany, with twisted stripes that embellished its surface.

The rest of the private room was padded much with cushion and hollow walls, and pockets brimmed with fancy, branded goods all wrapped in their gorgeous wrappers or boxes with cushioned insides, gilded gold outside and decorated or even studded with crystals that must have costed half of the item's price.

Food had not come yet, the ostentatious snacks that he had been saving his stomach for... it could be that he had slept through service. Lucas frowned. He knew they would be too polite... or scared to disturb a customer, but he now wished they did. Unlike the other rich passengers in this aisle, this wasn't routine for him.

Didn't matter, he would ask for his food later, and they had better hand it to him. In the meantime, he could snack on premier grade nuts and crackers, most of them flavored with rich and expensive spices. And there was a fridge packed with drinks below; not that he would touch them, Yruf had drilled in a habit not to touch those sorts of trash.

Yruf had once called the act of drinking such garbage profane, like gulping down sewage water. It had become so ingrained in Lucas that he winced if he even touched the stuff. The effervescence from it made him feel like it was dissolving him away.

The first-class seat was more than a seat, he was accorded his own little cabin that could be enclosed with a sliding door if he so preferred his privacy… or if he loathed his neighbors. It was his first time, so he had decided to give his neighbors a fair chance. So far, he had not thought it necessary to close it fully, though the verdict wasn't conclusive; most of the time he had spent here was asleep.

Outside, the plane was cutting through fluffy white clouds made of evaporated milk. The sky was an azure calmness that spanned as far as Lucas could see, and he was so high up that even the horizon was yet to be seen below, covered up by distance and a mist formed by so many layers of sky and cloud. The sun was nowhere to be seen, but that hateful thing was far from welcome to shoot its rays into Lucas' windows. He had been seared enough in the airport to yearn for more torment.

The sky was illuminated exactly right, with enough light to appreciate the infinite, boundless sky and not enough to feel uncomfortably hot.

He felt the vestiges of the dream fading as quickly as his wits and memory coming back to him. He grabbed what he could and stored it into his head, replaying them as frequently so as to make sure it would not be lost to him. He could decipher the scene now, and his mind got to work promptly, now having been recently rebooted after a good rest.

"The voices," he murmured longingly. It could just be a trick of his mind, showing him what he wanted to find. The voices may have been warped to sound higher than they were, but the mannerisms and tone they used were all congruent to the voices he heard previously.

And it only made sense. The voices were only two, and here he only saw two. The people looked pretty much the same as he had deduced from their voices, except the man was taller and skinnier. He had the same ears as Lucas too, there was no mistaking those elephant ears. Lucas caressed his left ear tenderly as he thought about it. He expected warmth, but his fingers were frozen stiff and frigid. It gave several unpleasant jolts knifing through the rubbery flesh of the ear, rejuvenating the pain receptors he had been eager to play host to again. His ear was oily with wax.

They worked in the EMA? Why? Weren't they homeless? Conversely, they were alumni to me in the same organization. Then why would Yruf lie? It only made the lie more insidious. Yruf must have known his parents, then. Yruf prided himself as a science and technology advocate. He spent as much time as Overall Commander as an unofficial scientist. He would have known their names. *Then why couldn't he just tell me? And why would they give me up? They must have earned good money. What happened?*

So many questions bombarded him, more so than before when he had not a clue of what they looked like. And the Cube... his senses were jolted full blast when the ululating yell reached his ears, like a spear stabbing into his ear drums. It stung. Lucas bent down and covered his ears, instinct honed out of training.

The sound was one kissed... no, smooched in pure terror. *Somethings wrong,* Lucas thought. That was not the scream of one who had gotten into an accident. It could only have been something hostile. Whoever it was, it should not count its lucky stars to have chosen one with a groggy, peevish Lucas aboard. Lucas' eyes burst open in its deep blue that varnished them when he concentrated. He reached for his buckle and unlatched himself free of his seatbelt. Then he spun out from his seat and landed at the aisle beside it.

His eyes scoured the room at the direction of the voice, but there was no offensive scene in sight. Oddly, the other passengers didn't seem that disturbed. Which meant the scream came from another cabin, in the business or the economy classes cabins.

That's bad. Lucas had never been put in such a situation... Yruf wouldn't allow him to be put in such a situation. He was meant to be the storm to rain down on everything when commanded; foe or friend. A hostage situation was possibly the worst place he could be placed in.

But that was not to say he had not been trained for such a scenario. Yruf had made sure he was skilled in everything that included a hint of combat, but only placed him at where he specialized at. Yruf was good at sniffing out the strengths and weaknesses of people and giving them assignments that suited them.

This wasn't his element, so all the rules he was so used to before didn't apply. Lucas had to be careful where he attacked now, killing even one passenger was not a good look for his resume. He hated that restriction... but in a hostage situation, he had to consider the worst; there was more than one assailant and he had to play it safe.

Or... that could be another way. The soles of his feet sprang up into action and he darted through the corridor, shouldering past people and stewards and stewardess pushing carts. The sea of people in their seats merged into a blur. Time was of the essence in such a situation, giving too much time for the assailants or terrorists to act was only going to disadvantage him.

He came to the scene in a blink of an eye. It was fortunate, his worst fears had not been realized, but it did not lessen the offence he was seeing. It was nowhere worse than a terrorist, but it was not a poor description to call it a hostage situation.

A man on one of the seats had his arm around a stewardess' waist. She was clad in the same outfit as her other colleagues, but her face was gnarled in revulsion. She was trying to wrench free from his grasps but he kept snatching her back where she could get an inch away. His arm was thick with muscle, so hairy it formed a new layer of black fur on his forearm. His head was facing away from Lucas, but he decided he didn't like his face anyway.

The rest of the passengers were slicked with worry and outrage, but none of them were bold enough to challenge the burly man. *It's up to me then, it's always up to me.*

"Hey!" Lucas bellowed. Yruf once told him that when commanding troops or threatening the wicked, he had to use the tone of a commander to flaunt strength, to be unyielding and powerful. He channeled that advice to his voice now. "You get your grubby hand off her!"

The man turned around and released the stewardess instantly. "What?" the man howled incredulously. The stewardess hopped back in fright, and her lips trembled like she was about to say something. The man whirled around and stood upright. He loomed over Lucas, twice the size he was and with half the brains withering expression and beady eyes. He had a heavy, voluminous beard, lit up with red which was the same with his hair. He wore a thin checkered shirt that pressed close to his bulging figure. *I was right to hate this type, the browbeat lumberjack.*

The lumberjack was about to say something, but Lucas would not give him that chance.

You think I have not faced big guys like you? I've faced bigger, and will face bigger. But they always fall when they face me, and they all fall hard. He pounced forward without hesitation or waiting for the man to explain himself. He looked like he was about to, but Lucas didn't think it would involve an apology. "You picked the wrong plane to perform your lewd acts, you degenerate scum!" Lucas yelled as he leapt up to thrust a knee onto the lumberjack's neck.

The force was enough to topple him and he thudded onto the ground with a boom. He grunted, and tried to reach his brawny arms onto Lucas, but Lucas had predicted that. *Offense is the best defense.* He spared no effort to evade the snapping grasps. Instead, he flung his left arm behind. Immediately, the skin on that arm cracked and fissures slithered out from his fingertips, chasing all the way to his bicep. Then beneath the fissures surged a brilliant blue light.

The people around gasped, some might have peed their pants, others might have fainted. He wasn't paying any attention, but it was not an uncommon sight to Lucas when people first saw his powers activate. The skin on his arm seemed to shrivel and peel off, but they only protruded out with metal joints within his flesh to hold them out.

All at once, they splintered into a million tiny fragments of skin and then a spiral scaled them to blue. They made clanking noises as they did, a very satisfying, metallic noise Lucas was familiar to. It was too fast for the eye to see, but they locked into place one by one like a jigsaw puzzle. In a heartbeat, his arm wasn't an arm, his flesh wasn't flesh, it turned into a blade that gleamed silver under the light, one made of a material the mortals had not even discovered yet.

It was armored with black foremost, and then blue glowing stripes flowing down where the black, craggy material would not touch each other so it looked much like many splitting streams of water coming down a black slope of a mountain. When the blade was fully formed, the light show ended. He turned his arm and it turned back to its original blue, now that the blade was facing the light above and cutting out what shafts of luminescence that came towards it.

Expertly, he swerved the tip of the blade towards the lumberjack's neck, just shy of piercing the skin. It tapped onto his supple flesh, but Lucas would not kill him... not for this crime. The lumberjack may be vermin, but he scarcely compared to the other foes Lucas had fought with.

The lumberjack had paled like curdled milk and his eyes wide with equal parts awe and petrified. His forehead was clammy with dappled sweat. "What in the world?!" His hands had shifted to surrender. "Who... what are you?" A collective gasp rose into its crescendo as more people saw he was with a blade, and then silence broke in when they realized he wasn't holding the blade, the blade was part of him; like a mutation, a cancer tumor armored like solidified magma and then growing out into a clean, honed blade.

"You dare speak after what you have done?" Lucas seethed.

"Done what?" the man looked genuinely lost and by turns startled.

"You know what you had done!" Lucas' voice rose but his tone deepened until it came out a roar. He could feel the veins swelling out of his skin and throbbing, a lurid red had taken his face.

Lucas felt a tap on his shoulder and his other hand had almost shot out to parry what he thought was an oncoming blow when he saw the stewardess the lumberjack had harassed. She had pale golden hair flecked with white "I'm sorry," Lucas jerked his arm back and retracted it. His tone softened, "I'm sorry what you had to go through. It's alright now, I've got this."

The worry that was written plain on her face, Lucas had initially thought had been brought on by the lumberjack. But with each passing second Lucas' eyes were set one her, it was becoming more obvious that it was transforming to something else. It was more disquiet than petrified, and more leaden than screwed with daze. If there was any hint of fear in her look, it was for Lucas. It slowly dawned on him the situation was not what he had thought of. "What?" was the only word he could manage.

"You misunderstand, Mr.," she said in a dropping voice, her accent rich with the wiry and hasty oriental accent.

"You're afraid of me? But I saved you?"

"He was just teasing me," the stewardess explained in a trembling voice, sounds rubbed raw with fear at Lucas' marked change in tone.

"And that's alright? I saw how he held you. Such disgrace should not be the norm," Lucas put in pointedly, clenching his jaw.

"No," the stewardess said again, less timidly this time, "he is my husband. We do this all the time. We don't get to see each other often with my schedule, and..."

It was all Lucas could do not to slap himself. No wonder she and the lumberjack that was her husband had tried to say something. *You paranoid moron, what the hell have you put yourself into.* The tip of the blade jerked back. He quickly recoiled his arms. The mutation on his left arm whirled back into flesh much like the process previously, except in reverse. Then he rose and averted the leaden looks he got from everywhere. Bashful could hardly describe his embarrassment, he was aghast. *Oh, Yruf would have some work to do,* he thought. "I'm... sorry for the disruption folks, I truly am. I saw something that I thought was one thing but it turned out that... ah you get the idea."

He had to say something or the passengers might think he was not only a psychopath, but a mute one as well. Those were dangerous. "Please do not spread what you have seen today." He knew the comment was redundant, but hopefully some of the more sensible ones would have seen enough to think of him as a threat to comply. He looked down to the lumberjack and bobbed his head short of a bow. "I'm sorry, I shouldn't have done that," Lucas managed, soft and desultory.

The man was still recovering from the daze Lucas had put him in. He batted his eyes and used his hands to feel his body

68

for any other injuries. Then his eyes skewed towards Lucas. "Who are you?" If there was accusation in his voice, it wasn't pointed out.

"I'm a Halfy," Lucas said, loudly and confidently so if anyone were to prod or spread, the lie would sit better with everyone.

"A Halfy? So one parent is human, then the other? What is your other half?" there was more curiosity in his voice now.

"That, you do not need to know," Lucas said, perhaps a little too harshly to someone he just mistakenly beat up. But the man would understand, most Halfies liked to keep their heritage low-key. Lucas turned before he saw the man get up, then screwed his face with shame.

As he strode back to his seat, he could feel the weight of their stares tickling his shoulders and back, a hundred eyes at once glowering at him like he was some maniac. *I deserve that.*

He heard them mutter and utter among themselves, spreading rumors and speculations. As more of them got bolder and more joined in the prattle, suddenly the airplane was abuzz with a low, but incessant humming.

Luckily, he did not once hear of the dreaded word; Ace. He only hoped it would stay that way. He would still tell Yruf for good measure, and Yruf would initiate the proper protocols to protect Lucas' secret. He didn't think it would be necessary, but if it so happened someone put two and two together, the protocols would be handy. Most of the time, things could be settled with hush money, but the more bull-headed ones... Well, Yruf had his own ways of handling them. Yruf had his ways. They were legal, but legality didn't mean pretty.

But it was for the greater good.

When he finally got back from the aisle of glares, he had been nicely toasted by the intensity of them all. He sighed and swung himself back into his seat and he sunk in, the humiliation weighing him down. He ruffled his hair, it was slick with cold sweat and some strands had stuck themselves on his skin. This time, he decided to close the sliding door to provide him with some much-needed respite from the rest of the people on the plane. What actions he had intended to be a heroic, now made him public enemy number one.

It's as if I became the true terror, and not Mr. Lumberjack. The door closed and he was left in peace. A nice tranquility flowed in. Lucas decided he wasn't going to go out of his little cabin any time soon, and he would have to drop the request for his food to be served to him. *The voices are affecting my judgement, they're elevating my already skittish nerves.* He decided he would not visit any public places anytime soon too.

At least it gave him some much-needed quiet time for him to ponder on what he had dreamt. He began to recall back the dream he had. Fortunately, his mind worked differently than most and Lucas never once forgot something that he had synthesized into his head. *To be honest, that's most people, but they just forget where they put them.*

The Cube he saw reflected from the glass knew just too well, its appearance imprinted in his mind. He had never seen it for real till the vision he just experienced, but he had seen enough pictures to know what it was. It couldn't have been anything else. It was too unique to be.

The Cube had once been the talk of the scientific community. It came to Earth in a meteorite that fell somewhere in the Oriental Continent, but for a long time no one knew what

70

to do with it. Scientists had tried to trace its origin, but only ever failure greeted them. One thing was clear however, the thing had come from somewhere far. Further than Earth's solar system, the Milky Way, or millions... even billions of other galaxies closest to Earth. The scientist who got the furthest claimed that the thing had simply suddenly appeared and made its way to Earth, but it was common consensus he made it up to cover his failure, made more devastating when he had hyped it up to be the breakthrough of his career and the Era.

Interest for its origin fizzled away when people began thinking about fiddling with the thing instead. It was clear from the get-go that the thing was alien, a product of some intelligent lifeform. It had to be, this Cube was the most intelligent Earth had ever created. And it meant that there were other things out there. Of course, it scared the hell out of everyone on Earth, and it ushered in a great rush to figure out what the Cube held in case Earth ever needed to combat a foreign invasion.

The Cube was passed around from Region to Region in hopes that someone might find some use of it. Many hypotheses were conjured up, most along the lines of infinite power, a map to the universe, or a trove of technology far beyond even what humans thought possible; most of these fantasies that the mortals on Earth sorely needed to evolve. It was the next gold rush, people said, except no matter how much people dug, nothing was ever yielded.

No one ever found out what it truly contained... or if it contained everything they had wished for instead. That was the official statement by the EMA which had been responsible for managing the Cube.

One day, suddenly, the Cube vanished.

No one knew where it went... except for Yruf and a select few. He had done a good job covering it up with his vast network of influence and power, providing excuses and conclusions that pointed that the Cube was nothing but a measly, disappointing piece of rock.

Of course, it wasn't the case, not by a long shot. And so far, only Yruf and some of the top dogs and scientists knew where it had gone. Even so, Yruf had to keep his hands dirty when one of them had so much as a whiff of doubt for him. Mysterious disappearances were not rare in the EMA at one point to protect the secret. Every rumor snuffed out, every trace of defiance vanquished, Yruf was forced to play a heavy hand on that matter.

Most rumors were that the EMA had weaponized it, or Yruf had lost it. Of course, none of that was true. Yruf was not careless on such matters, and in the EMA, mistakes and coincidences were seldom no more than thickly veiled ploys.

It didn't take much to blanket the truth though, not one person had thought it would have been attached to an adolescent boy all this while. Until now, everyone had thought Lucas' powers were a mere breakthrough of technology.

There were many details kept under wraps even from Lucas himself, but the gist of it all was that Lucas had been abandoned and left for dead and the only way he could have survived was through an assimilation with the Cube. And so Yruf allowed it in his infinite generosity. Through some machinations and surgery, the Cube fused with Lucas and so brought about a new type of soldier, a terrifying one.

At least that was the narrative Yruf had given him, and he had been given no reason to doubt his mentor, superior, and guardian.

72

Are you sure? The voice came suddenly. It was his own voice, but this one… felt queer. It felt like something had taken over his mind and produced a thought not from himself. It was something else. He did not think of it, then whose?

The voice continued. *Does Yruf seem like the type of person that would just give such an important piece of technology to a mere boy, a boy he barely knew, a boy who has no name, a boy with no worth or family, no value to his eyes. You said it yourself, he does things for the greater good, all his actions are meticulously calculated. But does this seem like a smart move to you? And even so, why pick you? There are so many orphans around the world haunted with more horrible afflictions that you have, why you? Luck? Do you really believe in luck, Lucas? Are you so witless?*

It was nothing more than Lucas had suspected, but he cringed his face now that he was forced to face it. Yruf was not a genial man, not with his imposing personality and size. He was not exactly charitable either, but his actions always had a goal for good.

Why would he want to lie to me? I've been loyal, I will always be. There is nothing he would need to hide from me. Nothing he has done in the past will change how I see him… not after everything he had given me.

The voice came again, with an accent of anger. Its words rattled quickly. *But you saw, didn't you? You saw your parents? Did they look homeless to you? Did they look like they abandoned you? And a curious thing, isn't it… that they worked in the EMA.*

"I… I…"

Yruf had once languished that Lucas always seemed to have three answers to dispute Yruf's for every one command he had. But now he was lost for words. He could not argue with such obvious logic, he was loyal... but Yruf had taught him enough not to be delusional as well.

An uneasy feeling weighed down on Lucas' gut. He did not like this. He feared that if he unpeeled more of this, it would only cause him great hurt. *Why would Yruf lie to me? Do I ask him why? What if... what if...* A hundred scenarios perforated his mind, each one more brutal and awful than the last, and not one he liked.

Who are you? Lucas asked suddenly to his own head, giving no mind to how ridiculous it was. Maybe he had gone mad, if so then rational would not help him now. The best course of action was to move forward. *And why have you shown me this? How do you even have this?*

If the voice could snort, Lucas knew it would have. *Oh, dear Lucas, I'm sure you are not so lost to not damn well know who I am.*

Lucas gulped and leaned his head back to his headrest and closed his eyes, wanting a good sleep more than ever. He wished he could just sleep it all away in this serenity, to wake up and find out all this was just a nightmare. Or if it would not wash away, at least then he could sleep on it with a hope when he woke up the problems would become easier with a clearer head.

HELLO WORLD-4 (LUCAS)

The bus would not alight right before the EMA compound for security measures. It would not have had groups of curious tourists and civilians lined up along the walls outside the compound, curious at what this mysterious place was. So, the closest stop was quite a walk away, but it didn't matter to most of the agents recruited under the EMA since most lived in barracks in there

And if you have risen high enough to grant yourself freedom after work had ended, then the question wasn't if you had a car, it was which luxury brand you chose and whether you wanted a chauffeur to drive you about. The generals and scientists and non-combat Agents instated into the EMA were the top minds of the worlds, the elite of the elite, and so were their salaries.

A thorough turnaround from the homelessness I was told.

But it was a pleasant walk, nonetheless. The bus alighted at the end of a street of houses, an old District just a step away from being described as desolate. Nothing much happened here, and even the crows had left this place in peace from their squawking and flapping wings. The houses weren't dilapidated, but their paint had worn and cracked, their purity smirched with time; red became pink and white became yellow. Most were brick built, a messy red stack of blocks splotched a field of grey concrete. Some were laid bare originally, while others painted up, though small crevices told of its frame. It didn't matter though, age still punished all with the fissures that spread through them.

The window panes installed looked as if they had been preserved from a century back where their retro style was more popular. A curtain of moss infested their walls with a new shade of color and texture, some blended in with the vines and potted plants hung on windows and porches that Lucas could no longer tell if it was meant to be or the owners had just been too lazy to do something about the infestation.

The District even *smelled* frumpish, with the odor of diesel and wheels on tar and a suggestion of barbecue, old clothes pressed on iron and crafted furniture and accessories. The main city area was far from this secluded place, so this was a perfect place for retirees or new families wanting a home for cheap.

What simple amenities were provisioned for convenience, that was much to the relief of most people, Lucas supposed. But nothing too fancy for tourists to come by to visit. It was quiet, but far too mundane to be eerie. There wasn't even a haunted house. People still walked their dogs along the sidewalks and runners jogged along in their tight tracksuits or tank tops soaked with sweat.

Care here was a rare occurrence. And even if it came, you could see one from a mile away. This allowed children to play ball along the roads or what makeshift game their minds conjured up. Under the gloomy sky mottled with clouds, with not so much as a patch of blue peering out from the white fur, the children's laughter and joyful shrieks and smiles skinned back so far wide was a great diversion from all Lucas' troubles. *I should be with them. I shouldn't have grown up so quickly.*

Lucas made sure to keep a wary side eye at the kids so if the ball came flying towards him, he could dodge in time. He didn't fancy a rogue ball getting a cheap hit on him just because he wasn't paying attention. When he knew he was far from their throwing range and out of danger, he reverted his gaze back to the front so that stupid notion no longer could purloin his attention.

A low mutter droned around him, but it wasn't enough to annoy him. In fact, it was kind of relaxing. Muffled and crisp tones clashed but all at whispers at once to produce a calming, gentle stimulus in his ears, like the grinding of peppers or the light flow of a river.

It was broken by an adorable meow. Lucas smiled instinctively. He loved cats, especially this one. His steely eyes combed his environment for the origin of the sound. Dismay almost grabbed him by its cold, vicious talons but suddenly there was another "meow", more piercing, more distressed.

Once he found his target, he sped towards it. The meows came from an alleyway wedged between two shophouses and he went inside. The alley was wide enough for a full-grown man to trudge in without squeezing so Lucas had no trouble at all.

It was a dingy place. The sunlight coming in from the sky was shoddy at best, and here where it was flanked in by two close, high walls, only a smidgen of light was able to cast in. It had a reek of rubbish that had been given the recreation to fester for quite a while. Even the floor felt mucky and sticky. No wonder, it was covered in some black substance Lucas would rather not think about. Garbage bins and bags were piled along the sides of the alley, a collaboration of all the trash the shophouses along the row had so kindly donated to add to the mix of filth.

The cat was nowhere to be seen, and where the sound came from was an invalid sight of a group of children crowding into something. The first thought Lucas had was that the cat was being bullied when he saw the pack of boys. But there was a girl, and girls were rarely cruel, at least from his limited experience; albeit his experience had only been with girls twice his age where they might have matured.

Lucas' ears twitched for a more comprehensive inspection. The cat's meows were not unusual, after all. Its meows had always been this irritation. It seemed too leisurely to have been tormented. Lucas relaxed his hands and let the energy flowing in him from his powers, and the adrenaline coursing through his veins dissipate. If anyone were to hurt the cat, they would pay dearly; and he would not discriminate among anyone.

One of the kids turned. He was a head taller than even the second tallest kids, so Lucas knew at once he was their leader. A child's naivety made for simple dynamics among themselves. He was a pudgy boy, but to the scrawnier kids, it didn't matter if his size had been made of fat or muscle, he was king. Most of the time, such kids didn't know how to fight, but their sheer size alone made for a pretty good battering ram. Lucas drew that from experience, and it wasn't pretty.

His head was a tangle of golden curls cascading down till his neck, wet from play so that they stuck to his skin. Snot dripped from his nose and his eyes were large with contempt. "And who are you?" he asked curtly. The other kids huddled around him started to take notice of Lucas and they shifted to face him. The second-in-command folded his arms and stood forward with his leader protectively.

Cute, Lucas thought. The smaller kids would not forget this seemingly small gesture. But the sentiment of protection would cast a large shadow on the kids as they grew, knowing they were protected as they explored. It was one Lucas was immensely appreciative of Yruf for.

"You took the words right out of my mouth," Lucas smiled. It was more favorable to treat kids with care. They looked all tough, one wrong word and he feared they might cry. After the most recent blunder, he was unwilling to get any more negative attention. "What are you doing with Mr. Benjamin?"

"Who?" the boy craned his neck forward to get a better catch on Lucas' words.

"The cat."

The boy turned to Mr. Benjamin and then back to Lucas dubiously. "I'm sorry, do you own him?"

"Mr. Benjamin is not owned by anyone. He is a free spirit," Lucas explained kindly. "I should introduce him to you," Lucas eyed Mr. Benjamin. "But it seems you have already been all over him. Not that I mind." He looked back at the pudgy boy. "Don't worry about it."

Mr. Benjamin was a pretty ordinary feline, but one dear to Lucas' heart. He was white in his belly and toasted on the top, and his personality was what made him shine. He was a feisty little thing when you gave him too much attention, claws and all but was reduced to a cuddly cushion when its required affection fell below its threshold. It was an odd thing like that, almost comical, but Lucas loved him all the same.

His claws had retracted now, but judging from his increasingly wary eyes, the kids had stayed long enough to siphon almost enough affection for the day. Soon the cat would be swinging his claws about absurdly, relaying that it had reached its limit of sycophants.

"Oh," the large boy blurted. "Well, Mr. Benjamin is very kind. We saw him lurking in this alley and thought to play with him. He looked hungry so we bought some cat food to feed him."

Lucas snorted and took a first step to evaluate how comfortable the kids were with him. They didn't so much as flinch and he knew to saunter forward freely. "Well, I can see Mr. Benjamin likes you," Lucas grinned a warm grin and exchanged looks with the cat. It purred and licked its paws. "Though if I were you, I wouldn't feed him. He may not look like much, but Mr. Benjamin is a fierce hunter, and he catches more than plenty of his required prey for food. Feed him anymore, and you might just make him as plump as you," Lucas nudged the head boy's belly playfully. The boy sniggered.

"He's a hunter!" he exclaimed. "Wow, that's a cool cat." The kids softened their stance on Lucas considerably.

Lucas nodded. "Yes, he is." For some twisted, strange reason, he realized then that perhaps the reason he liked the cat so much was because he reminded Lucas so much of himself... like he was projecting his being on that brown little cat. The cat had the eyes of a stone-cold killer, like he did. He knew those eyes well when he looked into the mirror, sometimes too long that he frightened even himself.

The cat's golden eyes gleamed a watery finish, and Lucas could see his silhouette on him. But within the eyes, he also saw something concealed. The cat tried so hard to hide it, but it would never be buried deep enough, it was never enough. He wanted love, he didn't want to be a killer. He just wanted to lie on a comfy lap of someone he loved where he could snuggle and be all touchy feely.

It was a different love than Yruf had. Yruf had a hard, steadfast love that made you feel protected from the outside. But what Lucas yearned for is another sort of love and protection, from the inside. He wanted the fuzzy, warm feeling. And Yruf would be the last one to nuzzle with someone; it would undeniably feel like rubbing your face onto a stone statue.

He patted Mr. Benjamin on the head and the feline allowed it. He knew Lucas, and his threshold had not been fully filled yet. It purred again. Its fur was a mat of soft bristles, with a consistency that didn't allow Lucas' fingers to stroke the cat's fur from head to back as smoothly as he would like. It must have been the years of filth and grime on him, but Lucas didn't mind. Love transcended such trivialities.

Lucas gritted his teeth and realized he was staring too hard and too long at Mr. Benjamin that even the feline meowed again and turned aside from his creepy ogle. Life came back into Lucas' eyes and he turned as well to the kids, releasing Mr. Benjamin from his love.

Lucas continued. "But I'm glad you are here for Mr. Benjamin. I first met him some years ago, and he was already this big. So, I must assume he would be quite a senior, though sprightly for his age. And so far, my work... school has been keeping me pretty busy that I had not been able to see him for quite some time. I'm sure he had more friends... the furry sort he could relate better, but sometimes I just... feel guilty." His words came out genuine and brimmed with contrite. Lucas found himself scowling.

What am I doing? I'm supposed to be more careful than that. I've just met these kids and I'm pouring my life story to them?

But before he could say anymore, the pudgy boy went up to Lucas confrontationally. "Don't worry, Mr. I will take care of him from now on, you have my word. And the word of all my friends here, right guys?" the kids all nodded firmly. He continued in a voice with as much commitment Lucas could take seriously from such a young child. "I will make sure he is accompanied till... till..."

"Till he doesn't need it," Lucas finished it up for him. A child like this still regarded death as some sort of taboo and he knew even when he was their age, he couldn't wrap his head around the concept of an endless sleep. He didn't want to distress someone so young into his journey, he deserved to be blissful... at least for now. "Thank you in advance, then. And I'm sure if Mr. Benjamin can talk, he would too." The cat purred as if in response.

Lucas smiled. *That's good. When we grow, sometimes we have to forsake the past we hold on to, isn't that what Yruf always says? That to reap the greatest rewards, we have to put what we hold most dear on the line.* Amusingly, the symbolism was a cat, but Lucas could not think of a better symbol.

"Anyway, it's not like I'm never going to visit. It's just the frequency I do will dwindle rapidly." Lucas sighed. He turned back to Mr. Benjamin. "I never really told you why I called him that—" He directed the words to the kids. "—he just looked like a Benjamin." Lucas snorted and the kids laughed.

"Well, it's a goodbye, Mr. Benjamin... indefinitely, we shall meet again."

Lucas exited the alleyway rejuvenated with melancholy and a new vigor in him. Hopefully, the melancholy from the loss of something so dear might be enough sacrifice to solve the bigger one that gripped his very soul now. It made his chest feel heavy and tight just thinking about it. Behind, the kids chanted and the walls echoed the magnificent name of Mr. Benjamin.

Lucas almost shed a tear but wiped it before he could shame himself.

"Cry, but cry alone. If you are to one day replace me, then people must know they can count on you. Once you allow yourself to open yourself to them, then you lower yourself. And like it or not, no one will rely on you as steadily as before. They must worship you. Have you ever seen a king cry to his subjects? No, of course not. Imagine the dent in morale that will cause." Yruf had said that even when he was a mere child, in all his intimidating and booming rumble of his voice.

Child or not, Lucas heeded to that creed. He would grit his teeth and bear with the pain till his face was all flushed, but he would rather pass out then show his tears.

He looked forward to distract himself and hastened his pace to flee from the chants. It was a pleasant town, far from the chaos that he was used to. Sure, it didn't have the usual luxuries he was used to, but as he got older it dawned on him simplicity could just be a luxury as well. Oh, what he would give to be one of these people, living in oblivious bliss without a knowledge of the horrors that went on behind the scenes. Instead, he had to face sleepless nights inundated with worry.

I want to make Yruf proud, I want to rise, I want to take over him one day so that I can relieve him of this burden. Yet… I hate the never-ending missions and fatigue and pressure it brings. Is there a balance? Or will I have to choose one and forgo the other?

His thoughts were broken up by a child's howl. "Car!" a kid behind yelled and Lucas turned around to their voice. They were the same pack of boys who were skipping about the road he saw earlier.

The kids scattered from the road something zoomed past. It went at such velocity it was just a red blur on the road. As it streaked through, it seemed to elongate as the afterimage of its previous spot rushed to chase on its new position. As it passed Lucas, it brought forth a gust of wind on Lucas. It was a statement of his power, the breeze trailing behind was a nonchalant swoosh of a magnificent cape.

It couldn't have been owned by anyone here. Even if people here could afford it, it wasn't in their nature to drive something so showy. It was most likely owned by an EMA agent, a rather high-ranked one at that, to be able to come to work at such a tardy time. Perhaps the driver was a general, those puppets were only good for attending meetings, snubbing and pushing pencils and delegating work to their underlings and authorizing matters on businesses they had not a clue about.

Turns of jealousy and admirations unfolded in Lucas' gut. He pursed his lips and watched as the car raced down further and further. It had just overtaken him but suddenly the gap it left between them had expanded vastly.

Stunned, he planted himself there long enough to watch the car shrink into a mere dot and then disappear into the distance. From the EMA compound to the street was a small thicket of trees, and after the grand headquarters that housed the protectors of Earth stood; protectors for the Earthians... from itself.

84

Everyone called themselves Earthians now, to reinforce their identity that they were one and the same in heart, in hopes that a different mentality would help find enough common cause and diplomacy with each other to prevent future hostilities. It was too early to tell if it would remotely work, however. The practice had not spawned organically. It was one along with a couple more extensive directives issued and enforced as ramifications or penalties of the most recent war, depending on which way you looked at it.

Even when just a few seconds had passed, Lucas found himself going back to the memories when the car had passed. He was more awestruck than he should be. The engine in him was far superior, but for some reason he aspired to own one of those sleek and beautiful things. At least it gave him a dream. Nowadays, even impossible ones were hard to come by.

He hadn't flown high enough to draw an exorbitant paycheck, so he would have to make do with walking for now. *But one day I will, I will be wealthy,* he dreamt of a mansion as large as the EMA compound, with a large water feature in the middle of the entrance encircled with rocky tiles, a house of only the more opulent of decorations, and a whole garage of sports cars all to himself. There were going to be fountains, walkways, halls and a large swimming pool, all embellished with expensive filigrees. He would hire hundreds of servants to care for his house, and a hundred more at his disposal in case something else came up.

One day, he thought. Where the car had swept through, it was as if its gleam had peeled off whatever redeeming qualities the neighborhood once had. Its presence had brought such luster and brilliance to the place, that once it faded, its absence was remarkably felt. Suddenly the street he walked on looked more dismal than ever, and he began to notice the flaws that plagued it. He wondered what madness had taken him to ever appreciate this place.

His lips twisted in disgust and he picked up the pace. As the thoughts purged from his mind, the walk towards the EMA compound proved more expeditious than Lucas expected.

The palette of his surroundings whirled to change the hues on it. From the harsh red to blotchy, silken green, to the sturdy and mighty gloss of metal where the EMA compound unraveled itself.

Here it stood, the headquarters of the mighty EMA on First Federation land. Officially, it was an independent organization, but everyone knew nepotism and favoritism was rife in every sufficiently large organization, and it was no secret the First Federation was their staunchest ally and donator. The amounts they granted the EMA was no small thing, utterly triumphing over the next few largest donations from other Regions combined. The First Federation was powerful, stable, so choosing this Region as its headquarters was an obvious choice. Well, it was only to be expected. After all, the First Federation was supposed to climb over all the other Regions, it was made to.

The EMA headquarters was a fortified castle in by itself; forded by high ramparts all around it made of several inches of thick metal and watchtowers roosted at intervals along the walls mounted with turrets. The walls were manned by an alternating roster of agents, but always no less than a squadron guarded the compound. As usual, no one knew Lucas from sight and most thought he was just a lost kid wandering into the unknown.

He tried to play it cool and accorded them with the respect Yruf had taught him to give to all except evil people. But a good security sweep on him and a check on the ID and suddenly their tone changed drastically.

"Ace... I'm sorry, I mean Lieutenant Lucas, the orders of your promotion just came. Congratulations," was the usual reply every told him after each tedious checkpoint of security checks. They were empty courtesies, they wanted to have nothing and less to do with him. They were probably praying for him to get out of their sights as quick as possible, but Lucas conferred his gratitude to them all the same.

The compound was as large as a small city. Looming structures and stouter buildings rose up all around. There were fields and training grounds, dozens of buildings each with a specific purpose. Most of them looked ordinary, just a metal structure covered with glass. Some others looked sturdier and more barricaded, but they were often hidden away.

He had spent most of his life here, so he had seen the scene a gazillion times that nothing stood out that it seemed to blend with the clouds and sky like they were mere background. He went straight to the barracks where his things were kept. But no longer would he need to sleep there, he would not sleep in the furnished quarters befitting a Lieutenant.

There were twice as many barracks as there were buildings in the compound, they lined about in neat rows behind the rest of the impressive structures; and it was the only part that had any semblance to a military camp.

Each housed a different sort of soldier. The majority that occupied the barracks was split evenly between combatants and intelligence Agents. Among them, they were split further into their individual niches of weaponry or by the nature of their mission. About a quarter was set aside for visiting armies or foreign EMA contingents when they would perform joint training. The last corner of shelter was saved for the cadets in the command school, those who were chosen from the crème of the crop from each branch.

The rest of the EMA personnel would be irked if they were handed such destitute quarters, even if they were starkly more immaculate than the second-best barracks of the outside. With such copious amounts of money, it had become expected that their facilities matched their wealth.

Funds overflowed the EMA's coffers and sometimes they were given more than they could even think to spend. The money streamed in from business people and political leaders trying to do good or more like to curry favor from the EMA. It was supposed to be illegal, but once you called it lobbying, all was suddenly good apparently.

Yruf was tactical with such games, and ever careful with whom he accepted the funds and who he made enemies when he refused their generosity. He was not one to be pushed about with bribes, nor did he respond to threats.

The barracks were fashioned just a step away from luxury apartments, dressed in all that money and bling, the quality of their furniture and facilities were top notch. But it was never enough for the top dogs of the EMA. *It doesn't matter where you are, most people never look down, always up. And so no one really knows how high they have risen.*

When Lucas entered the barracks, the cadets were in their personal field just next to the apartments training. Each barrack was allocated a field on its own to save time travelling. They wore suits as white as snow, and as slender as their own taut skins. They probably didn't appreciate the costumes now. The sun was merciful today, and Lucas could feel the rain drawing near as the clouds turned heavy and the air smelling moist and smoldering with excited static. But when the sun glared down on most days, they would be gracious for such an attire.

They were split into groups at once, thronged in a circle while a pair picked among them battled it out. A trainer was assigned to each of the groups, arms akimbo and looking intently as they sought to bring each other down. The cadets were rowdy as they placed bets and cursed and cheered at the fighters. If the guise of uniforms was removed and it had not been held in a compound that demanded discipline, Lucas knew it was nothing more than a cage match.

Soldiers being soldiers, youths being youths, they were naturally drawn to such a wild and rough activity. They could spend a whole day like that and none of them minded. Every fighting style was allowed here, as was the unpredictable and unrestricted circumstance on the battlefield; except this one forbade any lethal moves.

Lucas looked at them with a nostalgic gaze. It was perhaps the activity Lucas enjoyed the most when he was still a cadet. The freedom to laugh and chatter with his friends there was a highlight of any day, and fighting was his forte. Paired together, it made the sweetest days.

He thought fondly of his time there, fondly and painfully. He winced. Many might have expected him to have been talented in such vicious ways from young after seeing how graceful, yet deadly he moved. But in truth, he was often beaten… badly in this activity aptly named the fighting pits. Yruf only dispatched the most unforgiving trainers. They often pit him against older, larger opponents. Even without the disadvantage of experience, his losses were almost assured.

Lucas had thought that it had just been a political move to show that he held no favoritism to Lucas. It wasn't like Lucas' advantages had even been overt compared to everyone else. He had to work for everything here. But just the connection to Yruf sent morons into a jealous frenzy.

Lucas hated him then, but only because he had not yet learnt the merit of effort for improvement. He knew now, through that, and that grudge had long dissipated. As Lucas thought, he was sure Yruf just wanted the best for him.

That was how he became so good, prowess whetted through struggle. Through scabs and bruises, cuts and gashes, he shoved through them and managed to come on top ultimately. His trainers, even the ones that didn't like him out of spite for Yruf's favoritism on him, had congratulated him then. It had been a glorious moment.

But it wasn't easy. Besides the usual schedule the cadets had to follow, Yruf had subscribed to him with other trainers he hired for his more… unique abilities. It was no use training a lion how to fight like a sheep when he was stronger and had far larger and sharper claws.

"You have far more potential than the lot of them combined, and I would be mad if I were to waste it. I will make full use of it, Lucas, and you had better to endure it if you are to win any battle in the future," Yruf had told him countless times when he had felt like quitting. He whined and wept, and no matter how severe or how persistent his excuses where, Yruf never budged. And so, the only way he knew now was to go forward.

He went towards the field and stopped at the metal net that barricaded the field. He clutched at them with his left hand, fingers feeling the holes like he was about to climb it and the strings so thin they were a hair away from razor blades. He shook them out of urge and a wave dispersed out, clattering the rest of the lattice.

90

He looked down upon his left hand. It was marred with thickened skin grown from years of punishment. He could not remember when it had been tender before. Yruf was harsh. He did not budge when it came to complaints and Lucas hated him at times, but he could never bring himself to hate him for long. He knew Yruf was just doing it to train him. He could be kind when he wanted to as well, to support and lend a listening ear.

He would never betray me, not after the years it took to foster me.

He looked towards the field once again. The boisterous mood had not battered even an octave down, nor would it soon. It was a constant clamor of exhilaration. The faces he was familiar with were few to none since the roster of cadets often changed. EMA courses were infamously ruthless to guarantee quality in their ranks, so people came and went often. The fact that Lucas wasn't particularly talkative didn't help either. Even if there was someone he recognized, chances were that it was just another vague face he barely knew in the sea of other faces.

"Hey elephant ears!" someone shouted at the distance. Lucas jolted awake and tried to ignore the jibe. "Do not respond to mockery. It makes you weak," Yruf told him often. Yruf could have easily stopped all such harassment, but he believed Lucas should fight his own battles. "If you wanted people to respect you, you couldn't depend on the big chief all the time. You must learn that in this world, you can only count on yourself to back you up. No one else will do it for you. Reliance is what separates the strong and the dead," was another saying Yruf liked to dispense.

Best thing was, Yruf never told him he couldn't fight back. *More often than not, I was punished for it though. But it was worth it.* A curl of his lips made the slightest hint of his satisfaction.

"Hey! Ace!" the voice was tenacious, annoyingly. He tried several more times to change the nickname as if it was *that* was what made Lucas to ignore him, each nickname vexing Lucas ever more.

That blubbering, mindless buffoon. Lucas finally gave in and turned. He had no such patience to play such passive games now. "What, Sam?" Lucas hissed, he made no such effort to hide his scorn. He knew the voice of that particular trainer well; a human, an embodiment of every degenerate quality ever known to Earthians all stirred up in a noxious concoction. That was Sam.

He was brusque, bull-headed, loved to push his way out of things through fists than brains… if he had any. He belittled what he didn't understand or did not believe in, refused to acknowledge anyone better than him… or lower than him… or anyone but himself. He was an ironic medley of delusion, arrogance and stupidity, and loved to boast when he had nothing whatsoever to boast about. He would run into the head of a volcano just because you dared him to.

Sam was the epitome of a jock, which also unfortunately meant he was flawless in every facet when it came to appearance. He was vascular to the smallest muscle, with so little body fat a paper cut would be all that was required to kill him. He towered over lesser people, which he liked to remind everyone often, muscles bulged out of the tank top he liked to flaunt. His features were sharp, a chiseled square jaw locked in to give him a strong look. And he had the most enthralling of eyes, two green ones that looked like jewels. His hair was shaved so thin only bristles spiked up from his head.

Hearing the words of defiance come out from Lucas' mouth was no shock at all to Sam. He was used to bickering with Lucas for anything under the sun down to the pettiest of things. Once Yruf had to break them up because they argued over whose hair was browner. But perhaps Sam was having a bad day… Whatever a bad day was like to a primate, or perhaps Lucas had injected more scorn into his tone than usual. "What did you say, you little squirt?" Sam howled, his face reddening.

Lucas rolled his eyes. "Go away Sam, you still have teaching to get into, if that's what you do," Lucas sneered, "I have more important things to do than the play with you."

"Like what?" Sam roared, the sarcasm of Lucas' earlier sentence had flown over his head.

"Like actual important things that need capable people, unlike you," Lucas spat. Their arguments didn't always escalate this quickly. There was usually gradual build up before things exploded. Lucas was sure Sam wasn't going to let the metal fence stop him from getting to Lucas, but a boldness had taken him.

It was too late to fan the flames Lucas ignited. Sam charged towards the fence, stopping right before it and then rattling it. Lucas did not flinch. He did not flinch to Sam anymore. They glowered at each other, silently daring each other to take the first swing. "You think you're so smart, huh? Twerp?!" he shook the fence in taunt. The metal clanged violently.

"Such creative insults," Lucas said sarcastically.

"Well, I'm smarter than you." As usual, it went right over Sam's head.

"Perhaps," Lucas snorted, "in bragging about things that don't exist. But you damn well know if this cage comes off, I will sweep the floor with you. You may be bigger than me, but I'm more skilled and more powerful than you," he threatened, narrowing his eyes. In the realm where the EMA was concerned, his powers were no secret.

"As if," Sam insisted. He released his thick fingers from the metal fence and Lucas noted the dents he had caused. His brute strength was nothing to laugh about. "But I've got a reputation to keep."

"Not if, when. Come Sam, I'm waiting. Or do you like being insulted that much in front of all your cadets? That whatever little they think of you will plunge even further."

"Don't take the bait Sam!" a voice called from behind.

There it was. "The dynamic duo reunites. I was wondering when you might come to defend your rabid dog," Lucas had to take a step to the side to see the person who spoke striding forward. Sam was too large to look over his shoulder. The person who walked over was a grim man with a face full of horrendous dry and angry rashes like he scrubbed his face clean with acid. The training attire sheathed his lean physique well, but his appearance was undone with his hideous face. His nose looked flattened on his face and his eyes were always a pair of languid things, a grey color with boredom never far from them.

He was Icarus. This man never once smiled no matter how thorough Lucas searched in his memory. He was the type that reckoned looking solemn every second of the day would bring himself more respect. But all it brought him was jests about how he could be a nice addition to the war museum the EMA had. The stone-faced fool thought it made him look powerful, but it was an opposite.

94

All these years, no one told him that being strong didn't mean you had to forgo your personality. It was sad, honestly, but at least it was funny. Lucas didn't think he would listen anyway. The man was pitifully stubborn, and had grown an ego as large as Sam after the silly notion that he was some sort of genius had inserted itself into his head. Then again, Lucas couldn't blame him. Anyone would feel like a genius while around Sam.

"What are you here for, Lucas? Haven't you learnt your lesson not to stare? You should have changed and joined us by now, or do we need to teach you yet another time? Were we too soft the last time?" Icarus sneered.

Lucas grinned. They obviously haven't gotten the news. *Wait till they find out.* He wanted to see how quick the blood drained from their faces.

"Why you grinning, boy? Are you so eager to add to your already high tally of rounds you have to run?" Icarus smirked wickedly. "You can erase all thoughts of sleeping tonight."

Lucas assumed a blank look; his head tilted and his brows puckered. "I'm sorry, but I don't understand?"

Icarus, being the dense fool he was, thought he had Lucas within his grasp. "What?" he shot curtly. "Do I need to teach you basic grammar for you to understand me, boy? You think just because you've come back from a mission, we're going to hold your hand, spoon-feed you, and give you comforting words? Well, you're sorely mistaken if we're going to give you any special accommodations."

"Has the order of my promotion not come yet?"

It was all worth it. Sam's face washed with a pallid shade, but Icarus did not even have the grace to admit his wrong. He tried to put it off as if it was nothing. "I'm sorry—" His voice trembled. "—but people like us have more important duties than to care of every trivial thing that goes on in this place," he said in the dignified, most eloquent timbre the man could manage. It made him sound much like a chump though.

"Yeah," Sam managed to whimper some defiance, spurred on by Icarus.

Lucas smiled. "Looks like my tally is about to be wiped out. Now, I will get a clean slate, but I'm not so sure about you." Lucas leaned in.

"What do you mean?" Icarus asked brusquely.

"I mean I can punish you, as is my right as a superior, no? You just talked back to me, insulted me with crude words even, is that not insubordination?"

Whatever composure was wiped away from Icarus immediately. He lurched back, frightened. "You're bluffing. You wouldn't dare, I—"

"Oh, I would, I can," Lucas cut him off. "But I am not without kindness. As my first day in my rank, it is only proper I let you off the hook with a measly warning." His face dropped. "So I have to warn you about running your mouth anymore. I got promoted two ranks effective immediately a day ago. From now on, you will address me as my rank stipulates. Got it?"

"Two... two ranks?" Sam lurched back but Icarus tried to return to solid stone. Icarus put on his mask of impassivity once more, smoothening his attire and cocking his head up, but Lucas could still smell the fear in him. "Well, if Yruf have dictated that you are far from our grasps now, there is no point punishing you either. You will never learn to be a good soldier."

"Where do you get your delusions from," Lucas mocked. "I changed my mind." He spoke with a markedly stiffer tone. "My first act as a power over you will be to see you to run one round along the track. Don't curse me for being ruthless, that is simple enough, isn't it?"

Icarus finally broke into a flush and Sam was stuttering. "You can't!" Sam yelled. "The act is simple, but your goal is in the very act itself. You will shame us in front of all the cadets!" his face turned to anger.

"Like you did me," Lucas seethed. "Good, at least you aren't dumb as you let on."

"I know you, you buttered up to our Overall Commander and finally you got what you wanted. I will not obey a nonsensical order by an officer I do not see deserving of his rank!" Icarus lashed out, pointing a finger at Lucas in outrage. His quivering made him look like he was wagging it.

"So now you admit to willfully disobeying me?" Lucas taunted.

"Yes," Icarus clenched his jaw in more a nervous bluff than mistaken confidence. "I refuse any punishment from a superior I do not acknowledge."

Just as I hoped. "If you won't let me use the powers granted to me, and you won't allow me to defend against your malicious slander, then the answer is clear, isn't it? You agree to settle this the old way" Lucas cracked his knuckles, skinning back his teeth to reveal all two ordered rows of pearly white smugness.

They knew what he was implying at once. Both of them reeled back, suddenly wary of Lucas' careful, deliberate tone. What little resistance they had sloughed off in place of a new stretched layer of fright. As foolish as the mismatched pair were, they knew that Lucas was not a person one should challenge against so thoughtlessly. All the spurs and honors, and most importantly, all the nicknames were not altruistically given to him.

Encouraged by their reactions, Lucas' eyes slicked with even more arrogance. "Come, I'll let you take the first strike. I won't even use my powers, for consideration of your families… not that it would make any difference to the outcome," Lucas craned forward and mocked in a whisper, as if he was telling them a secret.

The duo pursed their lips and shied away as Lucas jerked forward. "Scared, huh?" Lucas laughed a maniacal laugh. "Why don't I give you two an out? Just admit that I'm better than you. It shouldn't be hard, for it's true."

"Never," Icarus rasped, face washed with white.

Fury coursed through his body, enhanced by the youthful vigor produced from his hormones. And when that happened, his entire body glowed. Cracks raced down his skin, forming a web along his body, and from the cracks came the blue glow. Craggy structures as shiny and as black as obsidian grew out from them.

As they were about to engulf his body, a voice called. "Stop this madness, Lieutenant Lucas!" a commanding voice bellowed behind Lucas. The light fiesta ceased as once. He recognized that smoky voice. He turned and saw an old man with a bleak face walking leisurely towards him. The years had done him dirty. His hair was a sea of white with only strips of ash to hark back to better years. His cheeks were hollow and spotted with marks, wrinkles and lines blemished all over, but his eyes still shone with the same imposing radiance. Laugh lines sprouted beside his eyes.

His skin was dark, but his hair darker. He used to sport a mustache but his wife had told him that as he got older and became sloppier, it was a hygiene issue. He had told Lucas that once and had a good laugh about it.

He tapped his rank pinned at his waist, several chevrons onto an EMA logo, a cluttered thing Lucas could never make out what it was supposed to represent, "Lucas, you may have outranked them, but you haven't me," he said mildly. He was clad in the formal EMA uniform, a long-sleeved nightmare broached with dozens of honors and badges that made it impossible to go anywhere but an air-conditioned office unless you wanted to cook up a sweat.

"Sergeant Major," Lucas nodded reverently; but it was the person he regarded, not the rank. The senior levels of the non-commissioned branch only had honorary powers over burgeoning officers since their ranks didn't exactly precede over the officer branch. But everyone respected them either way. It was a custom. If you didn't, they might not be able to punish you directly, but their seniority made it so that they surely knew someone else who could.

But even if that courtesy had not been practiced between branches, Lucas could still have afforded this particular one with the same respect. It was the person and his actions that Lucas considered. Perhaps, that was the ultimate form of respect one could give.

Besides Yruf, there were several others in the EMA he *did* respect. If Yruf was the dad, the Sergeant Major was the cool uncle you went to for advice and talk to when your dad was busy; which since Yruf was the top dog, he was often. But one… or two bad apples often spoiled the impression of other soldiers for him. "You look dashing as always."

The Sergeant Major took the snarky comment with stride. "I would take that. But spare me more of your empty compliments, Lucas, you will not escape me, you have never. What will Yruf say when he sees this?" he stopped at a comfortable distance before Lucas, standing just half a head taller than Lucas was.

"Well, I think he will commend me on punishing incompetence."

The Sergeant Major was about to utter a remark but he turned and took one good look at Icarus and Sam and all that energy he wanted to argue with was blown out. "Well, I can't refute that. But not now, not here. They are my men, and it is up to me to punish them."

Lucas knew he was right. There was no point in arguing with the Sergeant Major, so he backed off. "As you wish, Sir," Lucas smiled. There was no reluctance of sarcasm there. It was a genuine smile. All that anger had washed away from Lucas' system by the elation he felt when he saw Sergeant Major Vishnu.

The Sergeant Major turned to the duo. "You two, stop staring. Go back to work. It's still crunch time," he dragged his hoarse voice to pain them all with the sound of sandpaper scraping at each other. The two darted away instantly, whether it was joy they were set free from Lucas or the Sergeant Major he wasn't sure. He glanced back to Lucas. "Ah, Lucas, when you left you were just a boy, now suddenly you're a striking, spunky new officer ready to take on the world you even started to dispense some of your justice here."

Lucas blushed and averted the Sergeant Major's glance abashedly. "I'm sorry."

"Do not be." He laughed and patted Lucas on the shoulder. "Today is a happy day. Come, I'm sure you have not come here just to reminisce of the good old days, you've come to pack your stuff, haven't you? Walk with me."

Lucas studied the Sergeant Major dubiously. "What? Why?"

"Oh, don't worry, my hips and my joints aren't so weak just yet," he mistook Lucas' intention but Lucas left it as that.

They took the lift up to the top level of the barrack where Lucas' bunk was. Cadets weren't supposed to be afforded such luxury, they had to take the stairs; but Lucas wasn't a cadet anymore. It almost seemed too good to be true, a big lie or a prank, that his first step was a tremulous, uncertain one. Habits cultivated by his sergeants did not die off easy. The wariness that clung to his shoulders would not fade soon enough.

"Did you see your roommates? Are you going to say your final farewell?" the Sergeant Major asked while they shot up. The lift reeked of sweat and odor, but it was expected of one in a military camp. The cleaners would have to clean the lift at the frequency of the cadets' training if the lift was to be maintained, but that would be too unreasonable. At least this one didn't creak or had any bare or rusted parts.

"No," Lucas replied sullenly, making his voice clear that it wasn't a pleasant choice. He would spare the Sergeant Major the tedious details. The Sergeant Major understood and nodded. "Not everything will be pleasant, I assure you even in your new role. The best thing we can do is take it with stride and move on."

He shared the room with three other cadets, two of them arrogant bums who belittled him often and taught him unworthy of his rank for being too young, and another liked to sit on the fence. He would feign concern and geniality when the two weren't around, but his modesty left him when the pair would come back, sometimes he would even join them.

Good riddance to them, Lucas didn't even feel a shred of hesitation leaving them. He didn't even want to see their faces or say his goodbyes; this was not a chapter in his life with a happy ending, or perhaps it ending was one already. Lucas was resolved to make the subsequent one a happy one.

The lift jerked to a halt and the pair strolled to Lucas' old bunk. His bunk was at the end of the corridor so there was plenty of time to talk. A low wall at the other side of the bunks unfurled the scenery below it. It wasn't pretty; just more barracks and field organized in rows. The other side would not have been different, but at least you could get a glimpse of the headquarters. The cadets and trainers were mere dots on the verdant field, and the barracks looked so pale and glum. The only saving grace was the smatterings of trees that grew at the distance from the walls of the EMA compound. The EMA wouldn't let the trees come near the walls or risk leaving an ideal hiding spot for potential intruders.

Their canopies were mottled green umbrellas that joined together to form one large one. And the barks that held them were rough-hewn. Little light limned the insides, and less as if went deeper inside.

"I practiced much restraint. Not once did I lash out or they would have silenced their bleating long ago," Lucas decided to unravel, it was seldom enough that you got to vent out your feelings with the right person.

The Sergeant Major smiled. "Well, many times I feel like this too." He prodded at his exposed hand left bare when the long sleeves of his uniform ended. "My skin is as dark as ink, and long ago it was a sign of inferiority. Did you think I really got here by pure intelligence or force? It was restraint, and you have done well in that subject."

"I'm sorry for that," Lucas muttered. "You shouldn't have been so unfairly treated."

The Sergeant Major snorted. "What they did to me was indeed foul, and I used to detest my tormentors, but now I seem to have a newfound appreciation for them," he rubbed the stubble under his chin.

"What do you mean?"

He laughed. "Well, I don't mean I am fond of them now. If I were to see one of them right this moment I would not be able to think of anything better than giving them a good punch on their face. But if I lashed out, then I would degrade myself to their standard, I would be exactly as they said I was, I would portray the exact failing they said I had; undeserving. And even without all these moralistic ideals, it would not help me in the future when the rumors spread. It was hard, mind you, you have felt it firsthand, but it was necessary for my superiors and underlings to know I am more than that. I lost more battles than I won, but in the end, it was the penultimate they had all led up to that counted towards the war."

"It is hard. Do you reckon Yruf would be pleased if I lop the head of one of them if by any chance I meet them again?" Lucas joked.

The Sergeant Major paled and then acquired a more serious look. "I sincerely hope you will keep that as a joke."

Lucas chuckled. "Nah, I won't be so rash. But a few pushups and rounds around the track will be good enough for me. Now you were getting to the part that you were fond of them?"

The Sergeant Major sighed. "Well, yes. It gave me perspective. As will you, perhaps you are too young to feel it now, but when you have become mature enough…"

"I am mature," Lucas whined indignantly.

The Sergeant Major's voice was unyielding this time, and he did not look at Lucas this time. His eyes were deadly still to the front. "You are powerful, you are intelligent, and many other things that make you a far more valuable asset and person than me, but you do not mistake that for wisdom, Lucas. Wisdom is not something you can train, it is something that you experience as time goes on."

Lucas winced and suddenly took interest in his shoes. "Fine."

"Fine. As I was saying, it gave me perspective when it came to dealing with the Purebloods. Since I knew how it felt like to be discriminated upon, I had a sense of empathy for them, something that was rare among my cohort of leaders. My decisions were based on fairness and impartiality to both parties while the others only cared for the interests of the humans. Thus, I was seen as soft, but I'm sure you'll understand I just wanted equality… for everyone."

"But the Purebloods are different. You are a human."

"Are they?" the Sergeant Major's eyes glimmered with mirth. He stopped his tracks. "They talk, they eat, they do everything we do. Sure, they're some differences, but why antagonize them and only yield suffering when we can collaborate and advance *together.*"

The Sergeant Major clenched his fists and shook them. Then he released and let them subside down. He sighed. "Your thinking is the same thinking as those racists decades back,

Lucas. The discrimination which my skin had faced is a lingering bitterness I can never get rid, but it is exactly that, just a memory; no more, nor less. Not so for the Purebloods. And so now it is up to your generation continue the fight of discrimination as mine did to people of difference. Yours will work towards uniting people with scales, hide of furs, horns and claws and a myriad more than mine had, but that is all the difference."

"You think they're good?" Lucas asked hollowly, "Yruf always said they were evil incarnations that we have to tolerate because the higher ups said so." He noticed his voice had taken a petulant turn.

"And Yruf is seldom wrong, but not for this," he answered in a worried tone. "He is half right at least. Some seek to undermine the humans, and we must stop them. However, we must be careful when drawing lines. We may think our side on the side of good with the latter on evil, but we are never aware the other side across the line thinks similarly of us. So, who is good and who is bad?"

Lucas narrowed his eyes. He hated riddles, but the Sergeant Major seldom spoke this much unless he had a lesson to share, a particularly important one. "That shouldn't be a question. It should be clear if that one is bad by counting the atrocities one commits."

"A fallacy," the Sergeant Major said in a clipped tone. "What are the criteria for atrocities then? Who decides on the criteria? Is there even a way?"

"There… is none."

"Yes. There is no side, there is only our imagination. There is no pure good as much as there is no pure evil. Sides are drawn when our desires tell us to; for survival, for lust, even enjoyment. It doesn't matter who started it, it doesn't matter who has the boldest or more righteous motive, it doesn't matter how much we sugar coat it, this is a ghastly business, a horrendous one for both the victors and the losers, all fighting for mortal constructs. Good and evil, they are what *we* define them to be, it is what *the majority* defines them to be."

"And the majority gets to proclaim which side is which," Lucas realized. "And who wants to be hated?"

The sergeant major nodded with an even smile. "That is the lesson I'm trying to teach Lucas. We never know whether we are on the side of good or evil. You don't see the discrimination of Purebloods as wrong, and yet I do. It's so clear to me that I might think you're stupid. But it is no use chiding you. You will only oppose me even more. You... we must acknowledge such a disparity exists. You must know that you are imperfect. And this new power you are given only burdens you with a larger responsibility to keep questioning which you are on. What you do after that is quite self-explanatory so I will not babble on anymore."

The sergeant major exhaled sharply out of habit. If his mustache was still there, it would ruffle and flare out in all its magnificence. "Come, let's walk. My joints aren't as well-oiled as before. They get stiff when unused." Lucas mulled on the sergeant major's words as he walked. It wasn't hard. The sergeant major had quite a thunderous voice, so the words hung around Lucas' ears like hovering bees to a flower.

They finally reached his room. Lucas fumbled his wallet for his keys and opened the door. Packing up was quick. He didn't own much. There were some mementos or emotional trinkets and pictures he carried, but they could all fit into a small metal box together with some other standard issue equipment he was provided.

The process was expedited with the fact that he could just stuff everything in a duffel bag and no one could chide him for being tardy now.

Sergeant Major Vishnu continued the conversation as he chucked everything in mindlessly. Lucas could tell he was trying hard not to comment on the way he handled his stuff. "You know, Captain Jerrick would be proud of you." If anyone else, Lucas might have sent sharp words flying to them, but the Sergeant Major resonated with his pain well.

Lucas paused his activity for a moment, letting his arms piled with folded clothes hover above the bag. The memories flashed past him. An explosion in a factory lined with metal plates and heavy equipment, dismal and dark, sirens screeching in the distance and winks of red light that cut his eyes. Then a boy with dark skin coming towards him. He was about to strike Lucas' face, his fist coming fast and hard, but Lucas blinked and everything went away. Lucas flinched, but it was all a trick of his eyes.

He gazed at his own clothes pensively. "Thank you. He meant much to me. Pity I did not see it that way the last time. And it took his…" Lucas choked up, "I should have cherished him more. How many commanders here are actually as virtuous as him? How many treated me like…"

"A human?"

Lucas gritted his teeth and let the sorrow flow through him. "Yes, a human. Instead, I was a petulant brat to him. I was rotten to the core. And…"

"It was not your fault, Lucas. Captain Jerrick would have said as much," the Sergeant Major consoled.

"How would you know?" Lucas moaned with a raucousness to his words he had not intended to be so. "You weren't there. And you can't speak to the dead." He regretted lashing out instantly. His flush turned from anger to embarrassment.

The Sergeant Major shrugged away the derisive words and did not raise his voice. "I don't. But I know him long enough to hear his words. Conversely, you should celebrate his life. He lived it the way he wanted to…"

"But didn't die the way he wanted to."

"Yes, but no one ever has, and no one ever will… unless you are a certain type of Pureblood. And if you are not persuaded, then do the same for your subordinates to honor his image. Let them come to you when they need a listening ear, let them rely on you, let them learn of the kindness Captain Jerrick imparted on you before the incident. Let the incident of the Risings be settled and let's not talk about it again. You know how people here… especially Yruf, are ticklish on that matter."

Lucas let go of the breath he had been holding in and let the matter be settled. It had been four years, and so much changed when that incident happened. The voices came, his friends were killed, he was betrayed, and he killed one of the rare beacons that cared for him.

The Risings were his home, a group of individuals of the same age as him Yruf had rallied as a trial for a new type of team, an idea for a soldier that people could accept more readily. Behind closed doors, Lucas also knew it had a purpose to keep him company and allow him to grow with kids his age. Yruf may be a dour person, but he knew the merits of growing with people your age, the merits of learning things only experience and interaction could teach you. A military camp was no place for a child. Yruf did not just want an emotionless powerhouse built in a lab and a military camp, but a leader with real feelings.

"A true mark of a leader is his ability to recognize his people. No one will die for you if they do not know who you are, much less if they do not see you," Yruf said once.

"Have you seen George recently?" Lucas broke the silence with a new topic, hoping it would distract him. The bitter taste in his mouth would not fade though.

"George? The one you said was so capable you basically piggybacked on him through half your cadet life?" the sergeant major smirked.

Lucas let himself smile. "Yeah him." George had been his closest friend when he was a cadet. George was a plump guy when Lucas first saw him, but after being commissioned, he had just been stocky. He never seemed to run out of kindness and often helped everyone during training in whatever way he could, not only reserved to Lucas. Even among the trainers he was popular, and it quickly was clear he was officer material to the Sergeant Major. "He graduated top of his cohort and commissioned two ranks up like I did. He was the true trailblazer."

He thought delightfully of the times he and George were together. He was a rare specimen among the Cadets who didn't fear him or loathe him, so Lucas was sure not to lose this chance to get close to him. They bonded quickly and Lucas' life had been less rough after that. The craggy roads resumed when he was commissioned a year ago and he was left alone.

"Ah yes, that man is doing fine, Lucas. He doesn't visit often, plagued by so many duties passed on to him by his higher ups, as expected of an up and coming officer. But I remember him sufficiently. You were so sad when he left. No one to pick after your rubbish anymore," the Sergeant Major sniggered.

Lucas rolled his eyes. "Yeah, I guess you could say that," he admitted.

"It's a good thing though, he was pampering you too much and Yruf and I could see that."

"Was that why…"

The Sergeant Major flapped his hand. "No, don't be ridiculous. Yruf may be crafty, but he dares not play with the sanctity of our ranks just for this ploy. It was true keeping him away from you was good for you, for you to learn what it is to get your hands dirty. You may be good at combat, Lucas, but there are other things that make a soldier, and only by doing it yourself would you register that. We promoted him simply because he was good, too good. I'm hearing he's even about to be promoted to captain soon. Even as we speak, he's taking on the workload of three people if I've not heard wrong."

"That doesn't surprise me," Lucas muttered admirably. "He's always been good. I'll need to see him soon. I've been away for too long settling the EMA's issues."

"I'm sure he'll be proud. He always was. Perhaps even envious of how you could attend an official EMA mission already without a rank on you."

Lucas let his lips skin back in the widest grin he had for a while. "I hope he'll be. If I'm posted to the same company as him, perhaps I can get him to continue his good work of picking up my slack."

The Sergeant Major snorted and shook his head. "Then I'll be sure to give the orders not to have that."

"Where's he now? It's too late for lunch, but perhaps we can meet for dinner. Would you like to join us?"

"I would love to, but alas I have other arrangements. I'm sorry Lucas, but as the years catch up to you, you realize that you would rather neglect work than your family. My daughters had grown to be beauties of their own right and have moved out. I've made a pact with my wife to have dinner with her every night ever since. I cannot bear the thought of her being lonely."

"I understand. How thoughtful," Lucas said.

"My wife would say otherwise," he grumbled. "But even if I could join, I'm afraid George will not be free to. He has been deployed for EMA business. Now that I think of it, I hear he's leading a squad for a combat operation."

"So quick? But I thought only Captains could take overall charge of a mission?"

The Sergeant Major winked. "I told you he's good, didn't I? Yes, the very first Lieutenant to plan and lead his own mission. You would be glad to hear he completely dominated the house when they voted. No one voted against him. That's how much faith they had on him."

A good subordinate does not mean you're a good soldier though. It is wild outside, you need a different sort of skill set. But Lucas would not say that to smirch George's name. Perhaps George would prove Lucas wrong as he always did, Lucas hoped he would. "That's good to hear," Lucas only said. "Well, then I guess I will be having dinner on my own then. A pity I'm not eligible for room service yet. But that won't stop me from eating in my comfortable new quarters."

"Oh, you will enjoy it, I'm sure. Dinner is good today."

HELLO WORLD-5 (LUCAS)

The Sergeant Major was right, dinner was good. But EMA catered meals were usually of a certain standard anyway. It wasn't some lavish feast, perhaps only the top generals and scientists were allowed such a luxury, but it was sumptuous enough. Granted with the overflowing chest of money the EMA had, they were allowed such an expense; a delectable menu that rotated every month, never in order, so Lucas' taste buds would not stale.

The EMA hired specialized cooks, some had worked in award winning restaurants even, to supervise the food prepared. Each meal, while delicious, had been put to some thought as well to the calories and the nutrients that went into them. It meant the food tasted *wrong* sometimes, confused at rarer times, but mostly they had done a good job substituting unhealthy ingredients with healthier variants.

It meant that their ingredients did not come from dubious sources. They used more spices than starch and dairy. Thickening agents and salts were used to a minimum since there were no other good alternatives. The cooks had tried cutting out all the unhealthy elements once, which had also cut out all the taste to it, and the EMA had verged into a riot then. Food was something everyone could put away their difference and rally for. Perhaps that was key to solving the discrimination towards the Purebloods that the Sergeant Major had described.

Once all the sins were taken away, it had probably been an uphill task to produce something of standard with such restrictions. Luckily their cooking team never failed. The meat was tender, the rice always fragrant, and vegetables sautéed nicely. Steak was never too firm or chewy. It was perfectly moist and bloodied.

The EMA agents were bestowed upon a myriad of cuisines to excite every palette there was in their ranks. No one could ever once complain that the cuisines they served was an affront to the culture associated with each. There were no shoddy imitations; each were as authentic as they could be, cooked by chefs who specialized in them. If there was one thing the EMA did well, it was they had no patience for shortcuts. There were even some who had joined them from other Regions who declared audaciously that the food served here was far better than the ones from home.

The food that night was no exception. They served Chinese that day; a platter of noodles, a choice between fried with black sauce or ones in a meaty broth, and beef briskets, fried rice, dumplings and trays after trays of more food. Another thing the EMA did well, they made so much food so none of the Agents could ever sleep hungry. They deserved it, after all, for the number of calories they burned in training sessions.

Out of habit, Lucas had almost gone to the cafeteria where the officer cadets ate, something he had done for years already. Since the EMA compound was so huge, it would be ridiculous to ask the lot of them to walk to a central location, so there were many scattered about instead.

At first, Lucas thought he would just head there for old times' sake, but he decided he had caused enough trouble there for that day. He would give Icarus and Sam a rest for now, and his mood wasn't particularly great either. Being in a large crammed hall with a deafening rowdiness would most certainly not help.

Yet, eating at the big boys table with the commanders in the headquarters he was posted to was not a particularly enticing proposition. It would be a posher atmosphere than he was used to, and it would be jarring to eat in such a different environment. He knew he wouldn't have been able to enjoy the food anyway, spending most of the time looking over his shoulder and about, worrying about if others were gossiping about him. He knew not one of them, save for Yruf, but it would be forlorn hope to think the Overall Commander would grace the cafeteria.

He was most likely holed up in his room doing work again. When you were responsible for the peace of the world, commanding an army that could rival even the First Federation and the five of its closest competitors combined, the stress must have been overwhelming.

So, he ate in his new cozy quarters. It was a lonely existence, but he would endure it for now in the name of reposing himself after all the madness. He spent a few days like that, slacking in his room and enjoying the new amenities that came with it. Though not by choice.

Yruf had given him leave for two weeks on account of his promotion and the good work he had done in the Orc Nation. He had half a mind to make use of the EMA's facilities during that time. When he was a cadet, his day was always dictated by routine and a superior. Now that he was a full-fledged officer, he had more leeway and he could finally truly enjoy the swimming pools, the gyms and the sports arenas that were made with the most sophisticated technology and materials money could buy.

But all his hopes came crashing down when exhaustion and soreness of his mission caught up to him. He had thought he had graduated from that and the jetlag that came from switching time Zones. It was not a ludicrous notion, he had completed such missions so many times he thought one day surely it would happen. He had thought this one was the one. Oh, he was wrong.

The sores only delayed themselves, and this one proved to be the worst out of all he had been through. He was reduced to nothing but a panda those few days, a crippled one at that. His muscles twitched and throbbed, they ached at places he didn't even know he could ache at, and once he got so frustrated he pressed one of them so hard he swore he dislodged something he shouldn't have. The pain swamped him quickly, so much so he fainted.

When he was not sleeping, it was only because his stomach growled for one of two things; he needed to eat or he needed to expel what he had eaten. Even so, he often ate alone, and did both businesses drowsy and half a zombie, fighting to keep awake. Otherwise, he had basically fast forwarded three days of his life.

It was only then he truly appreciated the autonomy of being an officer. There were no nosy roommates to disturb you and no activity he had to worry about, and no annoying Sergeants who picked on him and asked him to answer for things he did not do. On the groggy flashes that he was allowed when his eyes blinked to sweep the room as he went about his necessary businesses, he took notice of his room.

It was furnished lightly, with a monochrome color of white that Yruf loved. When he took reins of the EMA, he had revamped the entire compound, stripping away what colors and pretentiousness he said were inessential to one that exuded glamor through simplicity. His room was splashed with just that color, and so were the furniture; his bed and cushions and pillows and covers and quilts that made it, the frame of the bed, his desk, his wardrobe and everything else he could get his eyes on. If not white, then Yruf settled on black. Only stationeries and perhaps some bolts and pins that secured the furniture were of a unique shade of color.

His room was large to him, a thorough upgrade to the one before. As you went up the ladder of ranks, so did your floor and the size of your room. Which also meant Lucas was assigned on one of the lower floors. It was the first floor of the apartments, but also the fifth when you accounted for the first four floors of amenities. He had a good idea how much confusion it would cause when people asked for another's floor.

The higher floors were sometimes given to lower-priority guests when the higher officers did not need them or it was vacant. A separate building was erected for the more important visitors like when the President of the First Federation needed to do an official inspection of the compound; an inspection only in name, it was nothing more than a formal way of spending money for a celebration.

As such, he wasn't given a room with a view at all. Even if he had, the level wouldn't have been spectacular enough to warrant one anyway. The only one was at the side where his table was, a measly thing that looked out into yet another training field. The best ones looked into a water feature. But he guessed he should be lucky he wasn't facing the worst one, a room that only looked into another room of yet another apartment building.

And the side where the window was placed made it so that the sun would not come splattering in at the start of dawn to interrupt his sleep, and in the evening the faint ruddy glow was often soft enough for Lucas to leave the blinds open.

Every time he woke, he would look out from the window that was large enough to look at a sideway angle. From the tint of the sky, bruised purple or unsullied blue, he could usually tell what time it was. If he was muddled about whether dawn had started or dusk was coming, he would simply listen intently. If there were boots stomping and drill sergeants howling commands in derisive tones then it was morning, otherwise it was night. Without fail, there were soldiers training in the field.

It was no use recalling what his last meal was since sometimes he slept through some of them and sometimes he was too fatigued to even activate his mind to fetch that memory.

This time he woke, however, the window did not greet him. Something large was blocking his sight, something dark and large. He was puzzled for a moment, but when his wits began to sink back into his mind and the fog in his eyes rippled away, then it became clear. A massive block of a man towered above him. Lucas had wanted to pounce up to engage this supposed intruder, but when he saw the distinct rank he could not mistake pinned on his waist and his face, he flinched to a stop.

There was only one like that, a gold rank with a crown above crested over the usual EMA symbol; a symbol that hailed the Overall Commander of the EMA.

Yruf had grown much older than Lucas remembered. When he was still a child, Yruf had not a strand of white on his head.

Now there were only wisps of that color sparsely wreathed like a delicate bird's nest perched on his head. He had once been a robust man that stood broad of shoulders and tall as a leader should when he led the charge for battle. Only now did Lucas recognize the change. It had been so gradual he had not blinked twice about it before.

He sported a thick beard, one made with a mass of individual curls of hair. A large gash from his younger days now graced him with a scar down his nose that made him look like he was always incensed. He was older and scruffier than from his fighting days. His left knee made creaking noises when he walked and his arms were less muscular. The overwhelming strength he once boasted at his prime, had left him. He now had to use an exoskeleton attached to his body if he were to fight. He didn't actually need it for mundane daily activities, but he wore it all the time, under the large coat. It wasn't for protection. Yruf always told Lucas presence was the most important. It was how people respected or feared him. He may be weaker, but he just needed people to *think* he was still kicking.

He had many enemies after all, they surrounded Yruf like a waft of perfume. And if he still wanted them to keep them down from wherever they kept themselves, he had to put up an impression of intimidation through posture and expression. He needed them to know he hadn't softened. He was still the ruthless person all those years before.

There had been rumors. Rumors of his treachery to his own men, and his faults of his tenure. But some rumors were truths. When he 'lost' the Cube, and the ever-growing dissent for him grooming Lucas. He skirted so many rules by bringing Lucas up, arming a child for once was clearly illegal, and not to mention the cries of favoritism by his own men, but no one had yet grown the courage to say it to his face. Not even Yruf's superiors. They knew that it took strength to keep up the fight like Yruf did. Whatever his faults, he was too rare to pass up because of a few taints.

"I have given food, an education and I always made sure you were treated kindly. I'm sure you did not feel so much as a hint of malice from me, nor did you ever feel he needed to escape. Under the tutelage of me, you became the top EMA agent and a deadly killer," Yruf started to speak now that he knew he had Lucas' attention. Yruf's huge frame blocked whatever light it could bar, but it was not wide enough for some rays of them to silhouette his body in a gleaming aura. "Have I been unkind to you, Lucas?"

He tried to act nonchalant, ignoring the large bear of a man. Annoyance gurgled in his mind but he dared not lash out at Yruf. Yruf looked composed, but he had seen him lose his top once and told himself never again. "No," Lucas drawled.

"You have gained many 'Youngest member of' titles in the institution. You overtook my kill count long ago. You're probably the strongest Agent I have, and you know how I do not mince words Lucas… I do not exaggerate either. But that also means that you need to step up," he continued, "or what did you think the reason was for your promotion and this room." He waved his burly arms around Lucas' quarters. "Your pay has increased dramatically even, and I was sure to add a few more zeroes to encourage you to continue your good work. And that you deserve every cent. And this is how you repay me? With sloth?"

"Sloth is an animal, not a verb," he blurted just to spite Yruf even though he knew he was wrong. Lucas did not know what came over him to produce such defiance. Forget about

119

language, it was wrong to even speak, and he usually did not like to self-sabotage himself. Yruf hated his digression and even more when you did not take his main point seriously and nitpick on trivialities.

"I know you know it is," Yruf made a guttural noise. "If you think my vocabulary is limited to synonyms of strength and cowardliness, then I'm sorry to disappoint, boy. I am not as stupid as you think. And neither do I need to explain my achievements to you for you to understand you are still my subordinate no matter how much I love you." Yruf did not venture into his temper and spoke with a stony voice.

Yruf groaned and turned away, his hands locked behind his back, fingers tangled with each other into a giant ball. He always did this when he was getting into serious business as if it always repulsed him. *But he loves it, he loves the game, he loves war... as I do.*

"Three times, Lucas, three times!" His voice rose like a wave about to evolve into a tsunami.

"And what so special about that number?" Nothing rang a bell, that number had no special meaning to him.

"Three times I sent people to call for you and three times you sent them back," Yruf rebuked. "Has your rank gone so far up your ass that you forget your duty? Not to me, to the people."

Lucas's brows furrowed. "What?" But just as he said it, the memories came flooding back. He may have been groggy then, but Lucas did not just *forget.* Yes, he remembered now. Three times he had been knocked on the door. The first two he refused to answer... or he simply couldn't, too deep in sleep. The last he got so irked by the incessant knocking he threatened the poor secretary.

120

"I even scolded him for being shoddy, Lucas. Now how do you suppose I make it up to him? I never thought you would be so indifferent to my calls. But now I know it is not his fault. You must know what the horrible things you said to him."

"Yes. I know. I told him that I would use my rank against him, but I would perform a special service for him. I told him I would slice his tummy open and feed his organs into his mouth and watch it flow back down," Lucas grumbled faintly with some contrite.

"Yes," Yruf fumed. "Utterly distasteful. You know my secretary is not a fighting man, he's an officer worker. He would not know you jest. And truthfully, you scare everyone, even the combatants. I expect you to apologize to him when you are done with this mission."

"Mission? What mission?"

"Why did you think I sent him in the first place?" Yruf turned and glowered at Lucas with a sideways look. His beady eyes were dashed with silver from the light and his pupils scintillated.

"But you said…"

"I know what I said. And I am a person of my word. You have your two weeks break, and it is up to you to choose who you would spend it with, yes… but do you suppose lazing here is a good use of your time?"

"Well, if I choose to. You've fought before, you know how tiring it gets," Lucas moaned. "And you as you said, it's my choice."

"Yes. It is. I cannot command anything of you, but I can request a favor from you that might get you to choose… differently." Yruf turned fully to face Lucas now.

"And specifically, how would you do that?" Lucas chuckled. It was a nice feeling having the leverage against Yruf for once, the choice to do what he liked.

Yruf sighed. "Sometimes I wish you didn't take after my stubbornness. But as you are stubborn, I know you are loyal as well. It is the one redeeming quality that can come from that bull head of yours. You are fiercely loyal to your bones, and you would rather rot in the dirt from failure than to watch your friends suffer."

Lucas narrowed his eyes. Yruf was not one who spoke much and he hated riddles and symbolism as much as the Purebloods. If something would drive him to a monologue just to demonstrate the graveness of the situation, then that something had to be big. "What happened?"

"George. He's in trouble."

HELLO WORLD-6 (GEORGE)

George closed his eyes. *I should have known, I should have seen it coming.* He looked to the skies and took himself out of the chaos for just a second, just a second of respite he asked for, just a second away from this nightmare, as if that was all that was required to escape from this harsh reality, as if heavens would grant it to him. He had been a pious person, born into the right family and attended whatever religious duties was expected of him diligently, but that was all it was; duty.

The sun was a bright star in the lucid sky. Yes, sometimes he had to remind himself of that. No one ever thought stars were so big, they thought they were twinkly little specks in the sky. Who would have thought something so large as the damn sun was a star? He caught himself in his thoughts then, his mind was trying to distract him from the situation at hand, a common occurrence when despair and disorientation kicked in.

But did it matter? George purposely confined his gaze to the top.

The sun was so bright it seemed to melt into the sky and swell up twice its size, but it was just the blaze cloaking it that made it seem that way. In recognition of the sun authority, the clouds parted from it, leaving a bare blue at a huge radius from the sun. But still, they were too bright to look at directly. The clouds were streaks, so thin yet still puffy they looked like white chicken tenders. *Ah, I'm hungry.* The sensations that rushed through him was confusing as it was anticipated. A person marked for death would want to experience the things he loved for at least the last time.

It was calm and oblivious to the carnage below. Whatever blood was spilled here was of no concern to the heavens above. A blossom of hatred grew in George's heart. *Then what was the point of all that praying? If he cannot even answer when I needed him most.* The white clouds floated and the tranquil sky was a constant blue. Only the sun seemed to have any concept of vigor, shining down with shafts of light that pricked his eyes as much as a spear would have.

He knew it was a foolish hope to think of escape. He was done for. He tilted his head back down to the field. All the edges and sides that he could escape from had been sealed up by hordes of huge furry monsters. All his life, he had been taught to treat species with respect, to treat them how he wanted to be treated, so he had never once believed the prejudiced and barbarous views Yruf held. But more and more he felt as if he was being played for a fool. His thoughts slowly transitioned. *Yes, I see now. They cried wolf, when they were the wolves.*

The Werewolves all stood taller than even their tallest guy, bulkier than even their biggest guy who lifted the heaviest weights, and had fur pelt that would put even their hairiest man in shame. But above all that, they were vicious. Each of the EMA Agents had put in years of meticulous and disciplined hard work to get to where they were, and they showed that by earning their badges and honors.

But the Werewolves did not need such things. They were built for battle, with huge fangs they bared to intimidate their foes and tapered eyes that shone with malice. They had powerful muscles matched his claws as sharp and long as small daggers that tore through with such force it shattered the EMA formation like it was made of paper.

They moved quickly too, like normal wolves, but since they were so large, they were black smears racing across the field walloping all that came before them. And so especially frightening when you thought they were far, only to blink and catch them appear suddenly right in front of you, their disheveled fur cloaking everything else around, their beady, yellow eyes staring down on you. Then it was death.

Each swing, each slash, each wrestle delivered devastating effects to the agents. They were like paper shields being ripped apart, into half, into many more parts, decapitated, mutilated into a bag of blood flesh, gored till it was unrecognizable. No one survived under a full strike of a Werewolf. Some he had known since young, some he had come to enjoy the company of, some they were slowly opening up to him. Since he was young, he had been taught to help others where his abilities allowed, and value everyone he met with the same courtesy. Since he was a commander now, all the more he had to abide with that mantra.

But how? He was no Werewolf. He had none of the strength or ferocity. It hurt to be so helpless.

Each person that fell was like a slash on his heart, a hollow slash which left residue of bitter pain festering inside. That was the worst sort, like poison eating into his heart, burrowing and killing him slowly but surely long after the slash had found its place. It was as if the strikes also progressed onto him through some telekinetic magic the Werewolves were using. Though it couldn't be, Werewolves didn't use magic, not in these parts at least.

George had seen so many dead bodies by now he thought he was desensitized to them, but he made the mistake of thinking too deeply about them; their smiles, their banter, their goals and all the dreams that they had told him about when he made the effort to know them better. *If you do not even care about the people who work for you, then do not expect them to do the same for you.*

He found it was never any easier, and the fact that time seemed to slow as the slaughter got closer to him did not help either. He felt so lost, and this felt so surreal. Like all this was just a horrible nightmare that would pass. But no. Each second, he had to remind himself this was real. As with each outermost soldier who fell, the ranks shrunk towards George and his impending death.

The sight of him sent lances of pain into his heart, chills through his spine as he realized he would not be able to talk or laugh with them anymore. He could only imagine the sorrow their families would feel when it came to his obligation to tell them... if he survived this slaughter; which was not likely.

George had seen documentaries on how wolves hunt their prey, this was far worse. Losing was an understatement.

The agents stood no chance if they fought in single combat. Humans were the weakest of all the species that graced this brutal yet lavish Earth, they couldn't even hold their own against smaller species like the dwarves or the gnomes. And definitely not against full grown, humongous Werewolves.

Desperation propelled in George quickly, and took him by the neck. It didn't make him feel better that the agents were trained to take the hit for him; the commander always fell last in battle. As long as you had your head, you always had a fighting chance.

The soldiers around him knew, and they still remained composed, for now. It was the best they could do. Charging recklessly was a surefire way to die. Their only hope was in working together. But they were barely delaying their demise. George knew someone would break soon, he could see it in their faces and their posture, for little good it will do. He knew they knew they would still die even if they surrendered or tried to flee, but sometimes insanity was exactly what it was, illogical.

The EMA soldiers were all clad in thick vests of the toughest material money could buy, armored in half a dozen weapons sheathed around their bodies that most had taken out to use already.

They were left with their rifles slung around their necks, blasting as quickly as they could to take out the Werewolves. Thank heavens the Werewolves weren't immune to the special bullets they were supplied with. Yet, not only were their reflexes quick, they were durable. And it took dozens of shots just to bring down one of them. But losing ammo wasn't the primary concern. They were losing more men than he could care for ammo.

Under their helmets, their faces were a range of expression; dazed and despair were the most common ones. Their skin was slick with sweat and their eyes glistened pure terror. It wouldn't take long before one of them turned unhinged, and when that happened, that was all it took to break formation and cripple what already little defense they held up.

"Is help coming, Sir?" a trembling, petrified voice called behind him among all the chaos. It was a miracle he could hear so crisply under all the battle cries and yells and piercing screams. But he figured his mind was desperate to keep him away from despair.

He dared not turn behind or risk moving his eyes away from the nearer threat. In a battle, the commander had to have a keen eye and focus or his soldiers would move like little ants rather than one hive. "No," George answered regrettably. He didn't have the heart to lie to him. Usually, George would propose an alternative, there was always another way. Not this time. "I'm sorry," was all he could manage to say.

There was nothing he could do now but continue searching for potential chinks in the Werewolf offence. They were coming in at all sides, and since they prowled on all fours before leaping onto them, he couldn't gauge how many there truly were. Being in a cornfield, where the grass was as tall as he was, made natural camouflages for the Werewolves. The EMA side might have had better military capabilities and strategy, but all was for nothing when the Werewolves made it up in viciousness, numbers and on a disadvantageous turf for humans.

"Why? Couldn't you call an airstrike? I don't mind if we die. I've accepted it. But at least bring the werewolves with us." the words from the soldier's mouth had lost all civility and the usual courtesy George was used to when he wore his rank. But he couldn't blame him. His words were shaking as well. George gritted his teeth. "If I could I would have called it long ago." He was able to suppress his anger and disappointment at himself. A commander had to keep composed, he alone held up the crumbling morale of whatever was left of his squad.

128

"Then why? Why won't they come?"

"They... just can't. This mission is supposed to be kept under wraps, it was off the books. No one should know about this. If the EMA calls an airstrike it would blow up into an international incident."

"Is that all?!" the soldier questioned indignantly. "Then do you mean to say the commanders will just leave us to die like that?"

It wouldn't be the first time, George thought. Yruf was ruthless, a man who prided himself in seeing the bigger picture of things. When George's life wasn't the one on the line, he appreciated it, but now... "There are many more factors, but do you really want me to list them all or focus on the battle?"

"What's the point? No matter how long we hold up, we're going to die anyway!"

George sighed silently, mere hot air flitting over his lips. He would not show his fear, not till the end. He was backed into a corner by another hard question. *He will come, he must.* "Just hold it! Have faith!" George frowned. *Let's hope that's not my final order.*

The soldier seemed to understand George's predicament. He relented and leaned away from him. "Then it will have been an honor serving under you, sir."

"I share the sentiments," George replied grimly. *This was supposed to be an easy mission. We were supposed to come in and go out in a blink of an eye with no one in the Region the wiser.*

And worse, it was all his doing. George did not make mistakes, no he did not. Everyone praised him for it since young, he was the flawless paragon that made everything better with his presence. And so he tried to be, he had to be. For duty, for he had the power to and so he felt compelled to do it.

And of all times, he had to be proven wrong now. His only fault, and his last fault. He just had to overreach himself, had to turn complacent at his chance for glory. He had laid out an elaborate plan to defeat the enemy, but it soon became clear it was a fruitless endeavor to stick to it when the first hundred things started to go south. They always said when you were about to die, your life would flash before you. Well, George had that luxury now. He sure had more time than those who did not expect it. But wasn't his life that he saw, not the ones he experienced at least, but the life that could have been.

If only I...

The Werewolves closed in. Hordes that were once scattered joined into a wall of doom. One by one, his soldiers were dragged or flung out of formation and they were never seen again, their screams never lasted long. George didn't want to know what happened to those soldiers. It sent chills down his spine. Others were stabbed or ripped apart by the large, menacing claws, as if it was better.

Without warning, a Werewolf leaped towards George, ready to make the kill. Being targeted like that was bizarre, he couldn't move or react, nor did his body think it was real. And he got a good look at his would-be murderer. He... no, she, George realized the Werewolf was a she with bosoms bulging from her chest. She had bloodthirsty eyes that was merited. After all, the EMA had started it. She was lean but vascular, George was sure, under that layer of fur.

A high-pitched buzzing stabbed his ears first. George closed his eyes ready to make his maker. If this was the way he should die, he had to accept it. Besides, dying valiantly among his men was one of the best ways to go. Perhaps he would be promoted for his bravery after his death, maybe conferred a status to the Hall of Greats. Would they talk about George the Brave? George wasn't sure, but it was a nice thought. It was better to have a dopamine rush rather than paralyzing fear.

George waited for a second or a minute, or could he have already died that he was just waiting for nothing. He could not tell, but it did feel like an hour passed. Nothing happened. Perhaps, it happened so quickly he didn't feel it? He opened his eyes and was greeted to much of the same sight. But where the attacker should have been, hanging in midair with an arm stretched away and poised to swing, she had been completely erased from that space.

In replacement was the scene of battle and the sky sliding down to meet the land at the horizon.

Weird. I did not hear anything. He should have heard a bullet... or a hundred of them lodge into her, but there was no such thing. Yet, with the chaos all around him, the gunshots must have blended with the rest, he surmised. Yet the hypothesis of a singular accidental bullet was blown out of the water as soon as he looked down.

The remains of his attacker laid in front of him in a strewn of exploded flesh, viscera flowing out like little snakes and drowned in a cascade of thick crimson blood. It took a moment for him to understand she had been blown up. But by what? The EMA's side had run out of rocket launchers long ago, and there was no other artillery in his squad that could unleash such destruction. On closer inspection, however, everything came together. A blue glow throbbed on the flesh, like the embers coated on charcoal about to extinguish.

Confusion twisted on his face at first, then he started to recognize it. And more his senses tingled to find more clues of what he deduced. Then he heard it, he saw it, and he felt it. The drumming in his stomach, the blare of heavy artillery as metal clashed with metal, and gears clanked into place, and bullets erupted from their shells with a violent detonation. Yes, he recognized this feeling. This was a specific feeling he felt in only one specific instance... one specific person. He smiled and jolted his head up.

Perhaps all the pious prayer had not been for naught. Someone answered.

From the sky, a barrage of blue projectiles rained down on the mayhem. They seemed random at first, but they were able to maneuver and shoot down the advancing werewolves. None of the shots hit any of the EMA agents.

Something burst down from the clouds, leaving a gaping hole in the sky as it sped towards the ground. George squinted and could make out a person with his jetpack. Only one person he knew had the ability and arrogance and the childishness to execute such an unapologetic and brazen entrance. And only he had the arsenal that could dish out such carnage with deadly accuracy.

Yruf had told him that the chance for a rescue was slim, but he would try. George had taken it as that. That time he kind of knew his life had been forfeit already. Lucas had just returned from his own mission so he was the last person he expected to come for the rescue, but he wasn't complaining.

A few more homing projectiles ejected out of Lucas' cannons and bounded onto the field, slamming onto the field, indiscriminately clearing the Werewolves close to the EMA formation.

When it all but emptied out, only then he descended, halting his descent with a punch on the ground. The loud boom shockwaved throughout the field. As if a temporary truce had been agreed on silently, Werewolves and humans alike ceased their brawl for a moment and turned to where Lucas had been. A dust cloud billowed out where he had landed, and a strong breeze was sent forth to flutter the stalks of corn.

Silent swept the battlefield, every soul frozen in place in anticipation; whether to admire him or reprioritize their targets, George could not say. The blue smoke and sand dust cleared as Lucas' brown hair settled on his head. His jetpack folded itself into his body. The bright blue streaks on his armor glowed, a faint silhouette shivered with the markings in the dust. He straightened himself up and strolled out, his frame enlarged and cleared up as he exited the smoke cloud.

Lucas was a young chap, sprightly and insanely intelligent for his age. Many of the times he had touted that he wouldn't have survived without George's help, but George knew that wasn't true. Lucas was just being modest. Whatever he picked up for Lucas was only due to his laziness, and sometimes he wondered if helping Lucas was good for him at all. Still George did for the simple reason that he was just a kid; a poor kid without the childhood the rest of the people around Lucas had. And sometimes George would forget that by the way he spoke with such eloquence.

But the Lucas now had no suggestion of cheekiness or joy on his stony face. His eyes were resolute and dimmed, steely like a predator about to strike. But the signs of weariness poked him till he had an old man's dour look to him. *Something's not right.* Lucas usually had a smile to him, just to keep the morale of the soldiers up. *He's tired.* A seed of worry germinated in

133

George's heart, but he hoped nothing would befall on Lucas. *He's different,* he convinced himself. *He's going to be alright.*

"EMA Agents, stay put," he commanded, soft but firmly. That was Lucas' way of command, one he learnt well from Yruf. The loudest and brashest of the officers were feared and avoided, but types like him were respected and depended upon, types who had substance *and* charisma.

It didn't matter what tone he used, his presence was enough. George could not see every of his soldiers, but he could suddenly feel the mood brighten and the morale raise. Lucas had that effect, and in no small part contributed to his powers. Lucas had absurd statistics when it came to mission victories and men lost. He was basically worshipped among active combatants. His presence was not unlike one of a messiah, as if everyone knew everything was going to be alright once he was here. There was hope. The Ace was here.

Before the Werewolves could process, Lucas whisked up his hands then jerked both down to uncoil them. In an instant, both decomposed into a million fragments of skin, from beige to a harsh metal color it transformed into and then puzzled themselves together into shiny cyan blades. The sun splashed a silver glint at the edges of his blades and they shimmered and shifted as he moved them. Two hulking rocket launchers materialized on his shoulders. The guns recharged with a rattle of clicking, the guns lit up and alerted they were ready, he plunged into the chaos and began his massacre.

It all happened in an instant. Lucas was a tornado armed with an arsenal. He kicked, stabbed and shot down his enemies three… no five… no seven at a time. No, he was too fast for the eye to see. One time he was here, then the next he was at the other end of the field. George did not bother to blink, just a

134

heartbeat was enough to miss out on a chunk of juicy massacre. And after all the trouble, heartache and anxiety the Werewolves caused him, he would have to be mad to miss this.

So many times, George had seen him in action, and still countless more he knew he would look with the same dazed awe. He was a smear in the cornfield, a medley of blue and black streaks cutting and blasting at his enemies. His blades swept clean like a skilled butcher, limbs and waists were relieved from their attachments in swift, smooth strokes, with no such grotesque cracking or slushy sounds or ragged remains that pounded the floor.

There was a last color, red. Red danced around him like a flow of rivulets levitating up, curling around him, then splashing out sharply and bathing the cornfield with a new shade. He was the genius artist who painted with only a singular color, all slashing behind his own blades in fine arcs. When the arcs fell, the liquid that composed them flowered down at different speeds.

He knifed through the wall that seemed as impenetrable as it was deadly, making it seem like George and his squad was only making a mountain of a molehill. Inch by inch, he stormed through the Werewolf ranks and disintegrated what a full squad of full trained veteran soldiers could not. He was a hurricane, the scorn of all life that tried to stand before him. And thus, it didn't take long for the Werewolves to grow the notion of retreat in their minds.

They ran. Lucas gave chase to the low hanging fruits. Some stumbled in fear like they were bumbling fools who did not know how to walk properly. Lucas vanquished them all. He stabbed, sidestepped from attacks almost condescendingly easily, and then flipped and slashed and swung wildly. He parried claws and fangs, and then struck back, slicing them off.

Blade and cannon oscillated between each other, transitioning so fast his body was a constant swirl of fragments blanketing him. Never once did George see him stop, he kept moving. And if he did, he stopped only so long as a blink of an eye that George could not discern it.

Usually, Lucas wasn't so swift in his attacks. Most fights George saw him in he was so relaxed it almost seemed like he was heading to the beach than some war. Sometimes, George worried for him. But it was always unfounded. Sometimes George wondered if Lucas was just playing with George's nerves... or most likely the enemy's.

Most fights were nothing to Lucas. Most fights looked like a child played with his food, squashing and sloshing them and thinking nothing of them. Ultimately, he would munch them, however.

This time, he did not allow himself to be careless. For once, he was serious. His fight patterns were safe and meticulous as wild as they seemed, and his movements had a power to them he did not usually see. He was no longer trying his luck with soft strikes for the sake of conserving energy. Usually, he would leave no survivors either, but this time he did not give chase to those who had gone too far, or even spare an effort to shoot them down.

He looked them on sullenly as they retreated, his shoulders were slumped on his body and his legs trembled with adrenaline and the seeping fatigue. He was breathing hard, harder than George had ever seen. But as George looked around him, shock ran through his nerves as he saw the void the werewolves had left. The whole lot of Werewolves that had surrounded them in a pack, covering the cornfield in black patches like an infection, had suddenly disappeared.

"You're not going to give chase?" George asked. He knew it wasn't appropriate, beggars should not be choosers, but he had to greet Lucas somehow. Lucas turned and gave him a look that immediately made him wish he could rescind that statement. It was flushed with purple fury, a dour, weary snarl took him.

"After what you have done, and you dare ask me that?" Lucas flared. "You really think I don't want to? You really think so? Do you know I had just come back on a mission myself? I had barely a few days of rest and Yruf ordered…. requested me to come save your ass! Do you know I'm still on leave? Do you know I'm still recovering? Can you see?!"

The armored growth on his arms flitted back into supple skin in the same beautiful whirl of shards. His arms were veiny and throbbing, bruised and swollen. "Do you see, George? Do you think I'm capable of *giving* chase? Much less continuing the fight? I could barely chase them off to save your miserable lives and this is the thanks I get?"

George pursed his lips, knowing that Lucas was well entitled to his rant. Making snarky remarks was never George's strong suit, nor was knowing when to say them. He made a mental note never to say them again. He stared at Lucas' hand even when his mind felt repulsed by it. "I'm sorry. I didn't know. Thanks."

Lucas' glower lingered at George for a second before diverting them to his hands. He shook them to loosen them before dangling them beside his waist. "Seriously!" he blurted. "We're all alive only because I played my cards right. They knew who I was and the reputation that came along with it. They thought they were playing with the Ace at his full

137

strength." Lucas swung his hand to point at George, deep blue eyes accorded him once more. There was no light to them, only authority.

"But I wasn't. You're lucky my ruse paid off. Any second longer and they might have seen that I was severely underpowered, they would have seen the obvious clues of fatigue on me. Then it would only have spurred them even more. After all, who would miss out a chance to take out the Ace? We would have all died then!" Lucas flung out his arms furiously. "What the heck happened, George?"

Yes, what happened? The memories had all been jumbled and pricked with gaps when the Werewolves came onto them. But now the train of events was slowly coming back to him. He knew. The EMA had put their trust in him, all his superiors wagered a limb for him for his success, and they agreed to the first ever mission where a Lieutenant was put in overall charge.

George was pressured to make sure he shone in this. If he did this well, it wouldn't be long that they saw more potential in him and sent him for more higher-class missions, even his promotion to the next rank would be expedited. And the precedent he sent, would open the gates for more Lieutenants to be given trust to lead their missions.

So much for that.

The mission was simple. It was an in and out mission that would take no less than a day, and one Yruf had warned him to keep quiet on. The EMA heard a whisper that this Werewolf District was harboring international criminals knowingly, and being set up as a hidden base for them. The District was a mere front. Yruf has liaised with the Werewolf government himself but said this was still supposed to be kept under wraps or it might risk the criminals anticipating their attack. He was

138

supposed to level the District, burn it to the ground, do whatever it took to get rid of it. Whatever Werewolf he could capture would be put for interrogation, the rest would be put down.

It didn't matter, however. Once George landed, the Werewolves attacked. He had been too complacent, and set his camp too close to the District instead of the outskirts as discussed; desiring to complete the mission in half the time assigned to him. The werewolves knew he was coming, and he led half his squad to their deaths.

"I underestimated the Werewolves," he replied concisely, not much was there to be said. "They chased us and we headed to the cornfield where we thought we could lose them in the stalks. But we only headed into their trap. They knew, Lucas. They knew we were going to head there."

Lucas sighed and lowered himself down before his legs could crumble. He crossed his legs and arms and looked up to George, scrutinizing him. "And on your first mission too. For all the help you have given me throughout our cadet journey, I will not be so harsh on you, nor will I contend against you when Yruf or the other generals ask me. But George, you never make mistakes, what happened?"

George narrowed his eyes. "Greed happened. And it was no slap on the wrist. I paid for it dearly." Who would dare join his squad now? This mission will forever be a taint on his record as a reckless commander. The missions handed out to first timers were always low-level ones to blood the commanders, give them a boost of confidence with a good start to their record. Oh, he got bloodied alright. If already on his first mission it had been sullied with such failure and mortality rates, would anyone trust him for future one? His commanders trusted him, but now he only solidified the opposition's belief that they were too inexperienced and naïve. It made him both angry and disheartened at once.

So this is war. Without safety nets, without people to check and appraise you. A mistake is death.

"You did," Lucas combed through his squad with those blue eyes while slouching forward and resting his palms onto his kneecaps.

"Should we call the mission off and retreat? We can cut our losses like that. And we are in no position to continue our pursuit," George followed up.

Lucas shook his head. "We are already here, and the Werewolf horde is in tatters, we should continue the mission."

"Not in our state. And not in yours," George voiced his concern.

Lucas sighed. He gave George a look that ensured he was dead serious. "George, I don't need to tell you how precarious your situation is. If you leave now with half of your soldiers dead and the other half badly maimed, injured, gored and in dire need of therapy after the horrors they have been through today *and* with the mission uncompleted *and* alerting the enemy of our attack, you know what Yruf will do."

George narrowed his eyes. He wasn't that oblivious. He knew well. It wasn't rare to see Lieutenants demoted back to the life of a trifling cadet if Yruf deemed them inept. Or worse, they might get sent to become a trainer where they would be banished to train soldiers for the rest of their rotting lives. Or perhaps if Yruf particularly hated him, the overall commander could charge him as a suspected traitor. That penalty granted the culprit the particularly permanent affliction of death.

"I know, but," he looked around at his squad... or what was left of it. His men were worn, gaunt, and in far worse shape than the Werewolves would have been. Their uniforms and vests were soaked with blood and sweat, some could barely stand. It wouldn't be to their advantage if they gave chase. If anything, the Werewolves might have loaded another trap for them to be sprung again once they caught up to them.

"You speak truthfully, I cannot refute. But I think I'm far from able to redeem myself. My track record is past saving already. I will not let another bout of egotism cloud my judgement once more, I will not have more blood on my already guilty hands. I am still acting commander here, and I shall remain as such until it is confirmed I am stripped of my status. And I shall act as such until that time comes."

He had thought Lucas would have given him eyes that loathed him even more, but Lucas' pupils only shone with pride. "George. I think out of all the moments we had, this is your most genuine. You never once refused something of someone. And now you did. You stood up to yourself, and now I respect you even more."

George realized it as well. He thought saying no would make him feel repulsed at himself. But it felt good, it felt good to think for his own for once. "Isn't that what a commander should do?"

"Yes," Lucas gleaming eyes turned a shade darker, but still with a glint of cheekiness. "But it will not hide the fact I still have to complete this mission. You can stay here, George. For all that I owe you, I'm going to repay you back in full now." He smiled. "Deal?"

"It doesn't seem like I have any choice," George smiled back.

Lucas nodded and muttered 'good' several times. He groaned and got to his feet with much effort. He stumbled a little to find his balance and once he nearly looked like he was about to buckle and fall once more. But he did.

"You sure you're in a state to continue? It's a kind gesture from your part, but I will have no part in killing you. You are more important than my stupid track record, Lucas."

Lucas waved his hand, looking away so as to hide his panting. But George knew. Eventually, the act gave way and he had to bend down and press his hands onto his thighs to simmer his breathing. "It's alright. I may not look like much right now, and… there is truth in that, but the Werewolves don't know it. Besides, I don't have to be as good as I usually am, huh?" he assured and turned and feigned a confident smile. "I just have to be better than every of them. Which I am."

"Yruf will still kill me if you die here, you know? You're our most valuable asset. And I don't mean that metaphorically," George warned ominously. It was no secret those who opposed Yruf did not last long in the EMA. There had even been some mysterious disappearances from those who had actively snubbed him the next day when they spoke ill of him. Yruf did not tolerate any rivalry in the EMA, as was his motto that a body only functioned at its pinnacle when it only had one head.

Forbidding lines cast themselves onto Lucas' face. George knew he knew. Yruf was not one who had any qualms on getting his hands dirty, but Lucas didn't care. He idolized that man like he was a deity. "You are an officer of the EMA, George, entrusted by Yruf himself to perform what needs to be done. I thought you should know better. I will not do anything against you in consideration that you are my friend, but I advise that you are not so liberal with your words in the future."

You're wrong. I am pledged to keep the peace between all the realms of Earthians, not blindly follow Yruf. Aren't officers supposed to think critically about such things, if not why commission officers at all? It was in George's mind to argue, but he decided this was a battle he did not want to pick. He glanced away in false contrite and nodded. "I'm sorry. It's just I'm worried about you. You don't usually sweat so much. Not in your missions, even in war or your most heinous enemies…"

"Yeah well, if you guys had been more careful, I wouldn't have needed to step into the fray," Lucas complained. "Joking," he chuckled when he saw George's face turn redder than a tomato.

His expression dipped as he swung towards the direction where the Werewolves fled. "Wait here," he warned unsmiling, "I'll go. You just help the injured and call in reinforcements. I'm sure you know what to do. Set up a medial area and blah blah, I forgot. And it's not my job."

Yes, it's not yours, George recalled wistfully. That was the Lucas he knew. From the longest memory he had of Lucas George had, the boy always liked going solo. He had never intended to become an officer to command his own troop, rather he needed the rank just to keep other people from pestering him; people he had coined as low-lives who had no business bossing him around.

Lucas turned before George would give him a reply. He carried his body for a limp for several steps, until he finally found a better position to tilt his hips so he could walk with the same fluid and cautious grace he usually had.

143

HELLO WORLD-7 (LUCAS)

It was an understatement to say that Yruf had been furious with George.

"I put all my trust on him, everyone told me he was the smartest of the lot, the best of them, that he had never made a single mistake. And on this pivotal mission, he makes his first? Am I to believe such inanity? My luck must have run out if so, or something in the universe has spoilt. People have put out a limb for him, and now what am I to do?" Yruf had complained. "Chop them off? If so, half of the high officers would come out with an arm lacking by tomorrow."

Yruf had made it abundantly clear he was willing to let George and his squad wither out and he would not lose a night's sleep. "All the better. I can invoke the traitor's clause for George and deem that he had gone rogue. And I would even have one less fool in the organization thanks to the Werewolves. So much simpler to explain."

"You can't!" Lucas objected. He knew he had spoken out of hand, he had never opposed Yruf before and he sure knew Yruf did not appreciate it, but he could not leave his friend out to dry.

Yruf raised a brow with dry amusement. Then he furrowed it with the other all the same with a stern look. "I can and I will.

He called me for help, and I told him I will try my best to find him what he pleads for. But I also told him that it was unlikely and he should say his prayers now before he gets stomped. The only reason I came to you first is because I know you two are close."

Yruf was adamant against summoning any support from the EMA outpost near where the Werewolf Sanctuary was. The Werewolf Sanctuary, coined the Werewolves' Jungle, was located at the end of the Continent that also most prominently held the First Federation among other Regions and Sanctuaries.

It was called a jungle but only in name. It was far from it. Like any other human Region in the world, most Pureblood Sanctuaries had modernized at the same rate as the humans have. They had sprawling cities, tall and proud skyscrapers that pierced the clouds, malls, schools… everything. Technology was the language that most successfully perforated through the world, much thanks to the EMA after the last big event no one spoke of. But like all advanced Regions, there were their outskirts and desolate areas where people lived the lives of a century before.

And that was where Yruf had commanded George to strike. He had not activated the outpost near the Werewolves' Jungle for fear it might alert the criminals hiding in the District where they were using it as a base to consolidate strength. Sending George from the heart of the First Federation to the Werewolf District was a roundabout way, but it was strategically necessary.

George had one job after that hassle, and he just had to ruin it, he just had to force Yruf to summon Lucas and spoil his hard-earned rest.

It was the only way. Anything else would have caused an international incident.

Already, the Werewolves had been reluctant in allowing the EMA to intrude on their land, as all Purebloods were to human intervention, so Yruf was hard pressed sending a fleet of aircrafts there to aid George. Already they were teetering on tremulous terms at best, it would not be a good look for the EMA if they had bombed another's property without prior consent. The Werewolves would never consent even if there had been time.

If Yruf had disregarded it all and went ahead to help George with the many other resources he had at his disposal, the First Federation would only find it as another reason to clamp down on EMA power and shrink its already weakening jurisdiction around the world.

Without a second to lose, Lucas accepted the request and raced to help George, but he was in no illusion that Yruf had done this as a favor to him. Yruf was a shrewd man, every move was calculated even towards the people he claimed he loved. Yruf would never have spared a second thought on someone's life he thought was necessary, especially for a lowly Lieutenant. Normally, he would have said his goodbyes and moved on to his next agenda.

Sending Lucas, his Ace, meant that Yruf wanted this mission to succeed desperately. And Lucas was to meet that target after he saved his friend. Fortunately, he had gotten there in time, or at least before the whole squad had been completely wiped out.

They were battered and smudged with blood and dirt, they looked so defeated, like they had their souls dragged out from them, leaving living but hollow husks standing and swaying with the cornfield.

He had wanted to give George a big hug when all that gruesome business had been temporarily suspended. After all, this would be the first time George would have seen him commission, and it had been a long while since they had seen each other. After George was promoted, their schedules had clashed ever since and they eventually drifted apart save for some scarce text messages.

But he went against his desires. George had to know the gravity of his situation, and hugging him was most likely going to soften the situation.

Then duty called, he had to complete what Yruf had really sent him to do. Also, Lucas was curious to know what Yruf saw so much in this District. Yruf wouldn't have cared so much about an ordinary criminal to have sent Lucas. Yruf could simply have waited for a better time than risk sending his most valuable soldier so perilously tired. And this being off the records only piqued his interest even more. Lucas was sure preventing their enemies from being aware of their approach was only half the story. Each move Yruf made always had more than a single purpose.

There was something in here. But what? *Weapons? A secret so nefarious it can never be divulged to the world?*

He was still angry at George, but not enough to warrant leading George to his death. He and whatever that was left in his poor squad were too traumatized to continue. And even if they hadn't been, surely none of them would wish to relive the nightmare that had reduced them into such a poor state. The werewolves had torn through them like paper. And more people didn't necessarily mean a better outcome, not in Lucas' case anyway. He fought better when there was no one else he needed to care for, when there was nothing he had to worry about getting hurt or destroyed in his mayhem. The extra people will only be fodder, or worse, liabilities.

The cornfield stretched for miles, but Lucas knew that the distance he needed to traverse was only a fraction of the damn thing. George, at his mad moment of complacency, decided to set up camp half the distance away from the usual prescribed distance from their target. And that was how the silver lining came about, a silver lining with beads of blood flowing down the strand to form a necklace of interspersed red jewels, provided and paid for by the EMA agents George had led to their deaths.

The stalks of corn plants held a robust structure, with long leaves of a rich green color that sprouted out and drooped down from its stem. Among the green blades, a rarity of maize emerged out from their cocoons like a mottled banana out of its skin. The cocoon broke apart into slices and peeled off into ears as if to bow to its fruit, to unveil and flaunt what it had made. The maize flourished proudly with silks on its tip fluttering at Lucas jostled through.

He was shorter than most people in the EMA, attributing to his age, so he was fully used to having to squeeze himself through taller objects. But the leaves poked him and tickled at his waist where humans wouldn't, especially not ones who knew him. He tried to push them aside or hold them off till he passed, but once he let go, they would only swing back to prick him like the tips of spears. He was wearing his combat attire, but the pricks still stung a little, an itchy sensation rippling through that area.

After a while, he gave up for there were far too many. He would fly, but he preferred to conserve his energy.

He was sure he was walking into an ambush… or at least a fortified District. The werewolves were far from savage beasts. They had culture and language and intelligence, their technology and their ways had kept with the sophistication of the times. Perhaps with that sophistication, they would also decipher that their odds of beating him weren't good. Surely, they wouldn't want to risk calling out his bluff. It would be in their best interest to run and leave whatever Yruf was searching for.

And even if they hadn't… it was just a District. Why was he so afraid? *Ah yes, because Yruf has taken quite an interest on this place.* If so, then they might try to defend that item that was so precious. Lucas gritted his teeth, poising himself for a tough fight ahead.

The maze corn spanned further than he thought. But it gave him time to collect his thoughts and his body to recover from the fight earlier. Already, he was counting his lucky stars he had slept through most of the three days prior, or else he might well be in a worse condition than he was now. But time didn't help hunger, it worsened it. When the state of battle left him, hunger pangs set in. He was thirsty as well, his mouth tasted like a dry sewer slick with algae. He had forgotten to ask George for his canteen in his rush to pursue the Werewolves, and he would only waste valuable time to go back now.

There were cobs all around him, all puffy and ripe with such vibrant yellow they were practically screaming to get eaten. A bite or a good scrub of a cob would do him good. And that's what he did. It was technically stealing, but he didn't think the werewolves would find out that one among a gazillion was missing.

The Werewolves were gifted farmers, and harvesting was their main source of income. This Region was famed for having such swollen produce they exploded with juice at the tiniest prick. There were those who claimed some even exploded by themselves, but Lucas didn't believe them. The werewolves even had a neat trick of marketing their produce by having a label pasted on each one of their packaging warning of explosives.

But as the Region was small, like most other Pureblood Sanctuaries, there was not enough crop to go around, so the werewolves could barely keep up with the demand. Prices never stopped going up like that, so much so you couldn't find them in normal supermarkets anymore. You had to preorder them. Now they came in nice packages as exorbitant gifts you could show off on your display mantle if you wanted to. There had even been bidding wars for the crème of the crop, as if they were rare vintage wines.

The field was quiet but the flutter of leaves and stems from the breeze that swept through the verdant sea. All the birds that had been here had flapped and squawked away when George and the Werewolves clashed.

When he finally reached the District, the sun was at its zenith, shining thick shafts of light down to punish the field as if the stalks of corn had somehow disobeyed it. Heat distorted the air and waves radiated from the ground.

Fortunately for him, this outskirt District was shielded by a thick canopy of humongous trees as tall as apartment buildings, with barks as thick as pillars of a grand monument. They were old, Lucas could tell, the covering of their bark ancient and dry, patched and shriveled. But they still stood strong after all these years. Lucas had almost wanted to apologize to such ancients

150

for what they were about to witness. After all, enemy territory or not, they were to be respected just for surviving for so long. And yet, he had a sneaking suspicion that they had seen worse done in this land.

The branches of the trees had as much time as their bark to grow, so they elongated as wide as they were tall, a network of brown reaching out in gradually thinning fingers with thickets of leaves at a time. Then and again, a leaf would fall, ever so gently and gracefully, swaying in the air leisurely with all the time yet none of the worries in the world, before finally resting with one of the stacks of its other fallen brethren that had died before it.

The wide canopy of the trees joined up together to start the darkness and the District. Lucas' feet parked at the line partitioning light and dark. The sun's rays would not cut through their thick defense, and only the most persistent could find the perfect angle to slant in a slit where all the crevices between the leaves aligned. Even so, only slender beams could reach inside. They fanned and shattered into smaller beams at a time, sometimes splitting them into the rainbow color. And among them, even fewer could reach the floor without dissipating first.

Lucas sighed. This was where the thing was kept, and most likely where the werewolves would ambush him if that was their intent. They could be anywhere in the District, so once he stepped in, he could not afford to drop his guard upon any direction. It was battle time. He put on his battle face to unnerve his enemies if they thought to try their luck with him.

Translucent floating screens appeared before Lucas' eyes. They were monitors that displayed everything from his heart rate, to the ones of potential enemies. They didn't actually appear in front of him, they were all in his head. It was just a trick of perception his eyes believed.

His eyes arrowed most intently on sensors which tracked any signs of heat or movement. He flexed his arms as he had done countless times, and felt them surge with a hot, spiced feeling. His skin erupted into the miniscule pieces of skin that turned into metal and then formed up into cannons. He straightened one arm and pointed it in front of him, tilting his head towards it for better aim as he advanced. They winked when sudden threads of light pinpointed onto them from above, and then a line glinted silver down its barrel when he walked through an unusually girthy beam of light coming down.

Stepping in, the leaves crushed softly under his soles in moist texture Lucas found yucky. Lucas grumbled, trying to tiptoe his way through the patches of sogginess and onto safer, drier patches. He presumed he must have looked like an off-balance ballerina.

He would rather pick a terrain where the leaves crunched and cracked dryly. Here, the mud would slow him down. Since the sun was barred from this place, the place was cool. But it came at a cost of humidity. The soil had divulged it to him. Moist mud was worrisome since it made him more susceptible to slipping. His soles, no matter how good, would falter in the face of muddy land.

The Werewolves, however, had claws on their hind legs that could dig into the ground and spring them in their movements, so it was all the same to them. If anything, the dry, parched land in the cornfield was a disadvantage to them. And Lucas knew well still how that turned out for the EMA.

The fact that they might well fight with more vigor here troubled him. If this was their ploy, then Lucas would be

152

heading straight into a lion's... wolf's den. He didn't have a choice but to press on, however. Yruf was expecting this of him, and he told himself he had faced worse odds than this. If they came through with what he suspected, Lucas would only be able to salute them for its ingeniousness and then add another count to the ruts he had to push himself out.

Luckily it wasn't so bad his shoes would sink in. Yruf sent him once to the marshlands of the Lazarus, and it had been such a ghastly experience he vowed that if Yruf sent him there once more, he would cut off his leg and plead himself as disabled. There the muck would seep inside your shoes when your leg sank so deep it reached your kneecaps. It was hard to fight the Lazarus but harder to traverse through their land. The muck would stay inside his suit and weigh him down, and every step was a chore. The soil would make disgusting bubbling sounds and suck Lucas' leg in harder when he tried to remove it.

After that, Yruf relented and gave him his word. But only in jest, Lucas knew. Yruf did not respond to threats, and he had only said the words to be kind. If there was ever a vital mission that required Lucas' attention, Lucas would be hard pressed to reject it.

Here, his suit might get a little soiled, but that was it. He blinked. "I am no longer a cadet where I would need to wash his own clothes," he found himself taking comfort in the reminder. "All I would have to do was pass it to the cleaners where they would do all the brushing and scrubbing for me. Ah, the privilege."

They just keep stacking up and surprising me, don't they? Lucas managed a grin. He had almost forgotten that, and probably so many other privileges he had been awarded once his promotion had been set to order. He made a mental note to check them when he got back. But he had to admit that was a good problem to have.

"Maybe I can even get Icarus and Sam to do it. Oh, who knows," he said to himself wickedly. His tone trailed off when he remembered where he was. His eyes shifted back from reverie to sullen at once. A draft of wind slapped him and he was alert again, if not a little startled.

This is just a stroll in the park, he comforted himself. *I've been through worse.* Yet every moment, the trees seemed to scream at him that it was a trap, and the frequency only hurried the deeper he stepped inside. The trees seemed to come alive, and the soft swishing of leaves and branches seemed more like whispers than the random ramblings of nature.

His hair rose and goosebumps bulged. He could suddenly feel a thousand eyes on him. But there were none. His emotions and fears tried to cloud his judgment with cold, willowy fingers grasping into his spine and tickling through it.

They clashed but Lucas had been trained enough to have his judgement always come up on top. His senses heightened and suddenly invisible enemies were all around him, chanting, marching towards him, pressing close to swamp him. He spun around, back and forth, in panic, trying to gauge how many they were.

Everything became a whirl.

"Shut up!" he seethed, determined not to let his voice echo through the greenery and alert his prey… or predators… the line was getting blurred at every second. It took him a while to register the flurry of motion and the rustling of leaves came from him. It was him who spun and him who floundered his toes on the ground. The marching army had just been the rigid,

154

ancient brown sentinels armored in rough-hewn barks. They were still now, they had always been.

Stupid nerves, Lucas sighed. He was cold and his clothes uncomfortably damp, and probably looking quite ridiculous. His hands would have been clammy if they had not been cannons. Cannons did not sweat.

His sensors told him there was not a soul in sight. Not a heartbeat, not a breath... at least not one large enough to have been a threat. If there was a threat, he would know. He controlled his breath and calmed his palpitating heart.

He continued in easier now. He decided against holding up his guns in front of him not long after. There was no saying where they would come from. And if they did, he had enough confidence in his reflexes and the sensor screens in front of him to parry the surprise. It would also give him the pretense that he had dropped his guard. With hope, the Werewolves would see it as their finest chance to launch an attack, and their confidence would show with sloppiness.

After their skirmish with George, he was sure the Werewolves would have gotten it in their egos to try the same strategy with Lucas. They might try to encircle him like they did with George and hoped that numbers were sufficient to do it to him.

So be it. All the easier to kill them.

The houses came into sight. In such rural parts, most of the houses looked like cottages preserved from decades ago. They wouldn't even be fit to be called houses by the people who lived in more technologically advanced Zones, though even the rural Zones of the First Federation Region weren't so dismal looking.

Perhaps it was just bias to his enemies. Still, their structures were all strange and never were two the same. They were stout and brittle, built as it was convenient, and only meant to be shelter and no more. Classic brick and concrete structures were forced to be slotted in where there was space enough between the giant, grand trees standing in attention.

There was no official entrance to the District, but Lucas decided it was where the buildings started. Since the trees were so tall, it allowed buildings to be raised as high as five stories high, six if you were pushing it, though they might brush at the leaves on the canopy. But the little District hidden inside this forest had all its buildings sitting comfortably at the highest of four stories.

Streets slithered and branched out rapidly, as quickly as the space the houses took until it revealed the whole District in all its destitute, barren shame. There was not a soul in sight, not a movement, not a tremble in the air, not a heat signature on his monitors, much to Lucas' relief and to the dismay of the warrior inside him.

Either they were too disgraced to receive him, or they had run. Lucas heavily expected the latter. He had hoped the wolves had more spines than that, after their little victory against George. But the streets were so empty they felt eerie and a sharp chill ran through Lucas in his bones.

Birds still chirped above, zooming from one branch of a tree to the next in a flurry of flapping wings. An occasional breeze sang the song of fluttering leaves and shrubbery to break the silence and give the District some life. He could hear insects beeping incessantly, some periods at a time. And above, a hint of sunlight sparkled through from where the leaves swung and opened a gap for it to come true.

This was every kid's nightmare, especially after they had read just one bed time story about the time a bear, or a wolf, or a witch or a... some horrible creature came prowling for them in the woods not unlike this.

But he wasn't a child, not anymore, not for a long time. And he was not about to be swayed but such nonsensical phobias. Without those, this was surprisingly... nice. All his life, if he wasn't in the concrete compounds of the EMA headquarters, he would only come to such lovely places in times of turmoil... bad circumstances. There was always more red than green, and things happened so quickly one never could appreciate the beauty of such a setting in its most honest and organic state.

The missions never entitled him to a good look at the places that had been his battlefields, and he never lingered too long in them, thought and body. It was in bad taste to stay where the dead lay, especially ones he killed. Perhaps it was fatigue, or guilt, he could not say nor did he think too much of it. Yruf told him not to think too much of it, thinking too deeply ruined many a good soldier.

It was a pity those places only saw that side of him, only saw him raid the place, only saw him ringed in blood. Sometimes he had to destroy them.

"Big bad wolves, where are you?" Lucas whistled. He was getting bored. And that was never good. He dropped his guard and the fatigue and aches that his body had held back in tension would only rush back to his body, then his reaction would be compromised. "If any of you can hear me, surrender now. It'll make it so much easier for me, and less suffering on your part. I'm in a good, merciful mood too, so I'll spare you in exchange. You guys know who I am already, you know you can't beat me."

157

When he finally did enough sweeps of the place till he got tedious of it, he decided to conclude it as that. "They really ran," Lucas murmured in an uncertain voice, yet also amused as he took one more good sweep of the place in admiration. "I guess I should count myself lucky, it would be such a pity to spill blood on such a gorgeous land." He lifted up a foot to inspect on his soles. "Or not," his face turned when he saw flakes of leaves stuck onto it, with the mud driven deep into his soles. "Revolting," he scrunched his face and looked back up.

"So, no fight then. All the better." If so, he had full rein of this place. But what was the point? If the werewolves abandoned this place so readily, then there could not have been anything special here. As he was about to leave, something moved. Somewhere in the bushes, or somewhere far... Lucas could not tell where, his eyes combed the place so quickly that he wasn't sure where it came from. But he was positive something was out there. His eyes went to his displays once more. But it did not show any beating heart, at least anything large enough to be a threat. In the forest, the screen that notified him of movements all around him was useless since the wind came by every once in a while, and sent the screen to static.

Then something emerged, so fast it was a blur, its shadow thrown behind it. It was fast and smaller than Lucas had expected of what would come out for him. It was slender but vascular, and it was no Werewolf or grotesque beast. Lucas recognized her kind, he had crossed paths with them at more than once, and half of those times they had been at odds.

"An Elf?" he reeled back, startled. The Elves were a prickly, distrustful sort who didn't like EMA interference on their lands. They were getting better at allowing them in though... so coincidentally it happened when they had also needed the EMA's help to settle domestic terrorism in their Region.

158

But all that information that didn't matter. Why the hell was an Elf in Werewolf territory? Purebloods rarely crossed over to other Pureblood Sanctuaries, and even if they did, they surely would restrict themselves to the main Zones. Why would one come to somewhere so rural?

The Elves did not look much different from humans, save for more flushed skin and sharper features which gave them a bad reputation for acting all high and mighty. In truth, they were nothing like that. Personalities were rarely standardized on particular species at once.

She was of Lucas' height, but from her tired lines stretched across her face, she must have been at least five years his senior. Her ears perked up, twice the size from those of a human. Those were their most distinct traits… or about the same size with that of Lucas', except Lucas' ones were rounder.

The Elf nearly pounced on him, but Lucas swung away deftly. He studied the Elf. She did not so much as growl, and her face was a stony mask. Her eyes were vacant, though her pupils moved unnaturally keenly. It was like she was an automation more than she was an organic lifeform. On all fours, she poised herself towards Lucas once more and jumped again.

Lucas shied away. She was quick, and he was determined to keep a distance from her. He needed more information about her before he struck. "Who are you?" he yelled. But she did not answer, nor even twitch to acknowledge his speech. She continued leaping towards him. When she got close enough, she launched a barrage of punches and sweeping kicks at Lucas, but Lucas did not allow her to maintain that proximity for long.

Plus, they were easy to dodge. She exposed herself with so many inexperienced mistakes he almost evaded them lazily. Which only raised more questions. If she was so bad at fighting, why was she sent here? She wore a black suit from shoulder to toe, which was surprising since he always thought Elves fancied more ornate outfits.

Something else unnerved and shocked Lucas by turns. His eyes shifted to the displays once when he had gained enough leeway to drop his attention from the Elf, doubtful at how the sensors could have failed him. It still showed that there was nothing with a heart rate around him. And that only scared him further. *Could it be... the fairy tales were true?*

His eyes flicked back to her, disconcerted but focused. Her face still reported a blank look, and it would explain why she would not talk to him, or even grunt on instinct when she fell. She didn't even pant, or sweat, or showed any signs of fatigue a normal mortal would have shown after so long into the fight. And it would explain her sharp movements, and why she couldn't fight well. She wasn't a soldier... A chill shot through his spine, clammy sweat began to emerge, and he suddenly felt *cold.*

But her face was still flushed with life. It wasn't rare that Lucas doubted his own judgment, or thought to find fault in his powers, but now he did. Dismissing his conclusion as an ill-made child of shock and confusion, he studied her face once more, hoping well he was wrong.

Even the most battle-hardened of warriors flinched when he did that. He disbelieved when he saw that she didn't. Her eyes were tapered thin, and her nostrils flared out, but still no signs of life. Lucas gulped and made a stronger leap behind than usual, somersaulting through the air and then landing far from her. "What the hell are you?!" he dared not believe what his imagination conjured. He was rational, there was no such thing such as...

Behind, more leaves fluttered and Lucas squatted down and decided where he would aim to bounce away to. He could not run elsewhere. The Elf was in front of him, looking at him as hungrily as a de… as an expressionless thing would. She would carve him up once he got near enough.

Just in time he jumped up, when he saw a burly, hairy paw swipe below. Lucas' eyes widened and summoned his jetpack. It folded out at his back swiftly, having practiced so many times. The propulsion below rumbled and radiated before the circles underneath. Where fire was supposed to burst out beamed blue, air emanated below. Then he was hovering in the air. He floated higher to catch what was below.

A frightening sight unveiled below him. The Elf wasn't the end of it, not by a long shot. There were far more than he thought. There were more Elves of course, but there were other Purebloods as well. There were the Centaurs and the Satyrs, both had a human upper half and looked rather human save for some small horns that grew out their heads. It was their lower half that made them stand out. The Satyrs had hind legs of a goat, and the Centaurs had one of a horse with all four limbs.

Both species belonged to the Elven Empire as vassal Regions, to be called to arms if war ever necessitated their need. It was no surprise they were here with the Elf. But it was the Wildcats that puzzled him. The paw that tried to swipe at him before he evaded it too close for comfort belonged to that of the Wildcats.

They were burly creatures, as tall as the Werewolves. Lucas didn't know much of them, he had never had the pleasure to visit their Region properly. But he knew from the talk of the other EMA agents that they had a great party landscape there.

161

They weren't particularly violent in this Era as the need for soldiers waned, but they could be when they needed to. They were matted with a thick layer of fur over their huge frames. Their eyes were always rheumy as if they wanted to cry, but the menace in their eyes was not easily missed. They were large and easily mistaken as ungainly. But they were not. They moved with a deadly, smooth agility that was terrifying even to Lucas.

They had an easy tell when they wanted to attack. Their whiskers flitted beneath their flattened noses as if in warning. The one who almost had Lucas in his grasps tried to reach above at him with several more fruitless swipes, but he gave up eventually. And then came more Werewolves. Yet they were different than the Werewolves he fought on the cornfield just now. They had cast their expressions to match the other Purebloods around them.

All of them wore the same outfit, a completely black suit made with a thick fabric for comfort. If the situation wasn't so bizarre, Lucas would have laughed at the peculiar group that they made. Purebloods hated to mingle, especially not so many of them at once.

"Who are you!" he asked again. But there was no answer. They stopped all activity and stood in attention of him. It was a sinister sight. He counted twenty of them. He could fire at them from above and be done with them easily, seeing as how they did not have firearms, but he was too curious to. His mind was a whirl of activity trying to draw similarities among their races that would lead to such an odd gathering.

And then he knew. Their Regions all belonged to the Amel Continent where the First Federation also resided in. But it didn't answer why they would come together.

162

Their noses were frozen solid and their chests did not rise and fall. Lucas felt as if a thousand ants were creeping on his skin. He was being proved more right by the second, and for the first time he hated it. What was he to do? He could phone Yruf, then it struck him. *What if this is the secret he wanted to keep? No, it can't be, Yruf would never keep such a vile secret from me... especially me who he loves so much and knows I'm trustworthy. If not... I'm his Ace.*

Before he could, however, the mindless drones started to fidget. And then they lost interest in Lucas. They turned and walked away. There was no way in hell he would allow them to go. Not them, not abominations like them. If they were to reach a densely populated Region or Zone... he could only imagine the panic. *Yes,* he knew the answer now. Yruf would command the same of him. The original command. It all fit perfectly into place now. Yruf had most probably sent Lucas here to clear the threats these... *things* would pose to society. He had kept it all under wraps to prevent panic.

Lucas glided to a spot where it was vacant of them. He dropped and landed. For once, the drones reacted and they turned to him instantly. They charged with their freakish but swift, jerking and disturbing movements once again. Lucas jerked his hands and two blades sprung out amidst the tornado of blue specks.

He sprung.

They were no soldiers, he could say so with confidence. They fought like amateurs sent to a battlefield, but a different sort of amateurs. Most new soldiers had the skill but lacked the temperament, these drones were the opposite. The fight didn't last very long. His battle mind took over again and everything turned into a blur.

The Centaurs came charging towards him, faster than the rest. But speed came at a compromise of less control. Lucas only needed to duck their attempts at ramming him, then cut off their hooves. Then they fell easily and crumbled helplessly.

The Wildcats and the Werewolves posed more trouble, especially as a horde charging towards him at once. They had a speed and agility to them that their enormous bodies should not have granted.

Lucas transformed his blades into guns and blasted them, hoping to be done with them without more complications. The rest, he kicked and used them as a platform to spring himself off and whirl in the air, decapitating a handful at once. He rolled when the last Werewolf tried to hammer him with its brawny arms so its claws only burrowed in the moist soil. He brandished his blade once more; one good swing and it was done.

The Satyrs, unlike their cousins the Centaurs, weren't built for battle. The Centaurs at least could act as a cavalry unit just by themselves, but the Satyrs had no mutation to boast of. Their legs, though a touch varied from humans, were not that amazing. Besides an extra few points to their jump height, they were as inept as human bodies. They died quickly without special weapons, as did the Elves. Slender and nimble as they were, they were simply not to Lucas' match.

Having trained for so long against every possible type of opponent, his body just knew what to do. He cut them all. No matter how tough their skin was, Lucas knew nothing on Earth could stand up to his blades. The material that made them was far too sturdy.

After a few flips and spinning around with his two blades, dodging, parrying, kicking, jumping wildly, he unleashed a torrent of crimson on the woods. *Another promise that I broke.*

164

All around him, limbs and heads rolled. At least their deaths were quick and their limbs were severed cleanly. He always made sure of that so their enemies would be given a painless demise. Yruf always said that you should accord respect to your enemies, especially if they knew you were strong. It took courage to plunge into such odds.

But truth be told, Lucas did not think of that. He only wanted to get the battle done as quickly as possible. Their existence was unsightly. Entrails and blood spilled all over him, some splashed over the trees and congealed into a thick slime. Soon they will dry into red crust. Some blood still dripped from leaves, little streams had formed between the furrows where they folded. At least it was a sound, and that Lucas welcomed.

Lucas finally found it in him to crouch down and tap on the skin of a Wildcat body that was still mostly intact. The Wildcat had died through a deep gash in his neck so his head flapped out like the cap of a candy tube. Lucas' hands quivered as they lowered down, fearing that what he thought would become reality. But when his hand sunk into the fur, relief swept through him. "It's warm," he sighed. And the sweat they emitted was just too small to see. They weren't dead when they fought him. The chill in his spin retreated back to where it came from, then vanished entirely.

Good. He could rule out any supernatural elements. It wouldn't be the first if it had been, but history had shown how just dangerous enemies of that sort were, and Lucas was not eager to face them.

When he tapped it again just to make sure, however, his brows knitted. It wasn't cold like a corpse… but it wasn't warm enough to come from someone that had just fought.

Among the carnage of torn and mutilated limbs, splotches of blood welled and trickled out. He reached out a little to dap his fingers on a spot. It was warm and liquid. "It's not congealed. That means they had not died... until recently."

It was scarce relief to someone like him who needed an abundance of proof before he believed anything. He looked to his scanners for guidance once more. "X-ray," he muttered and the skin of the Wildcat sloughed off to Lucas' eyes, to cut into the Wildcat's innards till his vision reached the skeleton. His heart was missing, but in place of it was some sort of device. Here and there, wires were strewn about, and the next largest node of technology was in his brain.

"You're not a zombie, that's for sure," Lucas sighed, but he wasn't sure if it was one for relief or concern. This new piece of information only caused his eyebrows to furrow in further, like brown hairy caterpillars coming to kiss, only to have the patch of creased up skin in the middle to halt their union tragically.

"Where did you come from?" Lucas muttered to the Wildcat as if it would suddenly resurrect and answer him. "And what are you?" Instinct told him that if there were already so many of them, there would be more. Lucas' fingers flitted down the fibers of the suit the corpse wore.

It was a familiar material, but that did nothing to answer his question. This type of fiber was used throughout the world, renowned for being the best protective material money could buy...

Lucas narrowed his eyes. He had no choice but to take back his words about it not answering his question. "The best material money can buy... then someone armed, clad and sponsored you... even created you perhaps." An ominous dread built up in his chest. There was more to this than met the eye. He was certain there would be more of them, this was not some isolated incident.

When you are uncertain, take every incident as deliberate. Another piece of Yruf's advice.

"They were controlled," Lucas deduced. "It could only be." He looked around the field of bodies he had ripped apart. He remembered there were twenty of them, the Werewolves would not have been so lax in their surveillance not to have seen twenty zombies roam about idly. It was too large a group. Even if they were zombies, just the sight of other Purebloods, the Werewolves would have reported them in haste. The Werewolves were a territorial but nervous bunch.

So, they came from somewhere hidden, and it was no coincidence they came when Lucas came. "Someone sent them to face me," he concluded as he began to laugh dryly. "Why would anyone do that? To scare me? Either they are trying their luck with inexperienced drones or they don't know me at all. If it does not turn out to be the latter, then my pride is sorely hurt." The inflated confidence came back to him.

He glanced around with a deadly look. "But whoever it is, they can see me," he spoke more warily now. It could only be. Anyone with half a brain would have installed some sort of camera around here to keep watch of the bunch of Pureblood drones in their employ. And it was probably how they found him. He stood up.

"Nevertheless—" His voice rose to a threatening cadence. "You made a big mistake. You think you scared me, didn't you? My father always said that you know you are going in the right direction when you can see more enemies. Well, your little diversion only confirmed that there is a treasure in this District for me to find. And I will not stop till I find it, do you hear me? Now, I will generously give you a choice. Surrender and I will arrest you. I promise no harm will come to you. If I catch you, I will not be so gracious."

His voice rebounded through the forest in a series of echoes, each succeeding one growing ever softer till it was too soft to catch.

For the first time, his sensors awoke from its slumber and it showed something moving… something large enough to be a threat. Something inside one of the better-looking buildings was shifting, its heart thumping rapidly.

Lucas' eyes examined the house. It was no common house, it must have been an administrative building of sorts used as an office for the local government. It was small compared to even the smallest of buildings in the EMA compound, but it was a monstrosity here compared to its neighbors, growing five stories high and spanning as large as a basketball field. It was not common to see trees far apart, much less to leave so much space so conveniently. They must have cut one of the tall sentinels to build it.

Lucas' hopes propelled and fell almost at the same time. It meant it was not a drone. The thing had a heartbeat, and it could well be the conceding party coming out to wave the white flag and take up his offer.

But it was small, smaller than a full-grown Werewolf at least. Lucas sucked the saliva from his mouth and gulped it at once. Just because he experienced something odd today, it didn't mean there wouldn't be another. The world did not put a limit to the number of strange happenings that could happen. And Lucas had no lack of challengers. Small it might be, but

Goblins and Dwarves were small too. It didn't mean they were any less of a threat.

He whipped out one hand and it turned into a cannon after a brilliant blue flash. "Whoever you are, if you're here to surrender, drop your weapon and come out slowly. If I see any sudden movement or even a whiff of deceit, I will shoot. I would advise against trying anything funny or you will find that I have little patience for that sort. We can speak terms once I can see you clearly. Otherwise, if you're not here to surrender, continue as you please. I would be happy to indulge." Lucas' lips peeled back into a cruel smirk.

He was facing at the side just an edge away from the entrance. He crept closer as a warning to the thing that moved, but kept a safe distance where he still had a good view to be able to react if anything happened. He had the leverage now, and he did not want to lose it all due to presumption.

The leaves of the potted plants placed at the entrance rustled as the glass door creaked open cautiously. Lucas' hand flinched but he bid his emotions to simmer. He hated situations like this. An open field was a far easier proposition. You just had to kill on sight.

His eyes quivered at their sockets and squeezed forward as if it would heighten his vision. And out came a furry creature cloaked in white fur, with eyes red as blood. But when Lucas saw her expression, he could not decide if the fur was white because she was born with it or if it was because of her fright for him. She was dressed as any child would in the modern world, in a shirt and shorts, but they were frayed and soiled. She was barely three feet tall.

Her hands were raised, and her movements awkward and robotic. Tears welled in her eyes, some had escaped as rivulets flowing down her face, compressing and soaking her fur. "We surrender! We surrender!" she yelled, her words muffled and buried in cries. "Please don't hurt me!" One eye closed and her head jerked away when she saw Lucas' cannon pointing at her.

"A child?" Lucas blurted. *A Pureblood child,* Yruf would have said. *They can be no less dangerous than their adults if they are trained properly. Lucas, take it that all of them are scum. And even if they are not, they will soon shed their innocence and grow up to be one. Do you think they will forget what you did to their elders? It may not be now, or even a year later, or even ten years later, but mark my words, your little mercy will come and bite us back. A good Pureblood is a dead one. Wash your hands off any potential trouble, I say.* Lucas wasn't sure if he agreed with that ethos anymore, not when she took a good look at the girl. All devotion to that principle vanished.

"Who... why... why would you be here, in this battlefield? Wouldn't you have run with the rest? And if not, how could anyone be so despicable to send a child to do his bidding?"

"You are one, aren't you?" the girl retorted, though it sounded so pitiful her scorn was barely a smidge in her words.

"What?"

"A child."

Lucas flinched. She was right. He may be taller than her, but strictly speaking he was. "Well... yes," Lucas admitted. "But it's not the same. I'm trained to do this. But whoever sent you out knows you can't... and yet he still did. How despicable."

"What?" the Werewolf girl asked. Her body still quaked in terror. It was not hard to find that his cannon was scaring her.

170

Lucas quickly retracted his arm and folded the cannon back into his skin.

"I'm sorry… it's nothing. I'm not going to hurt you, I promise. You are brave to come out alone. Are you alone?" He realized he was just speaking to a young child. He had to be gentle and his words simple.

The girl shook her head, her fear showing no signs of resolving.

"And where are the others?" Lucas asked warily, his eyes peeking at the monitors ever so often to make sure this wasn't a diversion.

"They're downstairs."

"Then take me there."

HELLO WORLD-8 (LUCAS)

He let the girl lead him into the building first. As much as she was a child, Lucas could not wash off the doubt on her. If she hid even just a knife when she was behind him, a stab would be all it took to end him. He preferred to be cautious. And if there were any booby traps she would be going down with him so she would think twice before triggering any. And even if she planned to play the sacrifice, he would be able to react in time. In front of him, he could study her for even the smallest changes to her body language.

The lobby first greeted him when he was ushered inside. It was dark and dreary; the electricity had long been shut off judging from how humid it was. There was a foul odor clawing into his nostrils, a mix of sweat, clammy air, years of an uncleaned putrid stench that had always gone unnoticed because it was covered up by the aircon. Worse, the occupants and workers of the building had tried to remedy it by placing fragrances around the place instead of air fresheners, but the supposed solution only aggravated the repugnance of the smell when it blended with it. He was sure he was being poisoned at one point, the air soupy and astringent to trouble his breathing. Lucas' sensors did not sense anything amiss, but he didn't trust them today.

They went into the building, through corridors where the light that perforated through the entrance could no longer reach, thus turning markedly dimmer. Only eerie sounds resounded through the building, enhancing its already scary atmosphere. Water dripped from loose faucets, lights flickered. At some rooms, things shifted and buzzed, but their doors were closed to Lucas so he didn't need to see what was inside, nor did he want to know.

The only lights around to speak off were dingy exit green exit signs that glowed above some doors which actually made the place even shadier. They did its job to light up the place, but if it was up to Lucas, he wouldn't have installed the most ominous color one could find for when the place turned dark like this. Darkness and dingy elements made the most ordinary places petrifying. But not to Lucas. He was the Ace.

It didn't matter if the girl was trying to restrict his eyes so she could spring her trap; Lucas had night vision installed in his eyes. He was as deadly in the dark. But if she was planning something, Lucas could not tell from the way her body showed.

The girl showed no discomfort to the light. Small wonder. Werewolves could see in the dark as well. They finally ended up in a room deep in the building. It had not been the type of room without a door until recently, Lucas could see, from its jagged frame that was a sorry excuse for an entrance. The entrance had been forcibly ripped open by something. Gnarled metal jutted out from the door, they were pins hammered in that held something once. It didn't take long to find out what it was.

Before the entrance was a pool of sprawled twisted metal, as gnarled as barbs. He surmised it had once been planks that barred the door. A fight took place here, a very vicious one. And whoever came through the door was strong as well. *Well...*

before Lucas to deduce who had done it, he was reminded of where he was. He was no longer in the First Federation where humans roamed. Here, he was among beasts that could tear apart metal as easily as splitting a piece of bread.

Tossed away from the jagged entrance was what was left of the door, carved into pieces like butter scraps. "What the hell happened?"

"You'll see," the girl said, drastically calmer than when Lucas had first met her. It gave him some comfort. He was here to frighten monsters, not children. And more and more, he suspected less of her. Either she was truly innocent, which was most probable, or she had a very lucrative career in espionage waiting for her.

Lucas nodded. "So…" he looked into the room. It was dark as the rest of the environment, but it was so small even his mediocre human eyes could see what was inside. To be safe, however, his palm flipped into a torch and shone inside. It was nothing but a common janitor's room. Lined along the tiny room were shelves of cleaning equipment and bottles of soap. Perhaps the only thing amiss of the room was how dark it was and how clean the mops and brooms and dustpan was. They looked brand new, their bristles still straight and polished. Even the bottles of soap did not have their usual crust of dried soap surrounding its exterior. "So, it's just a janitor's room, a little clean, but what's there to give?" he questioned charily, hoping he did not miss something obvious that would make him seem like an idiot.

The girl gave him a derisive look. "Do you not see the metal bars?"

"Ah huh, so?"

She rolled her eyes and switched to an aloof expression to show she gave up on him. "I thought it would be clear to someone of your caliber. But I think not." She was markedly more precocious than when Lucas had first met her. She glanced into the room. "Does it look like there is anything worth stealing? Why would a mere janitor's room be defended? To make sure someone doesn't steal their soap and mops that costs about a few dollars?"

Lucas' eyes narrowed. He got her point. "Perhaps they stole it already."

"Fat chance."

"Why?"

She shrugged. "Because I was the one who broke in," she said without further explanation and walked into the room. Lucas could do nothing but trail behind her. "What do you mean? You broke apart these metal bars by yourself?"

"Not me, silly." She did not bother to face him now. "Someone strong enough. But that's beside the point, you'll meet them soon."

"Meet who? There are more of you?"

The girl rolled her eyes. "Later!" she insisted, irascible. Lucas narrowed his eyes to observe her when a ludicrous notion suddenly popped into his mind. He had watched horror movies that had gone like that as well. If you met the most unsuspecting little girl in a dingy place, it was most likely a ghost. And when she referred to others, she meant her shadowy friends cloaked in a white blanket. And then when she said you were going to meet someone, it usually was a convoluted way of saying you were going to die and gang up on you so you could go wherever dead people went to meet other dead people.

But the girl was far too immature and annoying to have been a century-aged ghost. "You will meet them later, once I'm done explaining."

"Fine, explain," Lucas resumed his formal courtesy, intent not to let her climb on his head any further.

She did not seem to have noticed his not-so-subtle change in tone. She looked back at him. "Have you also wondered why the items are so clean?"

"Yeah. They barely used them. But from the poorly-kept corridors I walked through just now, it speaks for itself."

The girl shook her head. "They *didn't* use them. They look new because they are," she said.

"What do you mean?" he wanted to laugh from how redundant the statement sounded. If there was a point she was making, he didn't get it.

She looked on the ground and tapped the floor with her feet, lightly at first as if it was supposed to be a hint, then she stomped. Where the floor outside was paved with an imitation marble with brown veins on a field of enameled white, this room was covered with carpet. "What sort of monster would carpet the floor of a janitor's room, huh? Of course this is not the real janitor's room."

"The real janitor's... room?" he said, confused.

She nearly slapped him, but restrained her swinging arm. "Gosh, you *are* dense, are all humans like that?"

"Well—" His eyes tapered. "—if you are going to speak to me like that, I'd rather you don't at all. And I would have you know I'm actually considered quite brilliant where I come from."

"*Quite brilliant where I come from,*" she repeated in a voice that mocked him.

"I don't speak like that!" Lucas denied.

"Yeah you do. Anyway, as I was saying, this is just a disguise for the real purpose."

"What?" he blurted. The irritation was not the furious sort, it was the itch you couldn't scratch. But it was still irritation nonetheless; not just by the girl's impudence, but how quickly she changed her personality.

She grinned a mischievous grin, baring her fangs though Lucas was certain it was not meant to be menacing. "Now!" she screamed at the floor. On cue, lights burst into the room and the floor shuddered. Suddenly the floor dislodged itself from the walls and it lowered, leaving the walls above him.

Lucas' limbs jarred into action. His ears were always attentive to such words. His arms jerked up and his skin flicked into metal, forming his cannons which pointed right at her. She gave him a bewildered look and jumped back. "What are you doing?" she snarled. The fear that she had before flushed into her face again.

"You're luring me into a trap, aren't you? I told you to bring me to the rest of your people, but you managed to distract me by bringing me into a janitor's room that you say is dubious!"

"What! No! I'm bringing you exactly where you asked me to!"

Lucas combed the room. Nothing had sprung up to attack him yet, so he was half inclined to believe her. There were no guns that emerged from the walls, no drones... not even another Werewolf. The walls of the janitor's room were now above him, and so were the shelves. It seemed they had been stuck onto the walls. No, the walls weren't' shifting up, *he* was coming down, he realized. The floor formed the platform of this makeshift lift and its journey down was surprisingly smooth. Whoever maintained it had done a good job oiling its gears.

He gazed at the girl once more and lowered his cannons warily. "Fine," he said as they formed back into flesh. "Where are you bringing me? And what is this?"

The turn of events answered his questions. The platform descended for about 2 whole floors before it stopped. He was greeted to a wide hallway filled with Werewolves. The hallway had arced ceilings rising and coming together from curved metal walls sprouting from the ground. Lucas' muscles tensed at first, but on further study he realized that if the werewolves had wanted to ambush him, this was not the generation they would send.

There were their seniors, some in wheelchairs, others clutching thin sticks to hold themselves up, others were too weak to even sit so they laid themselves on the ground or leaned against the wall. They were grizzled and weary, their fur shaggy and silvered from age. On the other side of the spectrum were the young, ranging from infants cradling on their mothers' arms or kids like the Werewolf girl beside him.

There was no way they were assembled to fight him. These were their most vulnerable, and they must have come here to seek shelter since they couldn't run as quickly as the rest of the population.

"We heard you were coming, howls and incessant chattering, but they all said the same thing. The Ace is coming. Quickly, run. The Ace is coming," the Werewolf girl suddenly spoke sullenly. "We knew we had no chance against you. Werewolves are headstrong at times, but even we know when to yield. Even the most ignorant of us are not so ignorant to challenge you. Your rumors were enough. The one-man army, the decimator, the widowmaker, the orphan's dismay, the Ace and lapdog of Yruf of the EMA. You who killed more than anyone can count, brutally and without hesitation, it's true isn't it?"

All of it and more, Lucas reflected solemnly, bowing his head down, taking new interest on the floor. Pulses of shame coursed through Lucas, awfully slowly as if to let him fully bear through the sting it brought. He had once been so proud of those titles, but now that he was facing a victim of those actions, he wasn't so sure he should be all that pleased with it anymore.

"It is," he only said.

"Well, I hated you for it, even till when I first saw what you look like. But when I started speaking to you, I didn't believe it anymore." The words were unexpected, but Lucas only scrunched up more in guilt than felt relieved about it.

"No," he blurted, "you still should. It's an act, girl. I'm a monster when I want to be."

"A monster would have shot me at sight. But you didn't shoot me. I thought you would."

Lucas raised a brow. "You took a risk. Why, when you were afraid of the outcome?"

"Everyone's scared," she replied. "I was no less scared." She gripped one hand onto her other arm. Lucas had not known why she did it, until he saw her hands quivering. Had they been quivering all this while? "But just because you are scared doesn't mean you cannot help."

"And why is that?" Lucas couldn't decide if this girl was brave or stupid. Perhaps both. Adolescence had queer, innocent

179

notions of how the world worked. He hoped she would outgrow soon if she wanted to survive in this harsh world.

"To protect my people. As you are now."

"With no power? You're just a child. And don't refute your age, it will make you seem more naive than defiant."

"I'm not, I agree," the girl said. "It doesn't matter. It does not excuse me from helping others in need."

"Others in need. How noble," Lucas mocked. She was getting tired of the girl's glowing but foolish ideals. He was angry at her, he found, he was angry because he had once been like her. *When did I become so cynical?* Perhaps it was when he first killed a person.

"What's your name?"

"My name's Reesha."

Lucas nodded respectfully. "Nice name."

Just when he said it, a voice boomed at the opposite end of the hallway. "Reesha! Thank goodness you're safe!" A wave of black fur came bounding forward, rising and falling like an actual one. Lucas initially wasn't sure what he was seeing, but he quickly recognized them as Werewolves; the large and strong and in a combat ready age. They sprinted on fours to get to Lucas and the girl faster.

When they reached the platform, they stood upright and quickly encircled the platform. They were not the drones he encountered at least, their fluid actions and twisted expressions made it abundantly clear. They wore blue uniforms with sleeves that ran tight around their biceps and stuck to their hairy torso. Name tags were pinned on their right chest, and along the shoulders and collars and sleeves and chest, they each had a different plethora of honors and badges pinned on as well. They were policemen.

"The Ace," the one in the middle seethed, his lips skinned back to reveal his fangs. He bared them threateningly. "You have the audacity to use a child against us?" He must have been the leader. He wasn't the largest of the bunch, but he looked the fiercest and assertive.

"Use her? You were the one who sent her!" Lucas retorted.

"Ludicrous. Why would I send a job only fit for an adult? And why would I send one to surrender to the likes of you?" he spat with much scorn. "We know how you murder and silence people, and without authority or morals but your weak connection to the EMA."

"I silence people with my weapons, not anything else," Lucas brushed off contemptuously, "and if you would like a taste so much, just give the word."

The Werewolf narrowed his eyes. "You may be what you are, but I do not sense a lie from you." He turned to the Werewolf girl named Reesha. "Did you…" he only needed to take one look at her smug face and the Werewolf knew. "How could you!" his indignance flowed in his raging words. "You didn't even consult me and you decided to make this decision for all of us?"

"I did! And you refused because you're too proud to. Can pride save us? You heard him, he would have killed us if we did not surrender."

"He would have killed us either way!" the large Werewolf argued, not withholding his rage on the account that it was directed at a child.

181

"Are we? Dead?" Reesha flung her arms up to make her point. "He is not who you think! He's true to what he says!"

"How do you know? You just met him and now you're defending him?" the large Werewolf's lips parted to fully reveal his fangs.

"You saw how he killed our people like it was nothing. You saw how he obliterated those abominations that you sent! If he wanted to, he could kill us all at this instant. But he hasn't, has he?"

"Wait, *you* guys sent those drones?" Lucas bellowed incredulously.

Reesha's words stumped the police leader. He gulped, leaned back and proceeded to a more passive posture. "I... I..."

"Don't worry, she does that to me too," Lucas jested. He wasn't even mad, only amused at the absurdity of this scenario. He still had no clue what was going on, and every second seemed to pour more confusion into the air. The police leader glared at him. "Is this some trick, Ace?"

"This is no trick," Lucas assured. He looked at Reesha warmly. "And this girl has more sense than the whole lot of you combined," he directed his harsh words at the ruffians that surrounded him. "You come at me with what... a little more than a dozen able soldiers, did you really think that would be enough to stop me?"

The police leader growled. "No," he admitted.

"Then?"

"We meant to hide. Those who could run were bid to run, seek the help of nearby Districts. Perhaps they could enlist the help of other police forces there to bring you down, you scum.

182

The rest who couldn't have no choice but to hide here," he snarled with poison glazed thick on his tongue. "You could never have found this place unless one of us told you." He eyed Reesha with a nasty look.

Lucas could not refute that. Never in a million years could he have guessed the rest of the Werewolves were hiding underneath a paltry janitor room. "No, but nevertheless, here we are. You were a fool to have sent those drones against me. It only alerted me of your presence. And that brings me to my point, what the hell are they? How did you create them? If you did, then you are no better than me, you do not have the moral high ground here. Capturing other Purebloods… even your own kind to enslave them breaks far too many rules than I can keep track of, even that fact is not lost on you I'm sure. And you still have the audacity to lecture me? I should detain you right this moment."

"You would have done so the first you saw me if you wanted to. You do not delay, if the rumors are true."

"They are," Lucas said stiffly.

"Good for you. Taunt and mock me all you want Ace," the Werewolf seethed, "but my intelligence is not dependent on your recognition. It may be able to stoop low to send them against you to try to drive you away, but I did not create those vile abominations. Hell, I did not even create this place!"

"Then who? You do know how suspicious it is to see the pack of you in here and claim that you did not own this place. This little dungeon of yours is sitting right beneath your District, and you say you don't know? Really?"

"Believe us or not, I am past caring. But we found this place only recently too," the Werewolf said.

There didn't seem to be a trace of a lie in his words, and his onyx eyes did once avert from Lucas' gaze. "If you would have me believe that far-fetched story, then you will have to tell me more."

The Werewolf gave Lucas a look that said he was comfortable with the idea "I understand," he said distantly. "Follow me, but be prepared."

"For what?" Lucas accorded the Werewolf with his own chilly courtesy.

The Werewolf one upped him and ignored him. His gaze screened around for his people. "The rest of you, don't follow us, I know the way. I would like to spare whoever I can from what the Ace is about to see." Lucas pursed his lips. *What am I about to see?*

"Is it so gruesome?" Lucas asked. The Werewolf nodded curtly.

"But, sir," another beside him bleated, worried eyes making furtive gestures at Lucas.

"My words final," the Werewolf police leader commanded. "Besides, Reesha has the right of it. If he wanted to, he would have killed us already. Stay." He led the way, sauntering through the hallway. Lucas followed, cautiously at first, but slowly his guard fell.

Pressed against the two sides of the hallway, the Werewolves glared with a mixed bag of emotions at Lucas as he passed through them. It didn't bother Lucas much. He was used to that, it was not unlike the treatment he received from jealous agents in the EMA.

Their eyes followed him till their line no longer caught up with the hallway.

And at the same time, the Werewolf decided to speak. "My name is Captain Mitch of the fourth division—"

"You're a policeman, that's all I need to know. I wouldn't understand a word of what you said anyway," Lucas brushed him off. "Just give me the details I would understand without all your tear-jerking backstory."

Captain Mitch pursed his lips, his body tensed. "I can respect that. I had wanted to make small talk out of respect, but I guess I don't have to pretend to like you anymore. Thanks for doing me that favor."

Lucas sighed. "I did not mean it like that. I only didn't want you to go straight to the point instead of blabbering about irrelevant topics. You may think I'm the enemy, Captain Mitch, but all I want is just peace, same as all the EMA."

"Really?" Captain Mitch smirked, "I think you might have a change of heart after you see what you're about to see."

"Very well," Lucas said with icy courtesy.

"You want a truce? You want to play the nice guy? Easy for someone staring down at his opponent with a dozen and more options to kill him." the Captain admitted.

"If it had been the other way around, you would have ripped me apart by now. I'm glad I have them," Lucas insisted defiantly.

"Yes, to murder. You like it don't you?"

"I do what I do to protect the world. You included, believe it or not," Lucas blurted, he could no longer stand Captain Mitch's slander. "And who is staring down onto who?"

The Werewolf snorted. "It was figurative, but I guess you know that already. Admit it, you have faced larger than me and won. Fighting a dozen policemen and a horde of the vulnerable of society stands at far better odds than even your average day. You think you protect us. But is that really your primary objective? Is it really your choice? Or are you really some lapdog? When you came down here, was it a command or by choice? Are you really a guardian or a dog to be deployed?"

By choice, Lucas wanted to say, but deep down he knew it wasn't the case. Yruf manipulated him through his devotion to George. He *knew* Lucas would accept it. "Be that as it may, you cannot say we have not done good for you."

"You mean by bringing us to heel?" the Werewolf snorted.

"I mean by any means necessary," Lucas fired back with a tinge of annoyance. The brashness had arrived, and it had molded his tongue forked. "Sometimes people need to be dealt an iron hand before they would listen. Even you must admit not everything can be settled with logic. You can't argue with stupid, and stupidity is rife. We must contain it or it will bring everyone down."

"I agree with that... for the most part. I'm a policeman for heaven's sake, I've been through my fair share of vile criminals and sometimes I wish I could be the one who executes them. But your ravings about the EMA only stands if you guys have our interests to heart. Which you do not."

Lucas' face flared. "How can you say that!? Your damned backwater Region is the one who keeps calling for EMA assistance, not the other way around. We tolerate you because that's our jobs. Otherwise, we couldn't have bothered to set foot on your Zones and cleaned up all those messes you made! We aided you, some gratitude would be nice!"

"Gratitude?" the Werewolf laughed. "You did that for the purpose of looking good to the world and your damn resume, to gain people's blind trust, to expand your reach, to gain favors on our administration. The help was just an afterthought. Don't even try to argue about that. It's common knowledge," he sneered.

"Careful," Lucas warned with suppressed anger littered in his tone, "I come to you in peace and I don't mean to break that peace, I can even suffer some insults, but if this is how our conversation will continue, then I will not be so kind anymore."

"See."

"I…" Lucas' thoughts went back to the conversation he had with the sergeant major those days back and he paused. *Why side are you on, Lucas? Of good? Of course, you want to. But how do you know? If I were to set things right, then I must start now. By listening.*

"I'm… sorry. You're right."

"I am?" the Werewolf asked, uncertain if this was simply a lead up to another jape.

Lucas nodded. "You are."

The Werewolf glared at Lucas with dubious eyes for a moment, before he grunted. "Well, then I'm sorry as well," he said, the petulance still present in his voice. You have been nothing but polite to me. And the Werewolves you killed in the cornfield… we were enemies, and aggrieved as I may be, but even I must admit it was war. You saw your friends being harmed and you acted. I would have done the same."

"They didn't have to die in vain, both Werewolves and humans," Lucas insisted and Captain Mitch nodded in agreement.

"I was mad at the EMA. What may have been decades ago, but the consequences of their actions still linger deep in the scars and wounds of every man, woman and child here. During their reign..." his eyes narrowed, "I'm sorry, I spoke out of hand. We have all had a proxy pact not to speak of it anymore, didn't we?" he laughed dryly. "It's just... you seem so much like them."

Lucas sighed. "I do, don't I."

"No you are not. I see that now. At least you heard us out. Those... your predecessors would have turned this place into flint by now," the Captain spoke in a muffled, secretive voice. He bared his fangs in a wince. "Let's not speak of such evils, let's get back to the matter at hand. I'm sorry about the drones I sent. I did it in panic when I saw you coming for us."

"You had to do something," Lucas sympathized. "You had your people to protect. Even I can respect that."

"To be honest, I had no clue what I was doing."

"How did you find this place? What is this place?" Lucas asked, feeling that the Werewolf had become comfortable enough to entertain his question.

"All will be revealed soon," the Werewolf replied glumly. The corridors forked on last time, and the last passage he had to go wasn't so long at all. Finally, they were heading to a room that Lucas could see. Like the door to the false janitor's room above, this one had been peeled off violently. The frame was a battered mess of mangled metal bent around like ribbons. What was once the door had been turned into tatters of frayed and crumpled plates around the foot of the door.

"What happened?"

"There was a fight. But before that, you must understand the backstory which you had been so adamant not to listen to. Well, ultimately you have to. Don't feel so smart now, huh?" the Werewolf mocked.

"Go on," Lucas groaned.

"A few months ago, there was the first case. Then then the next, then the next. Of course, fools we were, we thought we were finding a simple kidnapper, or at best a serial one. They started small enough not to attract too much attention to them. They picked loners and outcasts that no one would remember or give a second look at. Then they became more daring. Each week the number of missing persons doubled and doubled and doubled. We thought it was just a very corrupt and depraved person we were facing." The Werewolf gritted his teeth. "But it was far worse. We slammed into so many dead ends, even my superiors were considering calling the specialized task force from the army to come into our little District to guard our streets and maintain what little control we had. But little did we know the other Districts were experiencing the same problems as well."

"And they depleted their army?"

Captain Mitch shook his head. "Not all."

"So, couldn't they have sent more?"

The Werewolf laughed. "Hmm, well, the government could have. But they had already been bought."

"Bought?"

Captain Mitch's eyes flashed a distressed hue. "Yes. You must understand, Ace. You live in the First Federation where things are relatively well for you there. But the Werewolves' Jungle, while relatively modern, is nowhere near the standard you enjoy there. We are a backwater land compared to your paradise there… as you said. Do you know just how many would love to shift there if not for the discrimination they here their friends and relatives over there face? Do you know just how many would pack up their things if they had the resources to?"

"No."

The Werewolf looked up and scratched his chin. "I reckon at least a quarter of the population. We don't even have to talk about luxuries, we can't even spend more than a month having not to worry about basic necessities like electricity and water and healthcare and our jobs. Our Government is corrupt to the core, bribery is rampant and so painfully obvious sometimes they do not even find the need to conceal their devious acts. And it was them that disallowed aid to us."

"Why?" Lucas furrowed his brows while taking a considerable concentration on the field of gnarled metal on the floor, hopping and taking huge strides to avoid stepping onto them and prodding on his soles.

"Because they were in on it too."

"What?" Lucas blurted, puzzled. "How? Why would they kidnap their own citizens?"

"Well, it is not likely they had a direct hand in this. But they were told by powers beyond us, the true puppeteers overseeing all of us pawns to do just that. They must have been paid a good sum too, to have the temerity to place their citizens in jeopardy like that. Eventually, I got so tired of requesting to pursue this mission I went it on my own with a few of my trusted friends. It was how I met Reesha too, that little animal. She is inquisitive, I'll give you that, but that almost got her killed. She was following the same trail I was going after her friend disappeared. She and a few of her other friends. They are a loud bunch. And then I found this place." He rapped a claw on Lucas' chest. "A few days later you and your friends came. And I thought, why not hide here and take the chance. It is big enough to hold the whole District in need, and I clung onto the fat hope you did not know of this place."

"Why would I know of this place? What is it?" Lucas asked, realizing it was about the dozenth time he had asked. "And how does this relate to other Purebloods?"

"You know," Captain Mitch continued as if Lucas had not spoken at all, "to think that I thought people who thought government conspiracies were lunatics. They were mild compared to what I found out. This is larger than any of us, larger than what I could have thought. Yet it is also so close to home, which makes it all the scarier. They lurk within us; the evil is within. A great deal worse than simply having to face an enemy head on. They are not aliens. They are not some ancient species long forgotten who recently awoke and are now bent on decimating us. They are among us, they are part of us. Their network has penetrated deep into every land and society this world has to offer, and they are powerful, very powerful."

"Who is it? Tell me Captain, I intend to make good of my words as a peacekeeper."

"If only you knew what I know, then you would recognize the irony of your words," the Werewolf said, taking the first step into the room. The room was dimly lit compared to the hallway. The light rods weren't as densely packed together in the room, though they radiated with the same power, so it resulted in intervals of darkness between each row of light, like the stripes of a zebra.

191

"Now you shall know. The one responsible is the one you are representing, the EMA," he turned to Lucas with unsmiling eyes and extended a hand out towards the interior of the room to welcome Lucas inside. Lucas' face kneaded as malleable as dough now, and it puckered terribly, with lines of worry slashed explicitly on his skin.

He was afraid of what he would see at first, his first step inside hovered a little above the floor. Eventually, he forced down the hesitation and took the step inside. His first thud onto the ground sent a louder than usual tremble in the air, as if it was something special. But it was just imagination. He peered inside and he had to blink to confirm what he was seeing.

No wonder there weren't any bodies outside. He had found it odd that while there were indications of a long-drawn and brutal battle plastered all over the hallways, he had not seen a drop of blood or body. Now he knew.

"What is the meaning of this? You did this?!" he accused. "You bring me to see a graveyard not yet dug? Of EMA agents!" His eyes barely believed what depravity he saw. The 'room' was far from a room. It was a humongous complex that spanned three football fields. A grid of giant metal cylinders erected from the ground and filled the complex, some ranging so far and so tall Lucas could not see what went on after even on an elevated platform. Equipment peppered the place; computers and screens, processors that were large and blocky, some medical equipment placed here and there. It was a lab, and the basic, conventional interior was frighteningly familiar to Lucas.

The floor of the complex plunged two stories below him so whoever who stood where he stood would have a good view of the entirety. But his eyes did not need to venture so far to notice what the Captain had plainly wanted him to see. Right below the entrance was a pile of bodies, both Werewolves and humans. A stink wafted the place and sought out Lucas' nostrils quickly.

After a few whiffs, his nostrils were clogged. And a blessing too, or else he was sure he would have retched there and then. The scent of the rotting dead, he could never get used to that stench. The frigid temperature of the lab did not help hide or even attempted to mitigate the smell.

They weren't fresh, some had rotten for days. But no insects lived in here, and so none came to crawl into the flesh heap to pester them. But other organisms naked to the eye did, and though small they were, they made their presence known with the overwhelming stench. The purple flesh they had festered on had turned ripe and swollen like a water balloon pumped up. If there were ever an intact body in the gruesome heap, Lucas couldn't find any.

It was a gallery of the complete collection of all that was grotesque. Severed limbs and head garnished the heap, while blood dressed the pale entrails and purple flesh, dripping down to form a pool below. Most of it had congealed into a jelly, while the ones at the fringes of the pool had completely frozen into a dash of dried, crusty blood wrought with craters by popped bubbles. Only the ones still congealing had the smooth, polished texture to it. Bones and tendons and viscera spilled out of the apertures where they had been severed like gummy worms.

It was obvious which ones were Werewolves and which were humans. The Werewolves were larger and thicker, and their pelts, though smudged and soaked and squashed under the wash of blood, still retained their girth.

193

"I did do this," the Werewolf admitted calmly.

Lucas was at a loss of what to say. He did not know whether to be angry or relieved, he did not know whose bodies they were, he did not know if they were enemies or allies.

"Now you see why I asked the rest to stay? I would have let you come alone if I didn't know better. Whatever you claim to try to be, I know you humans, I know what conclusions your mind will steer towards. Without me here to explain what you are seeing, I knew the first thing you would have thought was to blame us. But we did not," he declared.

"Explain," Lucas found his voice tremulous and devoid of warmth. He was scared. How funny. Lucas had not been scared for a long time. But not of the bodies, of what captain Mitch would say.

"It was a tough fight with the EMA, I admit, we lost many good people, but we eventually took control of this place," the Werewolf explained.

"I know," Lucas gave him a look. "What *is* this place? And if you dare have me ask another time, I would lose my mind," Lucas spat, aware the words had more truth in them than he intended. He had asked it so many times he was beginning to slacken the gates to his temper.

"As I said, it is the EMA. All the missing people link to here," the Werewolf said ponderously. His finger pointed to one of the cylinders at the far end of the complex, then he moved it in an arc toward the other. "You're looking at them now."

"They're kept in them?" Lucas exclaimed. "For what?"

"Why, I thought you would have pieced together everything by now." The captain gave a wry snigger. "Since you fought them."

194

What words he had prepared tripped over his tongue and fell into an abyss, wherever it was in his mouth. His jaw gaped open and his eyes bulged wide as ripen fruit. *You can't be...*

"When we first came here, we, like you, did not know what to make of it," the Captain continued, trudging down the staircase beside him. His footsteps ringed across the complex with a metallic reverberation, and it was especially loud and prolonged in the silence that blanketed the place. His fingers... or claws slid delicately on the railings. "What were the subjects for? Why would they need them? And more importantly, why bring in other Purebloods here instead of locating them in their own Sanctuaries? Well, the last question is easy enough to explain. The Werewolves' Jungle is the easiest to bribe, and the least expensive one. We are literally advertising ourselves for laundering dirty money. Other Regions have audits, more frequent and thorough police checks with more manpower, money and stability. We do not. Kidnapping and carrying people here under our noses was less than easy."

"But why?" Lucas' voice suddenly found its way out.

The Captain halted and turned to look at Lucas with those plaintive eyes. He swung back almost immediately. "Why indeed. Why do they need manpower? And why like this? There are countless other mercenary militias you can buy in the world. Why would they need this shoddy bunch who could not even hold up a minute against you? You could build a decent army without getting found out."

Lucas decided to follow the Werewolf down the steps. His footsteps were more rapid and nervous. "Unless, you couldn't. That's exactly the caveat that you're alluding to, isn't it? Unless you had to build such a large army, that calling on so many mercenary groups *would* stir some unrest."

"Exactly. The person who headed this project knew he couldn't just hire every mercenary group in the world. Word would spread, that is a given. And it is also a given that the powerhouses in the world would find out and seek to question him."

"Him? You know who he is?" Lucas asked.

The Werewolf's smirk was more condescending than Lucas liked. "Oh, I know. I think you do too. But you won't believe it. You're too devoted to him. You young and powerful ones always are with your innocent-tinted eyes. Not now at least," he continued his journey down. "And so, the only way to build an army undetected is when your soldiers do not speak. Cheap too, your resources were plenty all over the world; common, unaware civilians," his tone deepened with each word, letting his fury emerge. "How abhorrent," he ended his speech with a voice nothing more than a breath out.

"Someone's building an army for something big, someone's planning something big," he said shakily. It didn't need to be said, but Lucas found the need to let the information out of his head. He could feel it in his bones, an uneasy feeling fluttering under his skin.

"Yes, but before we get to that, I have a present for you," the Werewolf favored him a sly look before continuing on. Lucas' dubious glance only bounced off the Werewolf's back when he turned to walk forward. Captain Mitch continued down, past the heap of red, rotting flesh nonchalantly like it was nothing more than what he usually saw. Lucas grimaced when he passed it.

He wanted not so much as to catch a glimpse or a smell of it again, or anything whatsoever to do with that revolting mess. Unfortunately, curiosity got the better of him, curiosity he loathed, but one he had no choice to accept. He peered closer to inspect the bodies in intrigue, although he had seen countless corpses all his life before. His senses took in all the grisly details and choked up what threshold they possessed.

Flesh from different bodies sloughed off and melded together in a blend of red and textured, coagulated, obscene stir. Some had crusted blood sheathed on their limbs, and most were black and decomposing, leaving a dry, craggy texture, and the least still had liquid blood dripping down, slithering down, racing each other, before all of it joined with the large puddle below in splashes of soft plops.

He almost gagged, luckily he hurled only air. It wouldn't have created another mess, there was already much of it as is. But he knew he would not hear the end of it from Captain Mitch prattling of his humiliation.

Lucas took in all he had hoped not and quickly turned before Captain Mitch and his sanity had gone too far to be caught up with. He skipped past the flesh heap, avoiding what he could by leaping to patches of suspiciously empty ground and letting his soles soak in those he could not. They made nasty squishing sounds on them when his soles touched those nasty spots. He tried his best not to squirm when he felt its texture and chill his feet immersed in.

He bounded towards Captain Mitch and looked back no more. His eyes took interest in the cylinders now. They were all sealed with a sliding door made of a thick layer of metal, but Lucas didn't have to pry open them to know what lay inside. "How many are there in total?"

"Here?" the Werewolf asked.

"There's more?"

"If you're asking about harvesting complexes like this in the world, I don't know... honestly. I really hope there aren't more. But hope is a worthless thing, you can damn well expect more of these across the world, most likely in Regions just like this where the Government doesn't give two shits about their people," the Werewolf returned glumly. "It will not be like the EMA to stop at only one, fat chance. If its operations had already burrowed so deep here, then you can be sure its network of roots is as broad as well. But if you're asking about more of these rooms in this complex, then there are more. This is but one of dozens of rooms. And each cylinder holds about four captives... dead... drones, I don't even know what to classify them as, and each room holds about a five hundred of them. You add them all up..."

"Thousands," Lucas narrowed his eyes. But why would the EMA need these... drones? They had enough agents to conquer even a medium-sized Region. And in nowhere did Lucas see an EMA symbol. Then again, only an idiot would paste proof of his crime all around the scene.

"Yes, thousands," the Werewolf repeated coolly.

They finally approached the end of the complex where a human man in a white lab coat was shackled to an office chair. The chair was also handcuffed to a nearby railing in case it rolled around. The man's white coat and long pants had been sullied by splashes of blood, blossoming out like it was an intended design, but at least he did not lack any limbs. His mouth was taped, but his eyes were exposed; brown malicious things. He had so little hair, only thin and brittle white wisps spread thinly, his pink round head could be seen.

"This is your surprise?" Lucas asked.

198

The Werewolf nodded. "Yes, a good surprise. He told us everything. I'm sure you would be pleased to hear the things he has to spill," the Werewolf's lips curled ever so slightly. And that gave Lucas a stone weighing down in his heart. Lucas shuddered, now filled with a newfound reluctance. *What sort of secret?* His heavy heart weighed him down. Was he afraid of the contents of the secret? Or was he afraid that what he feared would come true?

Was blissful ignorance better than the harsh truth? He could turn back now if he wanted, he didn't have to hear it. Yruf was not unkind to him, why would Lucas have cause to doubt his actions even if it turned true this was his doing? What did it have to do with him? He didn't want any part in this. He was just a soldier meant to follow orders. *No, you wouldn't forgive yourself for this. This day will forever haunt you if you don't.*

The Werewolf was unaware of Lucas' ignorant struggle. He went ahead to his own activity. He looked down on the man with contemptuous eyes. The human exchanged the glance with his own beady eyes. "Well, Howard, I've come to visit you again. How nice it is, isn't it? To have visitors. You should be grateful! What's with that attitude?" the Werewolf mocked, ripping off the tape on the human's mouth with deliberate force.

"Ouch! Damn you, you dumb animal!" the man howled. His hands wanted to burst out to rub on his face, but they only jerked when they caught on their cuffs. His lips were dry and slashes of blood came trickling down. Around his lips were flushed as well, from the small hairs ripped by the adhesive of the tape.

"Oh?" Captain Mitch sniggered, "when we first met you, I was damn sure you were begging for us not to kill you. You were on your knees and hands together imploring us to find it in ourselves to see each other as heaven's creatures and spare your life?"

The man gave a snort and turned away, humbled. "Well… that was before… that was before I knew you needed me."

The Werewolf gave a louder laugh. "Need you? My friend, Howard, it seems you have dire need of a reminder how our relationship works. We are not partners, not by a long shot. Not even boss and subordinate. How it works is you give me what I want and I don't…" Captain Mitch caressed the man's cheek with an extended claw. "And I don't lacerate you like the rest of your friends in the pile."

The man named Howard had eyes that still glinted with defiance, but he nodded grudgingly in the end, accepting Captain Mitch's terms. He made some intelligible noises after that.

"Good," the Werewolf leaned back so he was beside Lucas. "We didn't kill everyone. He was the only one who had the good sense to surrender. And we accepted it generously. We were desperate for answers. It was him who explained it to us."

"You…" Lucas inspected the man. He didn't so much have a bruise or a gash on him. "You didn't torture him?"

The Werewolf chuckled. "Oh, he didn't need none of that. He broke easily. This man has the bravery of a sewer rat. He leaked out everything before we needed to do any of that. We *had* hoped to give him a bruise or two, but look at him, isn't he precious, Ace?"

Lucas rolled his eyes. But he saw the scientist suddenly stare at him with novel interest. "Streaks of glowing blue networking about a black suit, blue eyes, brown wavy hair, large ears, and a teenager to boot." The interest evolved into exhilaration, into hope. "There's no denying it... you're... the Ace," he mumbled.

Lucas nodded sullenly.

"Then why are you befriending this freak of nature? Kill him now! Kill him! We can get out of here and..."

Lucas's eyes shifted to Captain Mitch, reassuring him he had no intention to follow the man's chatter. "No," he asserted firmly and gave his attention back to the scientist. "I will not."

"But... why? We are on the same side! You are the Ace, our savior! Quick if you are fast then we can warn the EMA on this!"

Luca's heart plummeted. "Then it's true," he felt the air empty out of his lungs and it was hard to replenish it back. He leaned closer. "Let's get this clear, I'm on the side of the people. All people." His hand swung out to the cylinders. "And this... kidnapping innocents and then turning them into... monsters!? What sort of evil is this? This is not what the EMA stands for!" Lucas exclaimed.

Lucas made the briefest glance to Captain Mitch, then grimaced. "This is not what I thought the EMA stands for. And this is definitely not what I stand for. So you can damn well be sure I am not on your side. I urge caution on the words that are about to spill from your lips. If I get even a hint of deceit or something you are holding back, then I'm sure you have heard the stories about me of how I deal with my enemies," Lucas warned with a cold, soft, but dour tone.

"I..." the scientist looked at him with bulging, shaky eyes. "Of course," he stammered. "Just... just don't hurt me. What do you want to know?"

"For a start, what are these *things*? And don't act oblivious and vapid, we all know what we are referring to."

The scientist sighed and looked over Lucas' shoulder. "These... these are but just a part of Project Enslave. We may work outside the law, our actions may very well be questionable in any moralistic view, but I can swear we did this for the good of..."

"For the good of!" Lucas bellowed. "You killed them and you have the audacity to speak of good?" He could feel his veins finding the surface of his face, popping out like green worms. He felt heat wash over his face in a ruddy flush. "I saw what they are. They are nothing but dead. You lobotomized them, you killed them, whatever you did, they are not coming back, am I right?"

Jarred from the thunderous outburst, the scientist lurched back into the chair, hoping to sink back and get away from Lucas as far as possible. Even a few seconds later, Lucas' voice could be heard rebounding behind him through the walls of the cavernous complex. He shook his head stiffly.

"Oh, you done it. You've made him angry," Captain Mitch scoffed.

Lucas ignored him. "So why would you do that?"

"Which why?" the scientist whimpered.

"Fine. We got question by question. First. Why not just plant mind control chips in them? You could have just stopped there, didn't you? Instead you just had to kill them and turn them into those *things.*"

"We tried," the scientist squeaked, still timid and trembling. "We tried. But they couldn't take the pain. Their bodies rejected the chips, the constant wrestle between them caused them a great deal of pain. Besides, even if we could stand their howling and writhing, they would not have been able to perform what they were intended for effectively like that. So, we killed them, and we supported their bodies through artificial means."

"Why go through all the trouble? Why not just recruit mercenaries?"

The scientist started to loosen himself when Lucas' voice simmered and the anger lines on his face grew faint. He tested the waters by extending his leg, Lucas allowed it, so he let his body elongate further till he was idle and slumped down. "I'm sure you know the answer to that. Movement of such a large force undetected would not have been possible. And we need a large force."

"Yes, I did know that." Lucas glanced cursorily at Captain Mitch again. "Why do you need such a large force then?"

Lucas could have sworn he saw the scientist's eyes gleam, a certain twisted pride emerged on his face, a far contrast than his previous meek personality. It was as if he had forgotten the predicament he was in, it was as if he had forgotten who he was.

"For the greater good, as I said, Ace," the scientist beamed. "The Earth has been infested with roaches for far too long. Our predecessors had hoped to propagate enough to overrun the Earth and extinguish the Purebloods for good. How pitiful, these creatures, they do not know the joy of being a superior being like us. No matter how we help them, they cannot understand our brilliance."

"That is a lie!" Captain Mitch growled behind Lucas.

A defiance birthed from madness took the scientist to complement his newfound arrogance. "That is not! It has been proven that you only have a fraction of our mental capacity!" the scientist insisted.

"Be that as it may, what gives you the right to solve this 'problem' for us? Did we ask for it? You act like generous benefactors, but in truth you are mere slavers!" Captain Mitch rebuffed.

"As I said, you don't understand. You can't see the world in our eyes! You do not have the capacity to," the scientist shot back acid that pricked and coaxed out Lucas' disgust. It was as if something possessed him and made him rattle all those horrible things, he was a completely different person.

"It must hurt knowing that you will always be inferior to us. We're just trying to free you from your fate!" he screamed so ardently Lucas almost believed that his vile words were of righteous intent. The scientist probably believed that he was. *No, it will never be.* There was no cause so crucial to justify such means. This was plainly evil.

Lucas found himself going back to the Sergeant Major's words. It didn't matter how far the scientist was chasing his ideal, he had neglected the very important duty to question which side he was standing on. The side one faced against had always been synonymous with evil. No one ever bothered to turn around to check if their own assemblage was as virtuous as they once thought.

"Alright, shut up!" Lucas ordered. The scientist obliged, but continued chanting with low, slurred words, body swaying and shivering frenziedly. "Tell me who is behind this so I can end this now," Lucas closed in on the scientist, letting his shadow cast down on the man as he loomed above.

"I told you, the EMA," the scientist said tonelessly.

"Yes, but who? Yruf may be conniving, and call him what you will, but I have faith he will not resort to this. He's been backstabbed, that's all! Someone's doing it behind his back. Tell me who turned on him? Only someone with a high enough rank would have the authority and audacity and resources to do this. Tell me! Who? I will tell him! And we will shut you down!" Lucas screamed, uncertain if his words were meant to interrogate or to reject what he feared would come true. Feelings that he would never usually feel, came over him. He was afraid now, frantic to get answers, frantic to be disproven.

The scientist froze and glared at him with genuine shock. "I thought the Ace would be more astute than that," he mumbled. Then the scientist's eyes tapered into a mocking smile. The trembling voice transitioned into honest confusion. "Your lack of faith in Yruf is disturbing, Ace. How can you say he would not dare come so far? Yruf is the best of us, he is our great leader who would lead us into the new world fashioned in his image. When no one else dared to do something about this debauched world, he was the only one willing to risk everything, to stand up against the entire world."

Lucas did not know when it happened. But the next moment he knew, the scientist was towering above him. His legs had buckled, all strength drained from them and he crumbled. He stared blankly at the scientist. "No... it can't be... you're tricking me, it has to be," he mumbled.

Captain Mitch tried to step in. He was fast, like a black whip snapping through the air, his fur fused together into a singular blur. But Lucas held up a hand to stop him and the Werewolf put an end to his movement. He glared at Lucas in bewilderment and indignance, but did nothing. Lucas' arm flopped down loosely and regarded the scientist once more.

"It is no trick," the scientist sniggered. He was still in chains, he could not hurt Lucas. No, even without the chains he couldn't have. But… a sharp tang of dread roiled in Lucas' stomach.

A shroud of confidence clad on the scientist like a thick coat as he spoke. "I shall forever live with the shame that I gave myself out to the werewolves. But I had done so without the hope for redemption. You! You are my redemption. Not for my actions, redemption for the cause! Let our cause carry on! You can fix the situation, Lucas."

Lucas narrowed his eyes and glowered at the man. "You were the one who alerted Yruf," Lucas said stiffly. "You were the one who requested for backup. And it was why they sent a mere Lieutenant." Lucas suddenly felt sick in his stomach. "He is small enough to be rid of easily, yet high enough on the ladder to justify dispatching. Even a small squad like George's should have been enough to vanquish a pack of ill-trained, ill-provisioned werewolves no matter their advantage of physiology. He was to destroy the base, but even if he had been just a little more curious… the EMA… Yruf would have accounted for that, wouldn't he? He would have killed George!"

The scientist shrugged. "I'll be frank with you—that is out of my knowledge."

Lucas ignored him. He was on a roll. "But he didn't count on George blundering even on such an easy mission. He had no choice but to send me. There was a risk I would find out about all this, but the risk of the world finding out was greater." Lucas found himself panting, his words muffled in his anger and bafflement.

Lucas could taste the cruel irony. He wanted to choke, he wanted to laugh. By slipping up and sending half of his squad and his reputation to their deaths, George had saved the other half of his squad and his life. Once Lucas had stepped in the fray, Yruf surely would not dare touch George and further trigger Lucas' suspicions.

"As I said, I had no idea of Yruf's plans, only that I had been sure my life was forfeit. Either the werewolves or Yruf would have taken me out with this place. But now it doesn't have to be. We can save this lab and all the soldiers it contains. Do your duty, Ace, this is your ultimate chance to prove your loyalty.

The scientist giggled even when faced so close to Captain Mitch's fangs and his claws just inches from his neck. All the fear he had shown just now had left him and flung onto Lucas. He usually loved being right, but now there wasn't anything he hated more. Could he risk his world to crumble down in flames, or should he do his duty as the scientist said.

Your duty. Yruf is my father, yes. What is my duty? To the EMA or to the pledge it stands for? The pledge which says I am to protect those who cannot for themselves, to uphold the law and justice to nurture peace among all races. He took one look at the Werewolf, Captain Mitch and then took another towards the scientist and made up his mind.

"Captain Mitch, please stand back," Lucas spoke in a dangerously soft voice as he got up to his feet. Captain Mitch recognized that unyielding tone and reeled back wisely and guardedly.

"I thought I had known you better, Ace," he only said, his tone dropped back into the original forbidding quality.

"Fat chance!" the scientist mocked. The old man was silenced with a look from Lucas. "Even till the end, you would uphold his dignity," Lucas sighed, locking eyes with the Werewolf.

"Yes." Then the Werewolf gave the scientist an icy look. "You have no right to speak of dignity. But yes, I know how futile and pathetic begging is. If you say that you would spare me, it would be a trick. I know too much."

Lucas glanced back to the scientist, eyes now flecked with pride. Lucas rose up and their roles exchanged. It was Lucas who now loomed over him now. "I never asked, what is your name?" Lucas regarded him.

"Howard, sir," the scientist added the 'sir' not long after his name to fawn over Lucas.

"It's a good name," Lucas raised an arm and clenched his fist, eyes still fixed at the Werewolf. His skin disintegrated and whirled into a blade. "May I ask, is there anyone else who has found out about this besides the Werewolves occupying this compound currently? Anyone else who is not supposed to know."

"No," the scientist whimpered.

"Lie," Lucas seethed. "Again and I won't be so kind," A clean drop of Lucas' blade was all it took to cut the mesh of chains confining the scientist. They swung down to hang below the chair, swaying chaotically to clang onto each other.

The scientist was a little startled, but he composed himself quickly. "I'm sorry, sir. Of course."

"Spit it," Lucas stood back and watched the scientist rise up. He clambered awkwardly at first, his legs sore from unused after sitting for so long.

"There were many. Of course, there will always be people who found out."

"Anyone around sixteen years ago?"

The scientist gave Lucas a dubious look but lapsed back into flattery immediately. "There are many, sir. I couldn't possibly have known them all. I only know of rumors and cheap gossip. I don't exactly have time to sieve through them all."

"I'll help you narrow the search. A man and a woman, scientists like you."

The scientist laughed nervously, scratching his chin, eyes darting all over in thought. "Sir. I'm afraid I don't understand the meaning of this exercise. That barely narrows it down. The scientists have a large fraternity as well. I can't—"

"Remember harder then," Lucas made sure to put severity in his words.

Then the scientist did. His eyes widened. He shot a finger up in the air. "Oh yes. I think I do. There were two people who found out around that time. Very promising, young scientists indeed. We had wanted to recruit them, but before we could ask…" the scientist's face darkened and he shook his head. "But they were misguided. In the end they were the same trash as the rest. Such a pity. They could have shone so bright. You see, they didn't exactly see the good work we have done the same way as we do."

"Who are they?"

"They were colleagues of mine. But you wouldn't know them even if I told you. They're no one. Heck, you couldn't even have met them. You were just an infant then."

"Tell me," Lucas' voice quivered.

"Colleen and Cole," the scientist grunted irascibly, as if the names were poison itself. The names were two skewers that pierced into Lucas' heart and they sent it drumming in full force, slamming onto his chest like it was about to burst out at any second. "Where are they?" Lucas asked sharply, but he could not conceal the urgency and nervousness underlying his tone.

"Why, rotting on the ground," the scientist bared his yellow, corroding teeth and smiled horribly. A foul stench wafted out of his mouth.

Lucas felt a stone wedge itself on his throat, and the chest that was drumming so hard previously had turned hollow. "Who... how... where..." Lucas murmured tremulously.

"Yruf did it himself. Then, when he was still active. They were killed in their own. Yruf made sure they died horribly, I heard. I also heard they had kids, but Yruf done them as well. There could not be any compromise for our glorious mission," the scientist said it nonchalantly, as if he thought none of the details were terrible or gruesome. "After that, Yruf tightened all measures, closing the labs in the headquarters and other labs around the world. Afraid of audits by the First Federation and more stringent Regions."

"Yruf killed them," Lucas murmured to himself. He could feel the beating in his chest coming back.

What did you expect? You knew it all along, but you just didn't want to admit it.

"He sure did," the scientist beamed. "It's rare to find a man who stays true to his words. That is Yruf, an unprejudiced, impartial leader."

210

"Yes he is," Lucas muttered, dangerously soft. It took just a second. A fluid flick of Lucas' blade and it sliced through the air with a terrifying zipping noise.

The force was so large the head flung over the end of the room and collided onto it. The point where the head detached sprayed out with blood like a broken faucet. The scientist had not even time to scream, to register he was dead, and he was shortened by a head.

The body flopped down on the floor. Lucas knelt down with the same indifference the scientist had when he spoke about murder. Lucas wiped his blade onto the scientist's lab coat. When he was done, he dropped the flap and let it continue to soak up the rest of the blood blossoming out on the floor. With his blade polished, he shook it once more and it receded into his skin in a seamless stroke.

Lucas faced Captain Mitch who he expected would present him with yet another snarky remark. But Captain Mitch's face was solemn. "You were never on his side, were you?"

"No."

"If you wanted to kill him, you could have done so at the get go. Was all that farce really necessary?"

"Of course." Lucas' voice had turned hoarse. There was no joy in it, and Lucas suspected he would have to get used to that for a while. "I had to let him think I was on his side to squeeze out the last of the information."

The Werewolf narrowed his eyes. "Fine. Colleen and Cole, who are they?"

The names sent another lance through Lucas' heart. Lucas looked away and said nothing.

"They mean something to you, don't they?"

"I don't know," Lucas's voice betrayed him as a muffled sound.

"You don't know, or you don't want to admit... just like before."

"I don't know," Lucas insisted with a sterner tone. His brows creased and he continued walking. "I'm sorry, Captain Mitch, your help has been invaluable... and enlightening. But this... this is far beyond you and your local police. I expect you have the sense not to further pursue this... especially with the EMA involved. I've just met you, but you seem like a good guy. I would hate to see you die for nothing."

"Pretty words of advice," the Werewolf sneered. "Fine. But at least tell me this, did you kill him because of what you saw here... or because of what he said about those two names?"

"This is personal, that is all" he allowed.

The captain shrugged, then tightened his shoulders. "So what do we do now?"

"I would suggest you evacuate your citizens and never speak of this incident anymore. I will come in to level your District in a day's time, there are no two ways about it. If I do not, people will suspect... Yruf will suspect, and I'm sure we are both in the mind to be rid of this outrage quickly. I will not report this incident and feign ignorance of your part in this. Your government, from what I heard, will drop the matter completely. The EMA... I will try... no, I will get the proper compensation for your District. The EMA is well-endowed. In return, I need you never to speak of this."

"Hush money," the Captain chuckled. But the Captain was oddly warm with the idea. "Not that I mind. If my government can receive bribes, then I don't see why I shouldn't take it."

"You mistake me, Captain," Lucas eyed the captain to make sure he knew the gravity of the situation. "I'm doing this out of compassion. I don't need you to seal your lips. If you don't, it won't be me who will come for you."

The Captain's lips ran taut. "I understand."

HELLO WORLD-9 (LUCAS)

Lucas waited a day for Captain Mitch to evacuate his people from the District. They had only been given a day, so most of it had just been ferrying people out of the District with their limited vehicles. Some of the werewolves tried demanding for more time, but Lucas wouldn't let them. Delaying a day to execute Yruf's orders was already plenty enough time for someone to get suspicious back in the EMA camp.

That was last he saw of the werewolves. He gave the precocious sprightly little thing, Reesha, a big hug before she left. He gave a more formal goodbye to Captain Mitch. The policeman may have warmed up to him a little, but not so much that to warrant more than a perfunctory, courteous goodbye. Then they left each other to go back to their individual lives, though not the ones that they had before. The incident earlier had changed too much of their lives to go back the way it was.

While Lucas left the werewolves to their own devices, he went back to George's camp. His absence would be missed if he stayed to supervise the werewolves. And it wasn't like he could do much, nor do the Werewolves seem to enjoy his presence after all the compromise they had given them. When asked by he hadn't finished the mission, he gave the excuse that he needed a breather. He told no one of what he had just learnt, not even George. It was easier and safer to think of everyone as enemies when it came to secrets. Everyone there accepted his excuse willingly enough. He *had* just accomplished another mission before this recently, and he saved their asses. He deserved that small benefit of the doubt.

He did what he could at George's camp, shifting crates and helping up with the medical team that George had brought along to the mission to nurse the soldiers back to recovery. A camp had been set up before the clash with the werewolves, but George decided to shift the camp another distance away, fearing a repeat of the same incident that transpired earlier.

It was simple enough since it was more a makeshift shelter than a proper military camp with metal poles and to erect pavilions, towers to warn of an incoming attack and other cool structures. They only had short tents, some crates to stack up into feeble walls, some sandbags to cushion any surprise fire.

There was really no need to shift or put in so much effort in their defenses. Whatever sizable force the werewolves had was scattered.

It would have been a prudent measure if George had thought of it before... or not. If George had followed all the right procedures and he succeeded in his mission, he might have found out about the lab. Knowing George, the good and loyal soldier in him would have him raise it up to Yruf. Then George would be done for.

Initially, Lucas was surprised that George still loitered in a land where he had just experienced such horror, but George explained to him the medical team wanted to stabilize the conditions of the soldiers before they made their way back home.

There was no hospital nearby that specialized in human physiology, and home was so far away. The medical team could not guarantee that some of his soldiers could survive for so long without at least some proper medical care.

Lucas was glad to hear that George would stay long enough for Lucas to complete his mission after the deadline he gave the werewolves was done. Lucas was already fatigued as it was, so didn't know how much juice he would be left to fly back after levelling the District. Out of good manners, Lucas had told George he did not need to wait if his team wanted to go back, but George said that the decision had been determined more by the suggestions of the medical team, and less of consideration of Lucas. Lucas didn't mind.

Lucas knew the time had come to go back to the District when the sun began to set at the western side, drawing its power with it to consolidate it there. That left the east neglected so darkness had already begun eating up huge chunks of the once brilliant light, leaving patches and streaks of ruddiness. The clouds were untouched as always, white clumps of wool that were eternal and ubiquitous as laws of physics.

He had garnered enough energy to fly there instead of trudging through the field of dense stalks. Still, it took time. When he first started soaring, the skies were still bruised with some hint of light, but when he had reached, the skies at the west had already retreated from the conquest of dusk. Lucas had to rely on the faint blue strips of lights banded along his suit and his weapons to give them a futuristic touch.

It was and wasn't like any other job. He had always acted as the destroyer since his induction in the EMA ranks. It seldom bothered him. Now it did, tremendously. Perhaps he had grown a conscience after all that he had gone through, sergeant major

Vishnu's words slowly spreading and setting in. Or perhaps he had always known it was wrong, and this intense guilt was just the culmination of all that he had procrastinated to think about.

It was heartbreaking to have to destroy such heritage. Ancient trees with gnarled barks and humongous canopies had occupied the land for Eras, watching a hundred rulers rise and reign and fall. And the charming little District Lucas had grown to love for its tranquility and purity. But it had to be done.

He burst into the sky, as high as possible so he wouldn't be able to see the District anymore. He would spare himself the horrible sight. The blustery wind did its best to fight against him, whips of them skirled onto his face, some slapping him so hard he winced. Drafts beat onto his ears like a furious drummer. The air was drastically colder on top, and drier such that saliva refused to refill in his mouth. His lips turned arid like a land suffering from a drought. It was harder to breathe as well, but he knew he wouldn't be there long enough to faint anyway.

By the time he stopped, the sky had nearly turned dark, a dark blue spilt in the sky. Streaks of clouds amassed below him in a sea of mist that he couldn't even see the vast verdant canopy overarching the District. It was peaceful here, and Lucas knew he was about to be guilty for breaking all that. The boundless sky rolled out further than he could see… or before the darkness completely took over. Even the horizon had been blurred between land and sky. If he squinted, he thought he could see specks of lights from a nearby city through the thick mist of clouds. But perhaps it was just his imagination.

He took a moment to take in the silence before getting to his work. He would be wise to finish it quickly before he froze or died from a lack of oxygen. It was resentful work, so he did it without a smile. Lucas clapped his hands together, and just like when his skin turned into two smaller cannons, now they whirled and locked together plates of metal at a time, forming something far larger and menacing.

Supple skin flaked into metal and expanded into a large cannon that would have put shame to any tank. Metal plates were latched on it lobster style, the crevices of them lighting up with his trademark blue glow. Parts flapped and extended, others were embossed in to form engraving patterns, patterns no one could yet decipher. It didn't matter now, he only needed the firepower from it to do his job.

Just like that, his two arms melded into one, one so large Lucas always found himself asking how it retrieved so much matter to expand into something like that.

Behind him, four large barrels of the same motif as all his weapons emerged from his back; a craggy obsidian over a polished blue, hulking and terrifying. Their muzzles lit up in flames and a blue halo hovered right below them. Metal flaps sprouted out everywhere to act as wings, they shifted and rotated to get into place, in preparation for the cannon that had joined his two arms. All that to support him. The blast was going to be big, he knew. He had experienced it so many times, and he needed all that and more to stop him from being flung out of Earth's atmosphere.

Lucas closed his eyes and waited till all the clanking and beeping and locking and sliding sounds were over. Then he knew it was ready. His lids continued blinding him. He didn't have to be accurate for this shot, as long as his muzzle pointed vaguely towards his target, it would destroy all around it. And he didn't want to see.

He took the shot with little hesitation. He pulled the trigger in his mind and that was all it took. At first, he thought he had become used to its aftershock. Unfortunately, he knew he was mistaken after the first jolt ran down his body, in his muscles and his bones. Time lagged when you closed your eyes. He would have been hurled up if not for the wings and the cannons behind him pushing him from the other side. They countered the blast with blasts of their own, though it was his body that would have to bear with both pulses of energy. It felt as if he was being squashed slowly.

Even blinded, he could see the beam of blue light launched out from the cannon's muzzle to punch into the Earth, splitting the mass of clouds below and whatever that was in its way. Even where the beam had not directly hit, its residual light erupted out at a tremendous radius and surged into Lucas' eyes and stung them.

He heard the explosion when it first struck the ground, a boom pealed across the sky. He could feel the heat from the cannon crawling into his body now, daring him to endure the agony. It only took a few seconds and it was done. By then, a mushroom of grey ash and smoke saturated the area where the green canopy was once at. Under its translucent layer, fires raged below, flickering from the insides of the mushroom. He could smell the fumes from here, billowing up like a long bunch of grapes. It was toxic and heavy, so he did not breathe for long.

Lucas closed his eyes.

"And you Lucas?" Yruf asked in an unusually irate tone. "Lucas? Lucas!" Lucas was jarred from his daydream and flinched to consciousness. He turned to Yruf. "I'm sorry, sir, I didn't catch your question."

Yruf groaned, and so did many of the other generals. They were in *the* meeting room, the situation vault of the EMA. It was located deep underneath the main towers of the headquarters, under floors of solid steel and concrete, and guarded so stringently a rat wouldn't have sneaked past undetected. Lucas had been in the room several times due to his special circumstance, otherwise it was an exclusive room where only the top generals were allowed in.

The situation vault was where the top EMA minds would gather to discuss topics that were attached with very real, catastrophic repercussions if left unaddressed or badly dealt with. Like that, the room never lost its tension, its security… or the basic white it was predominantly washed with, as per Yruf's aesthetic.

Yruf had convened an emergency meeting once the incident at the Werewolves' Jungle had been concluded. The mission had been off the records, so there was no better place in the world than the situation vault to discuss something like that with your cronies. Since Lucas had been the one who cleaned up their mess, he had secured a spot in there. Lucas was not about to pass up on an opportunity to learn more about Yruf's schemes.

Yruf took the helm of the long table as usual, while the generals gradually filled in the gaps in order of rank and the seniority that came with it. The generals took their places around Yruf. They were refined in their formal uniforms that had been ironed, pleated at all the proper places, then the look spoiled by the badges and ranks excessively pinned all over. They must have thought they looked all smart and honorable with them, but they only looked like a shimmering Christmas tree. The impeccably snobbish expressions they wore, completed their look.

They stared at Lucas now, some smirking, some grim. Yruf's patience ended after realizing Lucas intended to keep up his lack of response. "Look, Lucas," he spoke mildly, "I understand you are tired. You have finished important missions one after another with little rest before you were requested to go for another, but I would at least expect you not to daydream during a meeting as important as this... especially your first debrief as a commissioned officer."

Lucas did his best to show his remorse. It wasn't hard. Fatigue already clouded him like a thick mist, so he only had to cushion the staccato of his words. "I'm sorry Yruf, I really am. What were you saying again?"

Yruf nodded gingerly. "George informed us of his... stupidity. He has been duly reprimanded and he shall make amends," Yruf gave a cursory look to George. George tried averting his glance but regarded Yruf in the end with sorry eyes.

"Thank you, sir," George said sickly. "I will not forget this kindness."

"And you better not," Yruf grunted. "The only reason I am so is out of respect to Lucas who had salvaged this mission. I tell you, if it had been any other way, I would have skinned you alive by now."

George forced a shudder down and nodded. He sunk in deeper into his chair as if hoping to disappear completely. Yruf wasn't usually so magnanimous to faults, even with Lucas involved. Perhaps it was to get on Lucas' good graces, or to stump him for questioning later, or even to test him. It didn't matter, Lucas was adroit at making the expressions he wanted people to see. His whole life had been about that. He put on his most pleasant look and regarded Yruf. A person who had been befuddled by the earlier events surely wouldn't have that composure.

"Now," Yruf faced Lucas, "we get to your part in the matter." If Yruf was relieved by buying into Lucas' act, he didn't show it. Yruf's face was hard and austere as he always was, but Lucas was not fooled. Veiled in his genial eyes, was a mind analyzing Lucas down to the slightest twitch. But Lucas had expected this sort of deceitful reception before he came here. It was another reason he came here. Yruf surely had some suspicion, and if Lucas delayed meeting with Yruf, only more suspicion would fester. It was crucial to dispel any suspicion at the earliest time you could, or it would only proliferate and become too much to contain.

"I assume what I read on your report is true?" Yruf raised a brow as he slid forward a piece of paper on the table. He then lifted it up like a dirty sock. "The documentation is poor, but I can allow it since you had done it in haste as I ordered. Still, this is an official report, Lucas. Next time try to do better. I have no doubt you can."

Lucas folded his arms, kicked back his chair and rested his feet on the table. He had never been so brash in front of Yruf or in a formal meeting before. It might present Lucas with a talking down to later, but if it would allow Yruf to think that it was his rank that got into his head, and not trouble about the incident, then the distraction would ultimately play to his advantage. His polished boots gleamed so brilliantly under the lights it reflected Lucas' image back to himself. "I think you forgot about the part where I clean up your mess for you, sir. Shouldn't you guys be thanking me instead of harping about trivialities?"

One of the generals was about to blow, but Yruf raised a burly arm up to stop him. His other hand with the paper sunk down to the table. He gently laid the sheet flat and pinned it with his fist. It was a soft knock, on the wooden surface, but it resounded through the room to silence everyone in it.

"I will not have us reduce ourselves to shouting. Lucas, you would have to put your legs down if you do not want me to chase you out of the room. You must know how insolent that gesture is... more so in a place like this. Just because you have been promoted recently, doesn't mean you have to show it off at any second."

Lucas did as Yruf bid. He had expected Yruf to ask him to anyway, so he had been prepared to do so. The solid heel of his boots clapped onto the ground. Only then did Yruf continue speaking. "Documentation is a triviality now, yes. Compared to what you have done, yes. But it is convention that lets us run smoothly, Lucas. You would eventually come to appreciate that fact as you take on more responsibility."

"Yeah, yeah," Lucas flapped a hand dismissively.

Yruf scowled, but said nothing more of his disgruntlement. "Now, back to the content of your report." He rapped his fingers on the report under his palm. "You've done the job as well as I have come to expect, so I do not have anything to say there. But I have questions. Did you search the District before you destroyed it? And if so, care to tell us what you found?" Yruf's voice softened dangerously low, like a predator prowling and keeping low waiting for its prey. It startled Lucas to see Yruf resort to such blatant tactics, but Lucas contained it in him as always. Perhaps Yruf knew that Lucas was trained to deflect questions, and so all the tactics that would usually work on ordinary people would be wasted on him.

For a moment akin to madness, Lucas wanted to give it all up; of the werewolves, of the drones, of the laboratory complex, of the scientist and everything else. He was good at keeping secrets, but not towards Yruf. Yruf was his father, his mentor, the one who taught him everything. If even Yruf could not be trusted, then who could? But as hard as it was to believe Yruf would be part of all that, he had to.

Which side am I on? Good, Lucas resolved. And if that meant turning around flipping over whatever he once thought as truth, then so be it. He would not clear Yruf's name so easily, he would not live with a lie. Yruf was guilty, and probably for a lot more too. Until he found out the truth about everything, Lucas would not stop.

Lucas made sure the subtle curl of impudence was still visible to Yruf and the generals when he spoke. His words had been measured before they left his tongue, but he rolled them out with his trademark cockiness. "I did not search the District thoroughly sir. I merely made a sweep for heat signatures to verify that they had emptied out their District before I could arrive."

"And why were you so late?" a general put in.

Lucas frowned, an expression he did not have to contrive. "I was tired. I had just fought off a bunch of werewolves that tore into an EMA platoon with ease, and you expect me not to take a breather? If I had given chase, I would have lacked the energy to save even myself. You *would* understand if you were sent into a mission right after returning from one."

Good, he did not trip up. Nor was his tone too flat; which was one of the most telling rookie mistakes. A hollow tone was still a tone, and an immoderate lack of response was just as obvious to draw information from as a flustered one.

Yruf nodded, still doubtful, still studying Lucas with those golden, intelligent eyes. But when Yruf saw that he would not read past Lucas' smirk, he relented and tore away his eyes.

"Fine." He seemed disappointed. But his face lit up soon after. "It must have been a sight, huh?"

"Uh, what are you talking about?" Lucas raised a brow.

"To see you release your powers. To level the impoverished District. No one likes destruction, but I am sure it was spectacular. The cacophonous explosion, the lurid, exorbitant lights that came with it. What a pity, I should have been there to see it." Yruf's eyes addressed the people around the room. "We should all have been there," he muttered longingly. His eyes shifted back to Lucas. "It was, wasn't it?"

"It was," Lucas said remorseful at first, but his face sprung back to a cruel sneer in fear that Yruf would notice it. "The werewolves had it coming. Such lower species belong in the dirt anyway, I merely hastened the process for them."

Yruf laughed and that welcomed the generals beside him to do the same. "Well done, Lucas. You have come through once again. I would say your next promotion would be due soon. You did well in sealing up this incident so cleanly," Yruf said, heartened, and some of the generals nodded in approval, even those that wanted nothing more than to detest him. *Good. They seem content enough with my lies.* And yet, Lucas didn't think that would be the end of their little tests. There will be more to coax out the truth in him. He had to be ready. But besides that, he had to do more to shed off as much suspicion from him as possible first.

That meant being a little oblivious, a little curious. Easy enough.

Lucas dragged his chair back to his edge of the table and steepled his fingers under his chin. "I have a question, however." Lucas' voice was not enough to overpower all the voices, but once Yruf motioned for the generals to quieten, Lucas' voice was the only thing that bounced off the walls. "Who was it who I needed to chase and destroy a whole District for?"

Yruf eyed Lucas for what seemed like eternity, then he nodded. "We had gotten reports from the werewolves that an especially large weapons ring had been allowed to establish themselves in there by the corrupted local administration there." Yruf lied eloquently Lucas wouldn't have doubted Yruf if he didn't know otherwise. "You did you part in destroying all the weapons before they could cause any havoc in the Region."

"Destroyed a lot of homes along the way," Lucas sighed. "And wouldn't they just set up camp in another place? As I said, I scanned the area. They were gone."

"But they couldn't have brought all the weapons along. They wouldn't be able to recoup their losses easily, nor find such a conducive location to set up camp easily. In the meantime, scattered and weakened, the Werewolf government can close in on them and shut their whole operation down. You saved the Region more trouble than you caused it, Lucas. Don't fret. And it's not as if the EMA isn't willing to compensate the District reasonably. I think they might even find the exchange profitable for them, now that they can build actual homes than living in their squalor," Yruf said with such finesse it didn't sound rehearsed nor was there worry in it though Lucas knew both were true.

"Some people prefer to live in a squalor. You steal their choice away," Lucas said.

"Sacrifices have to be made, sometimes. Besides, it had all been approved by the Werewolf government," Yruf's brows furrowed, hard lines cut down his face. *Coerced, you mean?*

226

Bribed, you mean? But Lucas thought he had been just nosy enough to cull out suspicions that could come from both ends of the spectrum of trying too hard and being indifferent.

Accepting Lucas' silence as compliance, Yruf continued. "And so with this report about concluded, I would like to get on to the next topic. It is rare to find a convenient time to gather all us together, so we must as well settle another before it becomes in urgent need of our regard."

Yruf leaned forwards, resting his hefty weight on the table with his colossal hands. His watery eyes drank the light above. Lucas knew whenever he did that it wasn't to sob, Yruf was about to say something mean. "But—" The word came out suddenly like brakes to a car. "—to maintain our secrecy, I would hope all the Lieutenants and sergeants leave the room now," his eyes swept over to George and the three sergeants, who had been with him at the Werewolves' Jungle, he had brought along to the meeting.

They understood and collected their papers and folders before making a line to exit the room. Lucas bowed slightly to Yruf before heading out at the end of the line, but Yruf stopped him. "Not you," he said tenderly as he could manage with that rich voice of his.

"Alright." That never happened before. Lucas was usually lumped in with the rest of the lower ranks. He was only a soldier in the eyes of the EMA. He was only told details of missions he had to execute, he never participated in discussions about the missions. Had Lucas done enough to prove himself to earn a seat at Yruf's inner circle?

Lucas returned to his seat, once again suffering condescending gazes of indignant generals who thought his presence was unsuitable in this exclusive conversation. Lucas felt extremely out of place, but he didn't show it. It would only goad more dirty looks from the grizzled veterans. At least he had people of the same grade when George and the Sergeants were still around, now he was almost a dozen ranks lower than the lowest of them.

"You proved that your value is undisputed, Lucas, time and time again. It is my loss that I did not allow you in sooner. This shall be a good experience for you too, when you eventually take my place, which I have no doubt you would. I have yet to see a worthy contender to you in this room and out."

Some of the old people scowled and made guttural voices in their throats, but they dared not to voice their dissent.

"Thank you, sir," Lucas said.

Yruf gave him a warm nod and stood back upright. His face drooped to a grim one. "Now, we move on to the next project. I really shouldn't be calling it that, but we had other guests with us so I had to disguise it somehow."

Yruf folded his arms behind his back and paused for a while. "The Vampires are stirring," Yruf said simply and hoarsely. The words had the impact of a drum jolting Lucas' insides, a beat that had no noise but the gravity in Yruf's words. The generals forgot their hatred for Lucas as they suddenly jolted to sit up in attention and gritted teeth. Their squabbles seemed so frivolous now that a subject so dire had presented itself. For once, everyone's interests in the room aligned. There was no more effective way to rally hostile sides together than a foreign threat. All eyes fell on Yruf.

Even Lucas pursed his lips. The Vampires were no minor race. They were once an ancient superpower who had held dominion over the world. The only reason their influence dwindled was because humans came about when cross-breeding happened. But it would be a mistake to overlook them. However small their numbers, the blood of conquerors still ran in their veins, and it was only a matter of time they thought to reclaim their former glory. And even if they failed, they would cause enough trouble for the EMA to activate.

"Their ruler, the venerable ninth Progneitor, Cornelius, is onto something. I don't know what, I don't even have concrete proof... just whispers and gossips, but where there is smoke, there's fire," Yruf said ominously. The room exploded into a fluster of voices, each general desiring to say their piece.

"Are they not going to abide by the treaty? They do know they are bound by the treaty, so are the other Sanctuaries. If they do so, they will stand alone. Are they truly going to declare war on the whole world?" an old general doubted with a trembling voice, but his eyes still sharp as ever.

"If so, then we can simply call for an emergency world council with the world leaders. Without even considering the human forces, there are Pureblood Sanctuaries who would take this nothing less than a challenge to them. I'm sure the Elves and the Demons... perhaps even the Angels might have some choice words for them," another spoke, a young general with black eyes and hair falling down like melted gold.

"I doubt we can count on the Angels," another spoke, a female general with her hair tied into a bun, but it did nothing to mar her beauty. She had immaculate eyelashes and full pink lips with a slender whetted nose. "They may be proud as the rest, but they have taken themselves out of worldly issues for so long they might not even care."

Another female general spoke, one with beady eyes and horrible sagging jowls. Hammocks hung below her eyes, dark

229

and dry like pieces of charred meat. Her nose flared as she spoke "Have they not learnt from the previous war? Have they not been humiliated enough that we have to repeat the event decades ago? Couldn't we just call back the..." All it took was a harsh look from Yruf to silence her, but the judging from the other general's expressions, they all knew what she was about to say... oh, they only knew too well.

"No," Yruf finally spoke after a brief silence, "we will not call *them* back. And even if I could, the First Federation would never assent to it. We agreed to let them part from the EMA and it will stay like that. Besides, we no longer need them... at least for this particular issue. Decades of technological breakthroughs and advances have propelled our weapons to far greater heights than decades ago. Right now, we are equipped to handle them, I assure you."

"So, what is it that you heard that ruffles your feathers, Sir?" Lucas blurted. Even Lucas' ears were shocked when they heard it, and for a moment he scarcely believed it came from his lips. He didn't know what came over him, only a madman would dare confront Yruf so impulsively.

"You have quite the mouth today, Lucas," Yruf noted, more amused than irked. "Whatever. Since I've allowed you in and you have found it appropriate to chime in, continue." Yruf cocked up his head, pressing his fists more heavily on the table. "What do you know of the Vampires?"

"They are strong. Really strong," Lucas muttered, regretting his sudden jabber more than ever.

"That is an understatement." Yruf frowned. "Vampires have perhaps one of the most interesting physiologies among the Purebloods. They are immortal at birth, but once they mate and produce spawn, they lose their immortality... a poetic way of completing their cycle of life on this Earth I must say. I hate to admit... but a superior way too. They are given a choice when to leave, given certainty that they have enough time to complete whatever they choose to before they die."

"Not that they use it well, though." One general coughed. "Why else would they want to kill themselves? If I had such an ability, I would want to live forever. All the talk about immortality giving way to madness is ludicrous."

Yruf smirked. "Perhaps. But we can all agree it is a waste on such a witless species. They only know the ways of savagery. Those creatures from Hell, evil embodiments themselves."

"Yes," an old general rasped, craning forward with his back permanently hunched. He scratched the brown spots on his wrinkled head. "They also have a thoroughly repulsive and unnatural ability that we have to consider as well. One to change the very structure of our heaven-given body."

"Besides all the other powers they have already. Had evolution gone mad when it made the Vampires?" Someone else groaned. She looked like a shriveled fruit, lips were moist and fixed agape.

Yruf nodded glumly. "Unfortunately, General Mighor has the right of it. The Vampires can spawn through their Vampire Stain. They once preyed on other species to turn them, but they had preferred the human species to oppose our prolific growth. Sometimes they chose the dwarves, since they most resemble us. Even the Elves were deemed to dissimilar for their tastes just because their pointed ears, so we need not speak of the likes of the Angels with their wings and the Orcs with their green skin."

"Then I wouldn't be in any trouble," Lucas jested while gesturing to his large ears as he started to relax. *Own your flaws and no one can turn them against you.*

Yruf glanced at him coolly. "Joke all you want, Lucas, it does not take away their strength. Even though they have purported to cease spreading the stain, or even siphoning blood from victims… or even causing victims at all, I do not believe they have graduated from their primal ways even for a second. I would propose caution."

"Is it a rule for them now?" the general named Mighor mocked. "Or is it some societal custom? Is their civilization trying to catch up to us now?"

"I believe it is a custom now," Yruf said. "And they are trying to evolve, yes. They have deep culture, but they spent too long dwelling on it that they wasted enough time for the humans to overtake them," Yruf said.

"That's good and all, sir, but you haven't yet told us about the rumors that spawned this conversation. You only that Cornelius is onto something, but what? What is the circumstance that would require such urgency?" Lucas put in.

Yruf's eyes gleamed. "Yes, I was about to get to that. The Vampires have pride. They have illustrious ancestors after all. They would not easily forget a transgression laid down on them, and the lost pride from the previous war seems to have punctured deeper than I thought. The Vampires only resigned from the war because the wise progenitor Worlud was still there to advise caution and courtesy. I heard he's kicked the bucket recently, leaving only Druvman and Miswol and Judas as living Progneitor… that we know of; and all three of them did not exactly have peaceful tenures. They would surely influence the current Progenitor to act. Also, the last time we had…" Yruf's

232

face darkened. "You guys know, we had *them* at our side for the Vampires to exercise caution. The Vampires must see that we are no longer protected by *them*. They never cared for the brittle treaty, and the only thing that stopped them was for fear of more powerful races now apparently gone and courtesy to us... courtesy we have exhausted with that war decades back. You want to know what I heard, Lucas?"

Yruf cleared his throat and straightened his humongous frame, letting his arms swing to his sides loosely. "I heard they see now as an opportunity to strike. I don't intend to wait idly while they work to harm us. We will strike first, as is my prerogative as your overall commander. And once we have, they will expose themselves to the world as the scheming vermin they are."

"Fine. And since you have summoned me to join this meeting, am I to assume I will play a part in this operation?"

Yruf grinned. "I am glad you and I see eye to eye. Yes, Lucas, but unlike your previous missions, you will play a larger part now that you have been promoted. Rest assured, the planning for this mission is still in its crib." Yruf stretched out his arms. "In fact, this is the first I have spoken of this matter after I had been informed by the intelligence bureau, so you'll have more than enough time to recuperate before being sent out.

Someone raised her hand. "Yruf, I get where you are coming from, and no doubt Lieutenant Lucas has proven to be invaluable to us, but I would remind you that he is still just a Lieutenant. Exactly how much more responsibility would you have him shoulder?"

Yruf narrowed his eyes. He hated to be disagreed with, but Yruf knew the merits of opposing views. He spoke with careful politeness. "You forget, Isabelle, there has been a precedent set for Lucas to—"

"A precedent is not a precedent if it had been botched. In fact, it should be fair warning for us not to repeat the mistake!" the general cut him off. He was one of the stone-faced statues that had been giving Lucas dirty looks. It seemed he could no longer stand it, indignant at the favoritism a mere Lieutenant was receiving when he had spent decades of his life painstakingly climbing the ladder. A cacophony of slamming fists and indignant voices to support the view rose.

"Yes, and Lucas fixed it," Yruf's stately voice boomed through the room to overpower them all. "Spit all you want, Isabelle. Lucas is different, he is strong, and has never given me cause to doubt his abilities, so I have much faith that he will not give me a new reason to after this." There was no appeal to the tone Yruf had rebutted in.

Just like that, Yruf had reined them all in and they no longer prodded about Yruf's authority. The rest of the meeting was used simply to draw the barest scaffolds of their plans and discuss some technicalities of the mission and how the work would be split. Lucas excused himself from their ardent discussion by trying to look as invisible as possible. It wasn't as if the generals were actively inviting him to participate in their ramblings anyway. There was a fragile truce between them and Lucas, and he was not tempted in the slightest to poke at it.

Lucas sunk into his chair and kept still. He tried absorbing the contents of the meeting, but never could keep himself attentive at the terminologies they used or keep pace with the speed at which they spoke. Or it could just be that their old age gave them unintelligible, slobbery tongues.

He nearly dozed off. The rest of the meeting was probably exciting as it had turned to nothing less than a shouting match. But even with the heated arguing going about, Lucas never found it in himself to get back to track about what they spoke of. Eventually, Lucas liked to think that the Generals forgot about Lucas' existence in the room.

As usual, the meeting dragged on with many things spoken but with little done. Lucas grouched to himself that he had some errands in his mind to accomplish before he could get a rest, but seeing how the meeting dragged on longer than it should, he guessed he would have to call it a day and get to them tomorrow. The mysterious event in the Werewolf District would have to be answered later.

If this is what it means to be an officer, attending long, tedious meetings, then I'd rather be stripped of my rank, Lucas thought. Cadet life was regimental, but at least it was fun. At least there was action and exhilaration. Half of the people there hated him, and the other half ignored him routinely, but at least they kept each other company when they were forced on assignments together. When you were in a squad, you put away your petty quibbles or you would only be sabotaging yourself. Icarus and Sam may have been morons, but at least they were entertaining morons.

He was the lowest ranked officer by far here. He felt so lonely here. He couldn't even be bothered to hate on any of the generals who despised him outwardly. They were all bark with no bite. They wouldn't dare do anything with Yruf backing Lucas. And so there was only apathy towards them He couldn't find a cell in his body to concern himself with them. Heck, he wasn't even sure if he spoke the same language as the generals.

And so it was that Lucas' mind drifted off as the meeting persisted. His body had turned sore and stiff by the end of it. As was custom, they strutted out by descending ranks. Yruf marched out with an entourage of fawners hoping to curry favor. But Lucas knew it would make no matter how much they tried to flatter him, Yruf was not so easily moved by such empty gestures.

Lucas was the lowest there, so naturally, he did not bother to rise until the last of them left. He gave whoever looked at his direction an innocent smile back, whether they glowered or smiled at his first.

There was one especially annoying colonel who Lucas had to grant an exception for however. She had a freckled nose and pale skin like milk, her auburn hair flowed back lustrously. One would have mistaken her for an airhead damsel in distress if she were seen on the streets with her doe, clueless expression she always wore. But Lucas had a sneaking suspicion it was deliberate to cause people to underestimate her; a weakness turned armor which she wore. She was pretty if not for the giant scowl she hung on her face when she regarded Lucas. Lucas answered in kind, then feigned a pounce, but jerking to a stop almost immediately.

She flinched and slammed onto the wall behind her in shock, granting her several odd looks by her colleagues. Lucas sniggered. She hissed several harsh words at him, but Lucas made sure that she knew he thought nothing of it by rolling his eyes. All she could do turn away furiously and carry on walking in line.

Once the whole gang of them shuffled out, Lucas waited for a while before he pushed himself up and headed out. He didn't want to fit inside the same carriage as the rest of the generals who had just exited the room. The journey up was long since they were so deep underground, and surely it would be made longer by the awkward silence when he was crammed in a box full of people who hated him.

After the long corridor, he greeted the guards standing vigil outside the elevator. They looked bored. It was not surprising. Shifts were partitioned hours at a time, and in this empty silent place that was also too deep down for internet service to reach, they could do nothing but talk to each other. They didn't even have scenery to admire in this mundane box with only white as their reality. But in this line of duty, boredom was often the best thing you could get. It sure was better than dying.

He made the standard EMA small talk with them, then boarded the lift. He was grateful for the lack of jingles playing in the lift. It was silence he needed now after being in such a racket. The hammering headache that had been a product of the racket slowly waned as well. The only complaint Lucas had was the radiance of the light panels. The dazzle of the lights made the lift hard to look at. After being stung several times, Lucas gave up and closed his eyes.

The recent days had been a frenzied race. He deserved this time now to just rest. Tomorrow. Yes, tomorrow, he would get to the bottom of it.

HELLO WORLD-10 (LUCAS)

"Do you see? Now do you believe me?" the man said as he trudged through the aisle with so much effort he must as well be ploughing through a bog of thick slime and algae.

The woman's face was aghast, and paled even paler than her skin was already. Her voice had left her, her tongue stiffened to reduce her to a mute. Her eyes wandered quicker than the steps would take her. Her legs tapped forward in a slow tempo, the clash of her soles on the polished tiles on the ground rang through the cavernous room. She tried her best to take in whatever she could see, but her face made it clear that her efforts were proving fruitless. She could not believe what she was seeing.

Lucas' vision was blurry, something had fogged his sight or was it his sight at all? No, it couldn't be, something just didn't seem *right*. Lucas had long outgrown the height which he was looking around now, and he could vaguely see the fingertips of a hand edging out from the bottom of his vision. He rested on a hand.

It came to him quickly, slower this time, but the reflection on the floor helped. He was seeing visions through the lens of the Cube; an object with a shape of exactly what its name suggests, save for a jagged exterior and a network of blue streaks carved through its surface to give it its alien look.

He had experienced this before so it wasn't so jarring this. His poor vision owed to the man's clammy fingers, sweat trickling down on his sight. It was irritating, but he was just glad he could see enough to matter. He continued tilting his 'eyes' up and he studied the man holding him and the woman stalking beside him.

They wore their lab coats loosely on their bodies, the buttons running down the center of the coat unclasped. It allowed the coat to flap behind while they advanced forward. Lucas didn't have to hear them speak to one another before recognizing them. He knew their names.

The woman, with pupils flecked with gold and skin of flawless porcelain, with hair tied in a brown ponytail behind her, swinging side to side as she walked, was Colleen. And the lanky man holding him with the receding hairline was Cole.

They were dead, as the scientist he killed at the Werewolves' Jungle told him. So this *was* a memory, as he had concluded before. Not his, but the Cube's memory. Somehow, it recorded it all, and when it assimilated with Lucas, it must have integrated more than its abilities into him.

Lucas pursed his metaphorical lips. He shouldn't have been able to recognize this place... and it probably wasn't the same one, this was not his memory after all, but he found himself having a strange connection to this place. It was a frail sensation at first, then it strengthened as he remembered.

It was the lab complex... perhaps not the same one he saw in the Werewolves' Jungle, but one alike. Just like the lab in the

Werewolf District, the pods here were sealed shut with another column of metal over it, so whatever was inside was hidden.

The cocky and mad scientist, Howard, had told there were more of such complexes around the world, so it wouldn't have been far-fetched if this was another. This one looked the same as the other one, at least. The place was uncannily silent except for the clicking of heels on the ground. The cylinders that walled them in were as tall as pillars and thicker than even the barks of the great ancient trees in the Werewolf District.

"I don't believe this, how... how could he have hidden all this from us... and close to plain sight," Colleen spoke again, in equal parts wonder and fear. Lucas' eyes followed Colleen's voice and then followed her as she meandered around the aisle like a drunkard; taking small staggers or large strides at a time.

"I had the same feeling when I first discovered this place. But the awe fades, I assure you... though this sight should never have invoked awe," Cole spoke in a grim tone, "not after you see what's inside the cylinders."

Colleen gave a healthy amount of attention to Cole before speaking. "Okay, you don't have to keep me in suspense. Spit it. Why does this lab feel so... shady? Why would they need to hide this within a fake wall? Yruf is a strange man, but this is too ridiculous to be caution."

Cole shrugged. "Not too ridiculous. I was able to hack into it without sounding any alarms, right?"

Colleen gave Cole a deadly look, but felt it wasn't enough. Her lips quivered, then her pupils dilated and she went in for the kill, slapping Cole so hard on the back the smack echoed through the cavernous lab. Cole yelped, arching his back and stumbling forward. The momentum he was driven by was far

240

greater than it should have been. Then again, he had the physique of a scarecrow. The Cube fumbled in Cole's hand, and in effect, Lucas' vision shook violently. He almost dropped the Cube in the process.

"Can you be serious? I'm still a little apprehensive about this whole thing. How do you know we are undetected? You are brilliant but others are too. What if it's a trap?"

Cole snorted, the confidence in him never dipped once. "How disappointing that you have such little faith in me. Don't worry, it's fine. Now, let's get back to your question about what this damn lab is all about."

He stopped towards one of the cylinders. He tapped on the screen that every cylinder had before it. Lights popped up the signal that it had activated, displaying a plethora of information. Cole tapped it with his keycard dangling below his neck secured with a lanyard for security identification. A short dance of his fingers on the screen and it beeped to indicate the tab that emerged out.

The lab shook at once, so loud and so forceful it might have been an earthquake, but it had just been the combined rumble of the cylinders. Their metal joints and hinges creaked, high-pitched buzzes and screams erupted out from metal scraping on each other as the metal column over the insides of the cylinder scaled in to reveal egg-shaped pods inside encased with glass.

And inside those ordinary pods were Purebloods of a dozen species, all deathly still and their limbs all clumped firmly to their body. Colleen's eyes widened. "What? Wow... I've never seen some up close before," she exclaimed as she walked towards Cole, her steps were more uncertain this time.

"Yes," Cole said simply.

The collection this lab had was more extensive than the one at the Werewolf District.

There, Lucas saw Demons with their sinewy frame, Vampires with their pale milky... even enameled skin, Orcs with their green hue and fangs as thick and razor sharp as daggers, the Lazarus with their craggy hide as hard as metal. The Golems with their rocky composition and the Serperin with their glorious scales. There were those who existed as liquid, or could shapeshift or change their states, those were frozen solid. Some of those even hailed from underwater, Purebloods Lucas had not thought Yruf would be so audacious to capture, knowing how easy to rile the sea lords under the surface were. It would be understatement to say they would be livid given such flagrant slight to their species. No, not only them. If any of the Purebloods knew of this scheme, they would not think twice before declaring war; especially those who have been stalwart allies of the humans.

"They... were taken against their own will, I suppose," Colleen replied in a partially irate voice since most of her attention was still spent admiring the subjects. She turned to Cole. "Are they... dead?"

Cole's eyes met Colleen's eyes but also didn't at the same time. He was angled towards her, and he tried to look at her, but his eyes were withering to inexpression. "You're right about the first one. They *were* taken against their will. Even if this whole operation had good intentions, it would never be able to justify such evil. But no, they aren't dead... and that is what makes it worse. They are cocooned in stasis... but I don't know what for."

"So what do we do?" Colleen's tone was shaky.

"It is clear as day and night this cannot go on," Cole gritted his teeth and said.

"How? Who do we report to?"

"Not the EMA, that's for sure," Cole said sardonically. "If Yruf is behind this, then by going against him, we're effectively going against the entire EMA and... the vast network it has. You know how tight a grip Yruf has on the people here. He's got his brainwashed cronies all sprinkled about in plain sight."

"Wait. How do we know it's Yruf? What if someone is trying to frame him by using his card and doing all this? Perhaps we should report it to him?"

"You still don't believe me?" Cole threw his arms up incredulously. He glared at her like she was stupid. "After all this, and your conclusion is that Yruf got framed? Sure, he's an easy target, he's the bloody overall commander, but what do you think is more likely? Someone is attacking him for his power? Or he's using his very powers to fund for all this," Cole challenged. "You're not a dull person, I'm sure you can figure it out."

Colleen's face twisted in contemplation, it was clear she was still finding out possible scenarios to explain everything. But when she couldn't she closed her eyes and sighed. "Ok, I believe you. But don't patronize me again," she warned. Her eyes shot open again and they glanced at Cole. "How did you know, and how did you come across this lab?"

Cole's puckered forehead did not show that he was quite content with Colleen's answer, but his eyes skirted away anyway, back to the pod in front of him. "I only dared to show this place to you when Yruf was far from us. It would have raised some alarms if his card was activated in two locations.

Right now, he's on a mission at the Elven Realm." Cole raised the Cube on his hand. "Do you remember what we discovered last week?"

"The digitization technology?"

Cole nodded. "Exactly. Among all the uses we have found for it, this one was the one breakthrough that really counted, we felt it in our bones then and it came true. Except... it didn't come through the way we expected it to be."

"They wanted to rescind our ownership of it," Colleen recalled. "They ordered us to compile everything we have on it and surrender everything we have on it to them by this week."

"No," Cole grunted. "They wanted to confiscate it. They didn't want the world to know, and they even had us sign waivers to shut our mouths. This technology could benefit the whole world and improve our lives exponentially... the doors of science and research it opened to whole new worlds we never have dreamt about. But they want to keep it a secret? You can be sure that if it is not to improve the lives of Earthians... it will have repercussions... and its effects will be felt throughout. They want to weaponize it. Imagine the damage that could be done, Colleen. And now imagine the EMA having sole ownership of that power. Their authority would be undisputed. That power is too great for any one organization, and definitely not for the grubby hands of Yruf."

"And we're only talking about just one of its powers," Colleen mused. "Yes, you're right. But how?" Her voice was starkly more attentive than previously.

Cole sighed. "To be honest, I don't know who we can trust. Yruf's web of influence burrows deep in every society. But either way, we must move now. With the amount of noise those damn cylinders made, we can only assume they are on to us already. We must get out of the First Federation to perhaps one of the Oriental Regions... they have little fondness for the EMA. Rumor has it that they may even be building an organization of theirs that imitates the EMA, so we can be sure they will be staunch opposers to him... regardless of what they think of you and I."

Colleen nodded. "Alright. What about the documents we have on the Cube? We must bring them with us if we are to prove useful to the Oriental Regions. I will go back home and get our son. We'll rendezvous at the airport."

"Heck that! We have all the information we need... and the very object that our work is useful for," Cole jiggled the Cube. "Time is too tight. We go back home together and get Lucas. He's my son too, you know? Also, I think we've watched enough damn movies to know that splitting up... is never a good idea." Cole started bounding through the aisle towards the entrance of the lab. "Do you have the babysitter's number? Ah, never mind, I'll call her myself."

Lucas, who was watching everything in the eyes of the Cube, did not know if he should have felt relief or dread after Cole had confirmed his theory, that he was Lucas' father... and that Yruf had been up to this all along. He knew all along anyway, the explicit answer was redundant. But, for some reason... Lucas' heart felt heavier in his chest... it sunk for he also knew what would come next.

The pair had not advanced in too deep into the lab so it was a short walk. They started for the stairs soon enough, ringing the grilled metal steps. When they exited the lab, a blanket of light blinded Lucas' vision. And there he was something familiar. White walls with a white ceiling and white tiles lodged on the ground. And from the windows, a view of the outside spanned to reveal a training ground and more buildings huddled near each other to block the view partially.

Of course it was familiar, it was the EMA headquarters.

Out of the blue, Lucas felt a tap on his shoulder. Wait… how could he feel a tap on his shoulder? He was the Cube. And the insentient device had no shoulder to speak of, how could it have *felt* anything? Unless… the vision had shattered and he was back to real life.

He was at a brightly-lit office with rows of computers and agents, the quiet sort with few activities but the whooshing of the air-conditioner above, papers fluttering, hole punchers being slammed, staples crunching, pins clattering and pencils scribbling. Machines beeped and growled and made scraping noises. There was the occasional ringing of the phone, but it never rang long before someone would pick it up. The call was never long, and the words were few and muffled. The floor was a thin carpet, the windows were tinted blue with nothing much to see outside but more buildings and some trees, just like any other mundane office.

Lucas was standing at a corner near a metal cupboard, with his arms folded. He must have blanked out. Then he remembered the tap on his shoulder that had receded away by then. Lucas jerked to his feet and spun around, every strand of muscle in his body ready to strike.

"Wow! Hold it there cowboy, I'm on your side," George jumped back, startled. His hands were raised in concede, leaning back with bulging eyes.

Lucas retracted himself back to the spot before he leapt. "I'm sorry," he shook his head while dragging a hand down his face to refresh himself. "I… was daydreaming."

"Must have been a good one to keep you so still," George laughed through the creases at the side of his eyes.

Lucas nodded. "I guess it was," he forced a smile. He remembered why he was here. "So is it done? I can access it from my own desktop in my room?"

"Yeah, sure. Knock yourself out," George said. "I just had to set up a new account for you, and getting permission to the system was easy, no one thought it was weird for a Lieutenant to request for access to the past agent database. Those had just added Lieutenants to the list of people it was declassified to, so lucky for you. But even if they hadn't, I doubt they would dare impede you, huh Ace?" He slapped on Lucas' shoulder playfully.

"An insipid reputation I never wanted," Lucas reminded him, "but thanks, man, I don't know what I'll do without you. You've always been there for me."

"Hey," George nudged him at his ribs, "I would have far more to do if I were to finish paying back my debt to you. You did no less than to save my life back there. And now to see you as a striking young Lieutenant…" George studied Lucas from head to toe and rested his hands onto Lucas' shoulders.

He was a foot taller than Lucas so his hands slanted down at a comfortable angle. His wavy hair settled on his head like a wig, there seemed like a cushion of air slotted between his scalp and his hair. His hair had the miraculous ability to always stay away from his fringe. If they were any straighter, his eyes could have been covered and George would have just violated the

EMA's dressing policy. His eyes were jet black, determined yet marked with a kind quality. It paired well with his bushy brows raised above them.

"You know, of all the places, I never thought the first time we would meet as officers would be at a cornfield." He grinned so wide his teeth bared and the lower lids of his eyes swelled up to partially conceal his eyes. "I'm proud of you."

"Thank you, George. That means a lot. And thanks for this favor again."

George nodded and released his hands. His face suddenly crumpled to produce a smirk. "It was easy anyway. Though I have no idea what you would want to do with a database of all the past agents in the EMA."

Lucas shrugged. "You know me, I like my data. I'm… just interested." He then tried his best to churn out whatever smart-sounding gibberish he could. It would have been nice to tell George about the conflict in him, to tell anyway. But no. He could not trust anyone. The best way to keep a secret was if less people knew. *I cannot tell this to anyone… even you. I'm sorry.*

"I see, well, that's fanatical," George commented casually, "but you've always been a special one, haven't you? Go ahead then, I have work to do too. I have to finish up my side of the report regarding the incident at the Werewolf District. I've also taken the liberty to polish yours."

"Really?" Lucas beamed. It *was* a ton off his shoulders to know that he didn't have to worry about the report Yruf threw back to him to redo because of its shoddiness. At least now till his next mission he wouldn't have to worry about all the formatting nonsense.

248

George nodded. "All in a day's work. And I've always been good at it anyway."

"You're too nice George," Lucas lamented, then switched his tone to something snarkier. "Just don't be so on your next mission."

Where Lucas thought George would scowl, he sighed. "That's going to stick for a while, isn't it?" He shrugged. "Well, I guess I deserve it. I got off lightly. Now—" George's face turned serious as he brushed off his uniform in habit though there were no curls of hair or dirt on it. "—it's time we part. Sorry I can't have lunch with you later. Again... I've got my work cut out for me."

Lucas only nodded, then watched his friend turn and walk away in all the dignity of his uniform, metal badges shimmering under the light and clanking. It wasn't because he felt melancholy, it was that George had a peculiar way of walking Lucas was always amused about. Each step was a hop, so George looked like he was skipping through the corridor.

Once George turned into another corridor and out of sight, Lucas went his way back to his room. It was a weekend, so most of the Agents would have gone out. Even those still in the base were probably asleep in their bunks. Only critical personnel and shift platoons responsible for guard duty were required to attend to their posts. This office was responsible for the maintenance and support for many EMA servers, so it never closed.

As Lucas walked out, he mulled on the grim words his parents had said in his vision, and the events that had happened after that he didn't want to know but had to if he were to proceed. He had to know the truth. The visions would grant him that soon enough, Lucas was certain. Not often was fate merciful enough to spare him from this sort of abhorrence.

Once he barged into his room, he got to what he should have done once he had reached the First Federation. He fired up his computer and went searching away for those two people. When they did not come up in the database, he tried to adjust how the names were spelled. Perhaps he had heard it wrong or it was just created differently with an extra letter or a configuration that sounded the same. It presented him with some options, but even so, none matched the features of Cole and Colleen. Then he tried searching for them by cohort.

Lucas had been born before this incident, but he had been part of the EMA for as long as he could remember, so he couldn't have been more than an infant or a toddler then; which meant the incident had happened around sixteen years ago. Yet, when he scoured the lists with the new constraints, it was to no avail as well.

Finally, he was given no choice but to skim through the list line by line until he nearly went mad. By then, he had missed both lunch and dinner. Yet, oddly, his stomach did not protest. It sat obediently. Just the anticipation was enough to fuel him.

"What do you think was going to happen?" a voice called out, a soft voice that seemed near him. His battle instincts fired up. Lucas spun around and brandished the blue blade from his arm in one motion to slash out, but he only cut air. "Who was that?" Lucas growled, eyes combed through the room but there was no one but him.

"Tell me, Lucas, what did you think was going to happen?" the voice called again at his ears, this time it was but a fleeting whisper, much like one Lucas would expect coming from a ghost, so close he could *feel* the lips... or the wind caressing his ears in a tender touch. He spun around again, whisking the blade through the air, but again, he only attacked the air. A gust of wind he created ruffled his uniform.

"Who are you!?" Lucas seethed, this time he was sure to inject more frustration in his voice. "Are you some sort of ghost? Or are you using some sort of cloaking technology?" He did not wait for an answer. If this person had been doing that, his sensors would pick it up. Silently, he activated every sensor he had in front of his eyes. But there was nothing... only himself.

He knitted his brows. There could only be two possibilities... either he had gone mad and was hallucinating... no it couldn't be, the voices were too real, they weren't his own voice speaking, he *heard* them through his ears, or that a superior technology was in play so the Cube wasn't able to detect it. That wasn't possible... and yet he wasn't able to discount the theory.

"Oh, if only you knew how ridiculous that thought is. You think of all the possible scenarios except the one right in front of you."

Lucas' eyes flashed past his computer screen and his heart skipped a beat. Desperation was beginning to clasp its razor-sharp claws onto his neck. And it was cold. Goosebumps rose around his body and a chill lanced through his bones. *No one must know. If I let whoever learn of this... Yruf will surely see this as treason.* "You can read minds? Come out and fight, coward!" he taunted, quietly hoping this person would respond to it. "Show me your face, tell me your name if we are to fight!"

"Lucas... can you pause and listen to sense for once?" the voice ordered, screening past his ears once more, making the tiny hairs on his ears quivered.

"If you had thought giving me that warning was a good idea, show yourself and you would find out what a mistake that was. I assure you, you will not get another chance," Lucas threatened, baring his teeth and waiting through bated breath, his attention split between the screens in front of him and his environment. But nothing pounced at him.

"Alright. I see that words will not be able to get through your obstinate character. Then proof will. Look at your screens again, Lucas." Lucas' hair rose as if he had just touched a live wire. *How did he know? He can see my screens? It can't be, the screens aren't visible to anyone outside. So, he can see through my eyes? Or does he know my technology? He's studied me.* Still, he indulged the voice and turned to his screen. It displayed the same thing it did the previous second, and the second before that, and before that.

"Tell me what you see on your screens."

Lucas took another look at the screens. "It shows nothing, what are you leading me at?" he snarled. Lucas was absolutely sure this was not him talking now. He didn't conjure up those words. He wouldn't be so enigmatic to himself. Or would he? Lucas shook his head.

"Nowhere. My point is that if you see nothing, then there must be nothing. My systems are not so easily broken… and it is by no measure shoddy compared to the things you call technology on this planet."

It all came to Lucas instantly. His eyes widened. "So, I *was* talking to myself."

"Oh no," the voice said again, with a trace of mockery, "you are not capable of such eloquence. These thoughts, you can surely say they come from your thick skull of yours, but they are not from your mind."

Lucas' eyes quickly narrowed. "Nice to hear from you too, what makes this day so special that you would care to drop by?" he reciprocated with the same enthusiasm. "I did not know you could talk."

"Oh, I couldn't… at first. But as you know… I evolve. I'm sorry to disappoint that my purpose isn't merely to act as your personal arsenal."

"Well, that's the only thing I'm interested in."

The voice paused, then it decided to disregard Lucas. "I have far more layers and functions than you think. For example, art, speech, culture. Speech… well that's easy for me to perceive. Emotions are still a little ambiguous for me, but I'm learning."

"And with a pretty personality as an added bonus," Lucas grunted. "But I don't suppose you could devolve *that.*"

"A joke, I would laugh but you wouldn't appreciate it, it would only affirm your views of me," the voice said again.

"So what do I call you? And…" Lucas paused, he recognized something oddly familiar about the voice, but he couldn't put a finger on it then. Now he could. "And why are you using *my* voice? It's a little more monotone and mechanical but it's still *my* voice."

"You can simply call me as you think of me, Cube. Well, your voice is the only one I was exposed to for a long period to capture all the nuances of your accent. But if you don't like it…"

"Never mind," Lucas swung his hand down.

"Good. Now that we can put that aside, I did not come here to chatter. I have come bearing gifts, Lucas."

"What gifts?" Lucas asked hesitantly.

"I did ask a question just now. It is bad manners not to reply to someone who is so inclined to give you such a marvelous gift. Would you be so kind as to do that now?"

"What did I think was going to happen?" Lucas recalled, his eyes lifted the ceiling. "Well, I thought I would find their names."

"What made you think Yruf would be so careless, Lucas? You saw the visions and the voices I supplied you and you still thought to risk all for this one imbecilic task? Even without investigating, you should know that Yruf would have erased all trace of your parents from the computer once he found out," the Cube chided.

"So you were the ones who sent me all the visions?"

"You couldn't figure that out yourself?"

"I knew," Lucas blurted more eagerly than he wanted to, "was it deliberate, or are our minds melding?"

"Don't be ridiculous. We may be one physically, but you have but only a taste of my power. If I unleash everything to you now, you'll explode like a glass brimming full of liquid. Luckily, you, the glass, the vessel, can expand and as you do, I shall gradually give you what you can endure. Whatever you experience Lucas, it is deliberate. There are no mistakes when it comes to me, I have colonized your brain and everything is under my control."

"Whatever," Lucas was aloof, he figured as much when the scientists told him the Cube had merged with him. "So, what is the gift?"

"The gift of the end, the end of the chapter you were so fervently searching for," the Cube's voice dipped back into a whisper.

"What happened to my parents?" Lucas morphed it as more of a statement than a question. It tanged his tongue as the words rolled out.

"Yes. Lie down on your bed Lucas. You might not want to take all of this standing up. The previous time you were lucky to not have fallen. You might not be this time."

HELLO WORLD-11 (LUCAS)

"Are you ready?" Lucas' father, Cole trampled past a congregation of toys and other items strewn across the parquet floor. He was tall, so he had to duck his head down when he walked through the door. His face was a canvas of worry. It seemed as though he had aged ten years though Lucas was sure from the previous vision it had not even been a day. The pock marks on his cheeks were showing under the glisten of sweat and oil, and they were flushed like he was drunk. His eyes were two pinpricks, quivering in place.

He had just shrugged out of his lab coat and donned a simple checkered long-sleeved shirt and jeans. He hoisted up his luggage, aware the wheels wouldn't have been able to ply through the mess on the ground without much effort. "Honey! Are you done feeding the baby!" he yelled again. "I told you not to, but you insisted. I agreed, but I also told you to be snappy about it! Time is trickling away, and we both know how little we have of it left!" He continued speaking with a courtesy, though Lucas knew it was quickly waning, Cole's suppressed irritation was breaking out.

Cole's other hand had the Cube firmly clenched in clammy fingers. Cole did not trust it anywhere else but a place where he could see. Lucas knew... he had the same habit, except not for the Cube, that object was the least he needed to worry about. Cole groaned when there was no reply again. He slammed the luggage on the ground when he reached the front door in frustration. The wheels clanged and rolled a little, but the force was too much to bear and it toppled.

Lucas took the liberty to comb through the apartment while Cole stormed through it. It was a cozy place, with warm textures and earthy colors, potted plants pegged on walls had their leaves sprouted out so Cole had to dodge them as he walked past. "You were a good idea on paper, but now that I actually have to walk through you, I hate you," he whined at the plants as though they would hear him.

The apartment was designed with as many natural details as possible. There was a beautiful kitchen with wooden cupboards, lacquer still shone from them. Plates, bowls and utensils stacked up nicely on racks. A living room sat at the center of it all, with brown sofas and bean bags pressed in the mold of a bottom that 'remembered' the buttocks of the last user who sat in it. More furniture sparsely populated the place, along with potted plants. Streaks of black ran through the wood, some polished and some left to its craggy raw form.

A simple rug, frayed and shredded at their fringes laid below the coffee table and extended to the legs of the sofa and nearly till the television set. It could hide the blemishes toiled on the parquet there, but the other parts of the house weren't so lucky to be concealed so elegantly.

The floor, with nothing over it, was a sea of scars Lucas decided it was because of the toys scattered throughout. Their curtains were thinner than paper so that barely did anything to shield the sitting room from the surging sunlight bursting through and winking at Cole. Cole winced as his face caught a shower of it. He rushed through a short corridor and slammed his fists onto the door at the end of it. "Colleen! We have to go now! They might be coming for us this very second!" his words no longer hid his desperation. "Colleen!"

He only stopped when the door handle creaked. He stepped back as the door unlocked and the hinges released a soft dragging sound as it opened. The interior of the master bedroom was fashioned into the likeness of a fantastical wonderland with candy canes and pumpkins as furniture, a green carpet of tall bristles to imitate grass and so much pink Lucas would have vomited if he was really there.

Colleen shuffled out laggardly. Her face was pale and hollow like half her lifespan had been drained from her. Wrapped around her arm, tucked in at her bosom, was an infant sucking on a bottle of milk. Its eyes were an intense blue, attacking at the nipple of the bottle with vigor.

A visceral sensation flooded beneath Lucas' skin, it made him feel sick…. yet nostalgic at the same time. It was a new sensation, something he could not place a name on. At once he felt more connected with this reality, and he didn't want anything so much as to hug his parents there and then. But he knew this was just a vision.

"What's gone to you?!" Cole screamed. Lucas would have flinched if he wasn't an inorganic rock. "I told you that you can feed the baby in the taxi on the way to the airport, now look at how long we've wasted!"

Colleen did not rouse herself to answer. Her entire attention was fixed on the child. Her eyes, though gaunt, were filled with love. "Look at him, Cole. Look how handsome he is. He's going to break some hearts and rise into a dashing hero one day, I can

258

just feel it," she spoke softly. Lucas' heart fell. He did break some hearts... though definitely not the way she meant, and definitely not as a hero.

"What?" Cole shouted, incredulous. "How do you suppose this is the time for being sentimental when we are perhaps the most wanted in the EMA's fugitive list now? Am I the only here who's worried?"

Colleen shot at him with a deadly glower. "Oh, this is by far the best time to talk about it."

"About what?"

"About you! If we do an evil deed to stand up against another evil, are we cancelling out the evil or are we just creating another evil?"

"What?" Cole scrunched up his eyes, genuinely confused. The fear on his face was scant at first, but it rose like a tide.

"Do you see what we are doing, Cole? What we are doing is backstabbing, going behind people's back, performing deceitful, vile deeds. What we are doing is the very essence of evil. Two wrongs do not make a right."

"It's subjective." Reeling back his frustration and his posture, so as not to seem so confrontational.

"Robin hood stole from the rich to hand out to the poor. Do you suppose him to be a good guy then?" Colleen argued.

"Well, of course!" Cole yelled.

"Then what about the people who he stole from? Isn't stealing the most clear-cut form of offence?"

"But the people were starving, they needed the money!"

"So you suppose the majority wins, is that right? You told me just now that you didn't believe I was dull, well I ask the same of you now. Are you? Can the majority always discern what is right and wrong? Or are you going to tell me it's a matter of perspective?"

"I don't have time for riddles. You are obviously leading me somewhere. What is it? Colleen, what have you done?" Cole questioned, eyes glinting with by turns fear and fury. He knew his wife well, and he got straight to the point.

Colleen continued. "Where do you think we could have run, Cole? Where? Yruf's network runs deep in the whole world. There is not a corner obscure or dark enough where his hands can't reach. Even if the damn Oriental Regions can protect us, do you think they would risk it just for two of us? And even if we succeed, do you suppose we spend our whole lives hiding? What about our son? Have you thought about him? Have you thought about anything else than that damn Cube of yours? Can't you see not everyone wants to be in the history books exhibiting their acts of valor! I just want a normal life, a happy life!"

"Do you not think I want the same thing? But we do not choose the cards handed to us, Colleen! We can only make do! And currently, a happy life is not one of our options in our situation. But later... we could have worked it out!"

"No, Cole, we couldn't. You are smart, but sometimes your need to solve everything, to fix every right, to be the righteous man clouds your judgement, it turns you into an utter fool who is blind to the things right under his nose. Yruf... on the other hand... is smart... *and* ruthless. He'll kill us all if I didn't..."

Cole's eyes flared. "I ask you again, what did you do?" his voice trembled, working hard to force his fury in.

A coat of tears covered Colleen's eyes and turned them rheumy. "He promised me... that if we surrendered now, he would show mercy to us. I'm sorry, blame me all you want, I am scared. I just want things to turn out normal again. I just want all this to go away, I wish this is just some horrible nightmare that I will wake up from," tears watered down her cheeks.

A wry laugh came from Cole's lips as he turned hysterical. He staggered back and plopped himself against the wall. "What..." the words came out wispy and breathless, his eyes darted around the apartment, though Lucas wasn't sure if Cole knew what he was searching for. "This... this can't be... we're all going to die," he sobbed. He spun back to Colleen, his features writhing in utter hurt. "I don't even know you anymore," he spat the harshest words he could, as venomous as poison.

Colleen's face had turned into a mess of tears, red blossomed on her cheeks and she wept. From birth to now, the baby would have seen his parents as steady pillars he could always rely upon when *he* cried, so baby Lucas was perceptive enough to know something was very wrong when his parents did. He started bawling as well, the annoying, obnoxious sort. He thrashed about, pulling the nipple of the milk bottle out of his mouth and sending a rainfall of milk splashing about.

Lucas cringed at the mess it had suddenly turned out to, but he wasn't even given time enough for that. The entrance blasted open, sending the door flying across the room in three huge slabs of wood. Colleen and Cole jarred to alert at once. Their jaws stiffened and they spun towards the site of the explosion.

But the child was oblivious to such social cues, he continued ruining the silence.

Colleen and Cole rooted themselves on the ground, too afraid to speak. Then the rumbling came... no it wasn't rumbling, they were footsteps, heavy and hard. They had an ominously slow tempo to them and a giant of a man appeared before the corridor, smirking. The ceiling at the entrance was too short for him, so he had to curl his back when he got in, and then he was allowed to rise to his full, mountainous height when he reached the sitting room.

He wore a brown trench coat with a tail that reached his shoes. It was buttoned in a zigzag pattern. It must have been custom-made or else anyone would have been hard-pressed to find a trench coat that was twice the normal size of one. He wore boots, and on his hands were humongous gauntlets gilded with a burnished bronze hue. They clanked mechanically as he clenched and opened them, the gears exposed where the crevices of each joint rotated and rattled.

The man was huge. Cole was taller, but the man more than made up with his broad frame, corded in layers upon layers of muscle. His jaw brimmed with shaggy hair rising up to his sideburns and he sported a good shock of hair running down long till his neck. His chin protruded long and square and proud, and where his eyebrows were thin streaks of hair that he must have shaved to look all the more menacing. He still had his scar, but his skin was less flaky and dry and dewier, and no spots sullied it. It was a complete overhaul from the scruffy old man he was sixteen years later; though it was much to be expected, people in this line did not age well... if they were lucky enough to do it at all. Still, it was surreal to see Yruf so young.

His intelligent black eyes studied Cole and Colleen in a soft but intimidating manner. His lips were pressed together and a curl bordering on mischief rose on his lips. He took his time looking at them, all the while remaining deathly still with his usual control of the situation, the classic way Yruf squared a person. When his lips opened, they made a wet popping sound. "I admire your bravery Cole, but sometimes it comes off as annoying."

"Yruf," Cole seethed. "And I assume you were informed by this back-stabber behind me," Cole glowered at Colleen with disgust, though he didn't spend much time on her and turned back to Yruf as if he couldn't even bear to see her.

"Yes." Yruf grinned. "But you should thank your wife instead, she has far better judgement than you do, for a start. She must have told you her reason. Your cause may be noble, but are you truly able to stand aside and watch your dear child be plunged into madness of your own making? If you ask me, her cause is nobler. She did it for your child, don't you get it? I'm not without reason, Cole. Surrender and—"

"And you'll let us go?" Cole snorted. "I'm not *that* stupid, Yruf."

"No, work for me. I've always held your abilities to high regard."

"So that I can help you butcher innocents?! Is that the alternative you so rave about? You are the one who caused this dilemma, and you of all people has no say in this! And I won't let you run scot free either. You're going down."

Yruf sighed. "Are you so deluded you can't see reality, Cole? You don't have to answer that, I know you can't see. You scientists are so caught up with your microscopes it seems it has caused your vision to turn as myopic as one as well. But *if* you saw, you would agree... no all of you will flock to my cause. Mine is a noble one, it is for the greater good, it is for the survival of our race!" Yruf bellowed as he took a step forward.

His boot smashed onto the ground with a great tremble and Cole flinched.

Even petrified, Cole did not concede. "No."

"You were this close to greatness, Cole!" Yruf pinched his thumb and index finger together though they didn't touch. "Both in stopping me and joining me. Either way, you would have won. You know, going to the oriental Continent is not such a bad idea? The EMA and their side are in direct competition. And you hold the Cube! Oh, they would have snatched you in a heartbeat. But whether you live a good life is another matter. You'll be taken advantage of, treated like a slave, because they know you have no other option but to stay with them." Yruf's malicious sneer was a hateful thing.

"You should have joined me, you should have given up, you should have listened to rationality when you had the chance! Instead you lead your one-man foolish crusade against me! Even your wife doesn't have faith in you, did you really think you stood a chance? Did you really think you could hide, Cole? To be protected against me? From me?" Yruf cackled. "The underworld, the Regions fear me. Even in enemy territory, did you think I could not get to you? You lost before you had even begun playing. You could have lived bathing in glory." Yruf looked around and his eyes didn't like what they saw. He scrunched his mouth. "Instead you won't even have this drab you call home."

"You call kidnapping innocent people the greater good? No cause is great enough to justify that!"

"They are not people!" Yruf howled indignantly. "They are nothing but the lowest of society, mere dogs who should bow before our brilliance. Their time has long gone after they had birthed us... their most perfect creation. They have resisted the

264

natural order of the world for far too long. They should no longer exist!"

"They did nothing to you." Cole's voice came out as a plea. "They do not deserve such treatment!"

Yruf narrowed his eyes. "Then you do not know me at all." He started his march forward. "I will scourge every last one of them, burn their buildings and kill off their line like the weeds they are. I will make sure their cries fill the air like a chorus in the fields of hell. I will make them suffer long enough to have their sanity slip away." He raised his gauntlets as he advanced, closing and opening his fingers to stretch them. The metal, no matter how well oiled, still wailed.

The baby's cries did not stop, if anything it grew louder. Colleen jerked back. "Yruf, enough talk. You promised us mercy, didn't you? I... I... risked everything."

Yruf shot her a glum look. "I'm not going to make a joke of this solemn affair, Colleen. You know how much I hate wasting lives, especially two such brilliant scientists. I would have much use for you if it had been any other scenario. In fact, I had always sought for you to join me. Alas, no matter how powerful a tool is, if it turned rusty, then it is no more useful than a broken one."

His eyes turned to the infant. "No, I take back my words. Three. Such potential you hold in your arms, a pity it must all come to an end. A traitor's child will only make the same mistake as his parents made. It runs in your blood, there are no two ways around it. I cannot have you around. I lied," he spoke with a queer courtesy in his voice, though Lucas supposed relaying it plain to your victim was the politest one could go.

265

Yruf started scraping the paint off the walls with his gauntlets as they dug in. "Go on! Say your last words! I will at least give you that. No one can say I am not gracious. You deserve at least that for the deceit I pulled over you."

"Why... why..." Colleen started to shiver so wildly she looked like she was convulsing. "But... but..." It didn't take long for her to realize, and Lucas saw the exact moment she came to her senses. "I was a fool," her breath was wispy since she only had enough force to churn out breaths.

"Yes, you are," Cole's eyes were still fixed on Yruf when he said those words through his gritted teeth. He turned, but his eyes didn't gleam with hate this time, it was despair mixed in with pensiveness, his face wrinkled and spotted. "But here we are. There is no point crying over spilt milk, Colleen. We must die one day. But for you and Lucas, today shall not be that day," he spoke, full of resolution. He handed over the Cube to Colleen and she took it readily, in between intervals of smothering her hands on her weeping face to wipe away the constant flow of tears.

"Take it," he said, "and run."

"Run where?" she sniveled. "There is nowhere else to go."

He gestured to the Cube with his eyes. "Do you remember ability four?" he said with a forced smile.

Colleen's eyes widened. "The portal," she murmured.

Cole nodded. "We could never really find a use for it since there was no way of testing where everything we threw inside went, so we set it aside for other more useful capabilities. But now we have the perfect time to test it, don't we?"

Colleen's face scrunched up in pain. "I don't think we have a choice."

"So go."

"Go? How about you? Cole, I don't want to leave you, not after... not after what I've done! You can't! I will not make you sacrifice yourself! Look at him!" She pointed towards Yruf. Yruf heard it all, but he saw no need to inject more urgency into his advance.

"He will eat you up in less than a heartbeat! You would stall for no time at all!" She started flailing towards Cole in a fit of madness with no true idea of what she wanted to accomplish. Cole pushed her away, soft enough to not count as a shove, but hard enough to convey his warning.

"No! Colleen. We don't have time! You made the mistake, yes. I may not forgive you, and you may not either, but now is a chance to redeem yourself a little. For our son," his breath and his resolve weakened with every word, and soon he found himself barely holding back his tears as well. But he could not. The welled-up fluid trickled down continuously. "I love you Colleen. I hate you and love you. It's weird, but it is that. This is goodbye, with no better way of saying. It'll only make it harder if you linger, Colleen. Go!" He turned back to Yruf and ran before Colleen could say another word.

She closed her eyes and sprinted the other way, never once looking back. But Lucas could. He saw. He saw the stupid man, that looked like a skeleton compared to the brawny Yruf, charge unarmed and without a plan. Yruf would bulldoze over him like a twig.

Yruf welcomed the last act of valor and reciprocated. His charge shook the apartment, eyes sparkled with malevolence. Lucas wanted to shut his eyes, but he could not. Anticipation forced his eyelids up. He knew he had to look too, if he turned away, it would be a disservice to his father... his real father.

267

Fortunately, that choice was ultimately stolen from him when his mother dashed into the room and the wall that blocked the collision. But Lucas could still hear the sickening crunch and the ululating scream of Cole that sounded so primal no one would have recognized it as human as he was beaten... no pummeled, minced like a sag of meat. Colleen winced several times, but she dared not stop. She had to move on. She had to redeem herself by at least fulfilling Cole's last wish. He had so nobly sacrificed even after she had faltered, this was not her life she was fighting for... it was a matter of her what little honor she was worth now.

She threw the door of the bedroom to a close, and locked it for what little it would do. Perhaps it might buy her a second, she didn't know, she kept running. She leapt through the bedroom, her face quickly shriveling as her eyes screened the room and the fond memories she had inside fleeted through her mind and showed on her face. It was all but the past now, her life here was over like it or not.

She tripped over a pile of clothes on the way, sending them scattering about to straggle the floor behind her. She almost fell, but her willpower took over and she skipped for as many times as it took to continue her way. She rushed inside the toilet, again sliding the door and locking it.

The toilet was modern and white, with glass partitions for its shower and a big mirror at where the basin was. A plethora of products, creams and body care items were stockpiled beside the basin. She spun her head around looking for anything she could place the infant on. The basin would not do, the faucet was in the way if the infant bobbed his head up. She finally decided on the table where she placed her cosmetics and scents on. With no time to spare, she swept them off from the table and sent them clattering on the ground, glass shattering and plastic casings rolling on the ground. She placed the infant on the table gently.

"Stay here, Lucas," she urged in the most composed voice she could find in herself. "Mama's got to do this. Carrying you will only get in the way." She smiled sadly and bent down to work on the Cube. She fiddled with it, though Lucas had no clue what she was doing. In the distance, loud crashes echoed through and into the toilet. Yruf could be heard whistling blithely; somehow that was more terrifying than if he were to shout his way through.

The Cube beeped and Colleen hopped up in relief. Whatever she was doing had worked. But just as ecstasy coursed through her, so did the force on Yruf's punch on the door. The gauntlet slammed onto the door heavily. It was a miracle it withstood the first hit at all. The next tore a hole through it, the wood splintering and dust spewing out. "This would be far easier *and* painless if you would just give up!" Yruf grunted. "Or would you like to end up like your husband? Would you like to see how I battered him? You won't even recognize him now," he taunted hideously.

Colleen fought to fight back the tears as she rose, the Cube in hand. She made a brisk rush towards Lucas… but she was too slow. Yruf bashed through the door with his bulk and demolished the once slab of wood. "I would cripple you before I deal the final blow with you! I will kill your son before I am done with you! I will watch you beg as I inflict agony onto you!"

Before she could reach Lucas, she found herself blocked by the wall of the man, blood splattered on his brown trench coat… her husband's blood. Colleen's face twisted in the moment of helplessness, veins rising up her flushed face. "Get away from me, you scum!" she screamed. "You lied to me!"

At first, Yruf seemed confused as to why she might want to come towards him. Prey would not usually make a last stand so bravely, they would usually cower and lapse back as far and as long as possible from their demise.

It took but a second for him to understand. A mother's courage. Yruf grinned when his eyes lowered down to her arms. The sound of the infant's wailing took to the air once more. He turned desultorily, knowing Colleen had nowhere to run and never would become a threat to him. He scooped up the cry infant and looked at him with tender eyes that did not match the situation.

"What... are you going to do with him?" she said, half a cry and half an appeal.

Yruf's eyes turned sad as he tilted his head back to Colleen. "He is perfect, such a waste to lose such value. A human, a perfect lifeform evolved through generations to come to this," Yruf spoke regrettably. "Don't you see what I see, Colleen? He is barely grown, brimming with latent potential, and you want to trade his life for a bunch of lousy Purebloods, inbred and obsolete now in the stage of evolution? You may refuse to like me, but can you refuse his life? C'mon you chose the right option once, you *saw* the truth of it once, you can do it again."

Colleen made a cursory look at the Cube. She raised the hand with the Cube up. "You give me back my son or I'm going to throw this. All that you have done will be wasted for you."

Yruf laughed, a guttural noise belching out from his mouth. "And what? You do not think the Cube will break, do you? You have worked with it the most, you of all people know that it is far sturdier than that." His face darkened to a menacing snarl. "But it doesn't matter. No matter what I think of your son, I have my limits. You dare even put a scratch on the Cube and I will bash in your son's brains!" He raised a fist towards the infant, the metal and cogs clanking underneath the heavy plates of bronze.

Breath escaped from Lucas' mouth in an instant, his heart pumping tremendously. *This... this can't be,* he thought. It couldn't be.

Colleen only needed one peer at the infant and what determination she had so meticulously marshalled left her at an instant. She slouched down and let her defeated breath vent out. She chewed on one lip, eye bags and lids scrunching in to fold into creases, amassing into dark circles around her eyes. She raised the Cube up. "Please, Yruf, for the humanity that is left in you, for the little shred of mercy still available to you, let us go. I promise we will go far away. We will leave the First Federation, we will forget all that you have done, we will never set foot here again... no you'll never even hear or see from us ever again. Please Yruf," Colleen begged and cried, a larger surge of tears and emotions came cascading down her pale, distraught face. She lowered herself as she did, getting to her knees.

Yruf narrowed his eyes. "No." He spoke the word with a hard voice. "No, no, no." He bent down with her. This is not supposed to be the way it goes, Colleen. No, it shouldn't be." He jerked his fist and the bronze gauntlet came folding back into a device fastened at the back of his hand. It revealed his bare, calloused fingers, though they were surprisingly almost as huge as the gauntlet itself.

He held her chin and tilted her head back. "You are a human, I will not allow you to die in such disgrace. You should hold your head high, Colleen. You did the right thing calling me, you saved our race," he consoled, oddly doing well at it. "You should not die weeping; no human should die in such a dismal state." He studied her for a moment, considering. "Fine," he finally said. "I will not kill you. But what were you going to do with the Cube? You know your efforts would be futile against me, and still you try?"

"Escape," Colleen choked up, her voice a muffled note. "Ability four, the portal to the unknown."

"How inane," Yruf snorted. "You do not even have a clue on what the other side holds. You would place so much risk on yourself just to escape me?"

"Escape death."

Yruf's face hardened. "There are far worse things than death." He did not ask before he took hold of the Cube, gently enough. Colleen knew there was no need to struggle. "But… your proposal is tempting. Send you away." He played with the Cube. In his hand, it looked no more than the size of a tennis ball. The Cube in his hand finally stopped rotating when Yruf clenched it. "You are willing to swear that you will forgive me?"

Colleen could only nod reluctantly.

Yruf clenched on the Cube and something erupted behind Colleen. It sounded like someone zipped open something, a rip in reality, the gap widening from thin air. Its rim smoked like a brazier, ash emanating from it, trickling out continuously. It stopped expanding once it had grown into a door of crooked shape, large enough for a person to fit in.

Its insides were a swirl of colors, revolving towards the center of it like an artist had mixed every color in the palette. Pale fingers of breeze came from nowhere and rushed into the portal. Colleen's hair was thrown out, breathed with life, fluttering with the breeze wending through her hair.

"Tempting, I have to admit," Yruf spoke over the whir the portal made. "And I shall take it. However, it may well not be the way you want it to be," Yruf flashed a vile grin. Before Colleen could process, she was shoved into the portal. She could only scream, but even that was short-lived once her whole body had been eaten by the portal. "I hope you do forgive me," Yruf muttered, "and if you do survive, tell me what's on the other side."

He looked to the child longingly. "You have the traitor's blood," he told him in his deep raspy voice. "As much as what I yearn is important, the mission far outweighs my wants or needs. The greater good always requires sacrifice. So do forgive me." The infant continued crying but Yruf paid no heed to him. He turned to the portal. It was now slowly closing. He was about to fling the child when he suddenly twitched to a halt.

"Argh!" he screamed. Unbeknownst to Yruf, while he had so merrily activated the Cube as he liked, it glowed with a luminesce that spoke of much heat. He dropped both the child and the Cube at once.

"Damn it!" he seethed, bending down and clutching the wrist of the hand with the other. "What the hell was that?!" His flesh sizzled and tendrils of smoke with the miasma of charred meat perforated through the air. Sweat started to dapple his forehead and the trench coat tightened around his muscles as he flexed them, doing whatever he could to alleviate the pain. His once beige skin turned into a layer of black crusty coal, darker spots flecked at the patches where the Cube had touched his skin.

While Yruf was licking in his wounds, the infant who had been dropped on the ground was bawling as loud as he could. It only made Yruf more peevish. An urge told him to kick the child but he stopped at the last second, grunted, and stomped towards the basin, running water on his wound. The infant flailed about, face red at a tomato and howling at the top of his lungs as babies do with their poor social conscience. Suddenly Lucas' eye met baby Lucas… or the Cube and Lucas saw them twinkle with interest. The child reached over as Lucas yelled at him not to. He knew it was not real, he knew it was just a vision from the past, he knew no matter how loud he screamed, no sound would come out, but he did.

It didn't matter, the infant's fat hands clawed the Cube greedily while his chubby face reflected mild amusement, making unintelligible noises to show it. When Lucas felt the hands touch the Cube, everything darkened and a pause drew out as long as it did to torture Lucas.

The last thing Lucas heard was Yruf croaking laughter. "Ah, hope." Light streamed back into his eyes the next instant, and Lucas knew he was awake. He jolted to sit up, panting, his hair slick with sweat, and rivulets dripping down his face… or were they tears? His pillow was smeared with a spot, a shade of grey soaked with water on a field of white. "What… happened next?" he stammered, anxious to know if Cube was still there.

"It's obvious, don't you think? By touching me, you triggered a protocol in me, an ability your parents had not found out yet. Through luck… or fate as you humans like to call mere coincidences when it corresponds to your beliefs, we merged as one being."

274

Lucas did not have to ask to know the rest. He only needed to look at the mirror. There was none around him, but where the window at the side of one wall slanted out open, the rays of the sun reflected his image into his eyes. And he saw the most haggard, miserable boy he had ever seen. He did not know what to think, or what to feel... except he wished it had all been a dream. But it couldn't have been. The voice of the Cube convinced him as much.

Lucas could do nothing but lie back with a vacuous look. He wanted nothing so much as to sleep away the pain shooting through his body in sharp pulses, routing through his veins. But he could not, he would not allow himself to. He knew he would have to confront the pain soon or late, and it was not in his nature one to procrastinate. But it would be a lie to say he was ready for the burst of emotions. The vision had wrecked him far more than he realized. When he searched inside himself, all he found were ruins.

He could only cry. He yelled at the top of his lungs knowing that he could since the room was soundproof, he thrashed about in his bed though he knew it would solve nothing. But he didn't care about reason now, he didn't care about his training, about upholding his stupid status. He punched and kicked the bed as if it was the source of all his woes. He felt a network of tears racing each other down his face, some dripping onto the already soaked pillow, some curving into his lips. It tasted salty... or would have been if his taste buds had not numbed as well. "Yruf! Yruf! Yruf!" he screamed, in agony, in despair at first.

Lucas' sorrow churned and bore angry fangs, swirled into an intense hatred that felt like it was swallowing him from the inside. His blood boiled and his heart palpitated so fast it could have powered a car. It transitioned to hate steadily. "Yruf!" he roared the last time, injecting every sliver of fury he scraped

275

together in the word. "I will kill him! I will carve his heart out!" His throat felt like it had been scrubbed by acid, the words dry and barbed.

Almost instinctively, Lucas willed his right arm to shatter so that it could reform into the blue blade. It grew out from his arm in a line of white, reflecting the light above. His compulsion to kill grew with every passing second. He was going to end it all, and he was going to enjoy every moment of it. "I will end it all now," he seethed, lips skinned back to growl, cringing his face to cope with the pain.

"Be logical Lucas," Cube warned.

"What do you suppose I do?" Lucas screamed, face flushed and wrinkled. "I can think of a thousand ways to kill him right now! He's not guarded, even if he is, I would simply just spear my way through anyone who would dare obstruct me!"

"Yes," the Cube agreed, "no one would be quick or powerful enough to stop you from getting to him. It is certain you can kill him right now. But at what cost?"

"At what cost?!" Lucas howled incredulously. "You showed me everything and you ask that? My whole life has been a curated lie, my mentor and father who I had loved and respected was the murderer to my parents, a terrorist who is well responsible for genocides, some I may not even know of. He kidnaps people, he runs foul tests on them, turns them into the aberrations I saw. He is everything he had taught me not to stand for, he is everything he had taught me to hate and fight against. And that's not the worst of it…" he choked up, the words clogging at his throat. He had to hunch over to reel from the pain.

He made me believe I was abandoned. He made me believe my parents hated me when it was the opposite. He made me loathe them... all the while nurturing me. Cube, imagine the irony of being nurtured by the murderer who killed my parents. "You wouldn't understand even if I told you a million times, Cube. You are a machine... nothing more. Emotions as strong as this I assume are foreign, at best hazy to you," Lucas cursed with more bitterness than he would have liked.

"I may be so," the Cube said in a forgiving tone, ever the logical being. "I admit, I am still a long way from experiencing genuine emotion as you organic beings do so easily. I lack many other things as well, but I am rational. Lucas. The cost I speak of it is the one your parents held dearly too. And I dare say you would want to honor their lives, their legacy, don't you?"

"What cost?" Lucas finally relented.

"Your life, Lucas. Do you think that their sacrifices are for naught? Well it might look like it, but all sacrifices always seem like that. Look in the mirror, Lucas! You were the cause they gave up everything for! What you saw of humiliation and dread... I saw hope! I saw bravery, valor! I saw what they gave just for you! And while you may get a cheap victory at killing Yruf, what happens after?"

"Cheap victory?" Lucas challenged. "I would kill him. If that's not victory enough then I don't know what is. Everything would end then."

"I stand by the cheap victory," the Cube snapped. "Do you really think Yruf does not have measures ready for an untimely demise? Especially this conquest he deems so important, do you think he would let it stop at his death? No. He sees himself as the world's savior. You'll only be cutting out the symptoms of

277

the problem. Yruf would have entrusted his plans to his inner circle, his accomplices, his vast network."

"Yes, but I can expose him after that!" Lucas contended.

"And who will believe you? The only proof you have is a few werewolves. You blew up the lab, and you do not know where any of the others are. But Yruf's side? They will have concrete proof that you killed the overall commander of the EMA. Now, if that's not a severe offence, I do not know what is. And let's face it, Lucas, you do not have the best of reputations. The world has always seen you as a wildcard that could turn on it at any time. Do you think they will trust you? Or a group of powerful people who are established. You will be hunted by both sides."

"So be it. I will be able to escape here too. No one in this compound can stop me. I'm too powerful. That will be enough time to run and think."

"Let's not even talk about the world. You will not run far. You've seen the power Yruf has... or at least the ones you know. You'll be a fugitive of the EMA, at worst the world, with the influence Yruf has. He has powerful friends lurking about in high places, I assure you that. You can't run forever. The EMA has a personal army it can summon and provision in a week's time. And now you know they have Pureblood drones, yet another faction to supplement their numbers. And if they call the... his old partners, then you will be so outmatched you would barely leave a scratch. At their full strength, I doubt even you could handle them all."

Lucas clenched his fist. He knew the Cube was right, so his voice simmered down. "If I fail to run... then I would gladly serve as the martyr."

"A martyr? No one will see you as a martyr, only an ungrateful boy who had gone mad and killed his mentor. And even if you become a martyr, what good will that do? And if you die, tell me, is there anyone else in this world to stop them? Will the First Federation stop them? You know well they have weakened in influence over the years, and half their cabinet is made up of puppets to do Yruf's bidding. The Sea Lords who will not stop squabbling? Or the Purebloods who are either too proud to enter the fray or are too weak to augment the resistance?"

Lucas furrowed his brows. "No one can," he admitted grudgingly. "Most are still reeling from the previous war."

"Oh yes," Cube said wryly.

"So you're saying I should just drop it all?" Lucas' anger simmered, but in its place came anguish.

Helplessness was an emotion he did not feel often, but now it rose up to envelop him. It was a hollow feeling, as if a vacuum formed in his stomach was squeezing all of his innards into it. There once was a time where there was no mountain too tall, no ocean too wide, no enemy too strong for him. He prided himself in being the final guardian at the gate, the last resort the EMA had who had never failed. Nothing ever withstood his might, nor did it once occur to him it might happen one day.

But here it was. "No one is saying that. You are your parents' son. Fighting Yruf is not only the right thing to do, but it is also a way of continuing their good work."

Good work. The words triggered a flicker of memories before him, the images of the labs filled with pods upon pods of Purebloods forcibly operated on to be turned into something that could be barely called a lifeform.

"You speak sense, Cube. And yet, I can't shake the feeling that the longer I wait, the more Purebloods will fall into Yruf's hands. I must stop him with the earliest chance I have."

"If you charge blindly into him, you will die. And with no hope for a resistance, they still die."

"But if I wait… the conclusion is the same," Lucas uttered.

"Not so… you live. Did you not think Yruf has not been patient? It has been sixteen years. No, sixteen years that we know of. All that time to tend to his plans, as heinous as they are, do you really hope to pull it all down in an instant?"

Lucas stared at the door blankly, his breath gave way into a sigh, energy seeping out for him. He suddenly felt lousy and lethargic, every motivation, everything he thought he had figured out shrinking. "Why must it always be that people die so that I can live? Why can't I just end this misery? Why can't it be other people that relieves *me* of my burden?"

"Because it is easy to do that. It is easy to be strong when there is nothing to fear, just as it is easy to do something when you know you have nothing to lose. But you are different Lucas. You *are* a cut above the rest. Where has your usual arrogance gone? You hate easy, it is the way you are."

Lucas shook his head ponderously. "No. I'm no hero. You must know the things I've done. Sure, Yruf had been the one who gave the order... but *I* executed them with such efficiency, such blind loyalty… and you know what, Cube? A part of me has always known it was wrong, a nagging feeling. But not once did I bother to reflect on it. I've played a part in Yruf's scheme to be blamed as much as he, I'm not virtuous enough to champion such a cause."

"You really think the heroes you read about have squeaky-clean pasts? I'm sorry to burst your bubble, boy, but you are sorely wrong. Heroes are not exemplars of virtue, they are the ones who do enough good to offset the bad they have done. And that is exactly what you are going to do. Remember that you are only mortal. There is only so much you can do, there is no perfect. Where there is perfect... well... then I believe there will only be oblivion. Beauty and calamity are two sides of the coin, one cannot exist without the other. But that also means perfection can only be achieved if both do not exist. Now... if there's no variability in life... then where's the point in that?"

The blade receded into Lucas' arm and Lucas slumped down, nesting beside his bed. He folded his legs and curled over, lost and languid. "What's the point indeed? My parents are dead, and my whole life has been a lie. My guardian whom I am closest to is the antithesis of what I had once thought of him." He wanted to laugh. This whole scenario seemed like an especially cruel practical joke played by the heavens on him just for giggles. "This sucks, Cube... I'll admit. It... I am hurting very badly. I know you're right... but I can't help it. I guess no matter what, I'm just... as you said. Mortal."

"And it should. I for one would be more troubled if it didn't."

"Why? Wouldn't that prove I'm strong like Yruf is? Nothing seems to throw him off."

"Emotions prove you are human, and emotion the essence of sentience. Why else would I be programmed to learn it? I'm still in the budding stages of understanding it, it is difficult and I admire how you mortals perceive it so easily, but I know its value. It makes you empathize, it makes you happy. Control and conquering emotions are what makes you strong... not the lack of it. Yruf, by my standards... is weak."

"You just said he was strong," Lucas blurted passively.

"For now. Lucas, you'll be tenfold the person he is."

HELLO WORLD-12 (LUCAS)

Lucas fumbled as his toes, pinching, scratching, and sanding the more calloused parts that had hardened from burst blisters. On the other hand, he held up a tablet. He liked to sit on the bed while he read important stuff. The desk was too formal to skim through long documents like this, he would only get a neck ache if he did. He preferred to lie on the comforts of his bed, on his pillows and swathed under a thick blanket. He sat upright. While his other hand disappeared in the sheets to disturb his toes, the other hand was getting quite sore from holding the tablet up and hovering high enough so he didn't have to crane his neck down or strain his eyes.

He frowned and read the words displayed on the document with a sardonic voice. "And so the esteemed Lieutenant Lucas will be granted a seat on the main war council that usually only comprises of generals. He will be in charge of infiltration—" Lucas snorted. "—not even reconnaissance."

"Why is that bad?" Cube asked. For the past few days Lucas was slowly getting more used to Cube chiming in his ears. It was jarring at first. Lucas already had a pretty noisy internal voice, and a second one only sought to reduce the space in his mind meant for deep thought. At times it gave him bad migraines, a throbbing in his brain like it was fighting to explode out of his skull.

The past few days had been especially torturous for Lucas.

He was seldom awake, and when he was, it would only be short episodes at once. And he showered often. He felt chilly, not the cold sort, but the numbness in his very bones. Only showering would help thaw the cold out, but still it was only temporary relief to his frigid bones.

He would close his eyes and let the water run onto him. Streams would cascade on his goosebumps, though they always refused to subside even when his body heated up. He took comfort in whatever warmth enveloped him.

These days he found himself more thankful than grieved. He tried not to think, but that only exacerbated his feelings and the memories Cube had shown him. He only wanted to relax as he listened to the water trickle on the ground, getting gulped by the shower drain. He only wanted to feel the water flowing down on him, he only wanted to stand there for all of eternity in that state of peace. But his body would not allow it. So if he were to think, he must as well think of all the good that had happened.

He thought of his parents, trimming away all the bad parts. *At least I wasn't abandoned or sold like some dog. At least I was loved.* He took scarce comfort in that, but every sliver of it counted.

Yet, as Cube had told him, there could not be bliss without calamity. Now and again, the images of pain and torture flashed in his mind. He would grimace at them; his stomach would churn and his entirety would twist into a knot. He wished the water current was strong enough to wash that away just like how it scraped dirt away. But they wouldn't go so easily.

283

He spent most of the day napping. He took long naps at a time that would have put him on par with a hibernating bear. It was much alike the cycle he lost himself to right after the Orc and Serperin incident. It was eat and sleep and shower, then rinse and repeat. It was all he could do while processing and coming to terms with his new reality. He presumed he would not be able to walk through the corridors the same way as he did before everything got dug up. The EMA was now a completely different place to him, and if he even took a leisurely stroll down, he would not be able to vouch that he wouldn't belch.

Unfortunately, napping only proved marginally better than staying awake. Only in small bouts was he allowed an escape into some merry land where the grass was always verdant, the people were all honest, the sun was always bright and balmy, it was tranquil and joyful, and there was not a trace of worry in the world. It distracted him from the worries, but that was more an occasional treat than not.

Most of his dreams reared their heads into ugly nightmares, baring fangs and growing horns. They started mellow at first, but Lucas would soon find out their benign appearance was exactly that, an appearance.

The nightmares were pretty standard. Most of them were reruns of the scene where Yruf murdered his parents. No matter how many times it played in his head, it did not make it any easier to watch. Exhilaration would channel through him as his parents fought and when his mom ran from Yruf.

He knew how it would always end, but it never stopped him from hoping it wouldn't. He screamed at them; he flailed his arms to gesture to them not to make the mistakes that would be their last. He cursed his mom for being so foolish and his father for being so obstinate. He yelled at his mom not to turn to the toilet, and when she did, he hollered at her not to leave him next to the door where she would not have time to reach. And then dread when the inevitable eventuality came would delve its claws into his skin, sinking in and then wrenching out flesh and blood.

If he thought those were bad, his mind decided that it wasn't enough torture. It transitioned into the countless missions he had taken part in. Lucas started killing when he was eleven, barely even able to carry an ordinary pistol with his scrawny arms. But he didn't need to carry one anyway. He was the weapon.

He *was* good, very good. The way he killed, so swiftly, so mercilessly, one would have mistaken him as a tiny tornado. Nothing touched him but blood, splattered on him after they had flown around him in circles in a dance of red arcs.

He dreamt of all the villains he fought. Some were plainly evil, and Lucas would applaud himself at stopping what deprivation and horrid acts they performed of spread. Yet some... what deeds he had deemed evil last time... didn't seem so now. Good and evil blurred to a smear of grey and now he wasn't so sure. His missions weren't solely reserved to criminals. Some were rebels, though Yruf were categorized in the same group anyway.

He used to ignore them because he was indoctrinated to hate them. Yruf told him they deserved it. They were rebels after all, lower in the hierarchy of contempt than even soil stains below his shoes. Yet... what if they had just been where Lucas was at now, enlightened at the atrocities of the EMA. What if they had been right?

He might have just been the weapon to the mastermind, but it did not excuse him from the evil he had dished out. It was his blade and his bullets that were stained with their blood after all. His kill count that he had worn so proudly as if it was a badge was now only the measure of the sin he had committed.

He dreamt of their faces when he had them killed, some aloof, some indignant, some disdain, some begging. Most were resigned. Of course they would be. They were fighting the Ace, the unstoppable arsenal, the trump card of the EMA.

He always remembered their faces. For some queer principle, he thought it was the least he could do to honor them as he relieved their heads from their necks, every minute detail etched into his mind. Their faces told all, but their eyes told most of it. The way it gleamed under the light in a moist quality as the blade collapsed.

Some shrewd, some malicious to the core, but even combined, they would not have come close to the qualities Yruf possessed. They were embodiments of sin, Yruf was sin himself.

"Lucas, you hear me? I can see you drifting off. Don't dwell on it. It's not healthy," the Cube's voice shot through Lucas' thoughts to break him out.

Lucas crumpled in his eyes and shook his head wildly as if to fling those corrupted thoughts away. He knew that it was good advice, but sometimes… it was just so hard to "Yeah, you're right. You were saying?" He found the hand that was holding on to the tablet slumped on the blanket where his folded legs were at. It ached from exhaustion, and the tablet screen had blackened from disuse.

"To your earlier statement about infiltration. Why is it bad? You are still a proper commander on the field. You should be delighted, no?"

Lucas could not help but smile. He released the tablet and let it slide down the blanket formed where it ran taut at his kneecaps. The hand moved over to rest his forehead. "For a machine so intelligent, you sure are naïve."

"As I said, I still have a long way to go when it comes to understanding your mortal constructs. Some things that are not written or set in rules I cannot yet understand... it is just not obvious to me."

"It's just practice," Lucas consoled, "but you'll learn it soon from our tone and choice of words. Yes, well, coming back to your question. You're right, on paper, I am a distinguished commander, same as all the other old hags. But unofficially, the infiltration troupe is deemed the untouchables of the army. It was never actually an official faction until recently, only to persuade people that the job isn't so sordid and despicable as originally thought. Well, no one is fooled."

"Why?"

"Well, for one, they're called the suicide soldiers. Once they have speared through undetected into enemy soil, they would sow discourse in the Region or Zone about to be raided. Then when they are done and the vanguard comes swooping in, they would be reduced to mere time bombs. Their final acts of service would be meant to devastate society from within, driving chaos in their people and cluttering their defense."

"Oh, so I assume many would not come back from the squad he has granted you with," Cube said.

"If I'm given ten members to lead, I'd be lucky to even find a single recognizable body after we're done." Lucas groaned.

"Then how about you? Doesn't Yruf know he's sending his trump card to the most dangerous place?"

Lucas nodded peevishly. "He knows exactly what he's doing. If you were him, wouldn't you send your best soldier to the most troublesome area as well? He knows I won't die... not like that. And what better position than to place your trump card behind enemy lines where I can take them by surprise. Vampires are strong... but they have always been more durable than a threat. It's only because of their troublesome immortality that makes them so tenacious. But we have weapons, see."

"I see. Yruf played you. He's not giving you responsibility; he's only using you as he has always done."

"As a weapon. But that's how he's always been, hasn't it?" Lucas snorted cynically. "Manipulative."

"You seem sad," Cube noticed. "But shouldn't you have expected it? Is there anything else that is bothering you?"

"You can't read my mind?"

"I could, but I have studied you humans enough to know I would only be breaching your privacy if I did."

"I see," Lucas said. "Considerate."

"And I prefer not to. Adolescents your age... have your needs... and that means having thoughts with more detail and indecency than I like."

Lucas' cheeks went bright red. "Yeah, good call. Anyway, I'm not troubled. Just irritated that I wasn't given more information than this meagre report. Yruf said I was part of his little gang, so why do I get the feeling I have not been promoted at all?"

"If you had been given your information, what had you hoped to do?" the Cube asked.

Lucas lolled his tongue along the dry walls of his mouth. It tasted putrid. "I can wait and slowly cultivate my strength, but that doesn't mean I can't thwart Yruf's plans silently. I don't know what he's playing at long term, but I know this; he plans to add numbers to his army of drones with this attack on the Vampire Kingdom." Lucas gritted his teeth. "If he succeeds with this supplementation, his strength will be launched greatly."

"I see. And you need to know his play before you can react."

"Yes."

"I got an idea, but it might be you would not like it," Cube suggested.

Lucas sucked in his breath, it was all he could do not to say no. "Tell me," he spoke with a measured voice. "It's not like my ideas are coming in abundance now."

Made in the USA
Middletown, DE
04 November 2020

23286978R00166